# Light of the New Day

*And Other Stories*

*by*

*Darin Cozzens*

ZARAHEMLA BOOKS

Provo, Utah

*Earlier versions of the stories in this collection appeared as follows:*

"Alkali Coulee," *Windhover* (University of Mary Hardin-Baylor, Belton, Texas), vol. 8, January 2004.

"The Darlington Girls," *Irreantum*, Summer 2001.

"Elk on Chimborazo," originally titled "New Boots," *Weber Studies* (Weber State University, Ogden, Utah), vol. 10, no. 2, Spring/Summer 1993.

"Handshakes But No Hugs and Kisses," originally titled "All the Girls," *Coraddi* (University of North Carolina, Greensboro), Spring 1987.

"Light of the New Day," *Irreantum*, vol. 9, no. 1, 2007; reprinted in *Dispensation: Latter-Day Fiction*, ed. Angela Hallstrom (Provo, Utah: Zarahemla Books, 2010).

"No Say in the Matter," originally titled "Headgate," *Greensboro Review*, no. 41, Winter 1986–87.

"Oasis," *Greensboro Review*, no. 46, Summer 1989.

"Reap in Mercy," *Irreantum* (double volume), vol. 9, no. 2, 2007 and vol. 10, no. 1, 2008; reprinted in *The Best of Mormonism 2009*, ed. Stephen Carter (Salt Lake City: Curelom Books, 2009).

"Signs of the Times," *Cimarron Review* (Oklahoma State University, Stillwater), no. 101, October 1992.

"The Treading of Lesser Cattle," *Irreantum*, vol. 11, nos. 1 and 2, 2009.

"The Trees in Lyman," *Midland Review* (Oklahoma State University, Stillwater), no. 5, Winter 1989.

"Vigil," *Irreantum*, Summer 2002.




ISBN 978-0-9843603-2-1



Published by Zarahemla Books
869 East 2680 North
Provo, UT 84604
info@zarahemlabooks.com
ZarahemlaBooks.com

"Darin Cozzens's stories display all the vital elements of fictional craft. His narrative voices compel the reader's attention. His characters are varied and empathetic. His dialogue rings true. His landscapes are a felt presence. His prose is seamlessly professional. Seen as a whole, *Light of the New Day* is a panorama of rural Mormon culture, rich in earned pathos leavened now and then by eccentric humor. This is a book to delight serious readers, a book deserving a diverse and discriminating audience."

> — Gordon Weaver, winner of two Pushcart Prizes
> and the O. Henry Award, author of ten short-story
> collections and four novels, including *Count a Lonely Cadence*

"These stories hold the reader with their compelling characters, plots, conflicts, and deft use of language. They evoke Wyoming farm life, make it real, palpable, and human, including the Mormonism, when it appears. Above all the stories are honest, insightful as to what makes us mortal, and skillfully told."

> —Douglas Thayer, author of *Hooligan* and *The Tree House*

"*Light of the New Day* is one of the most admirable books I ever read. The tender, unsentimental respect it holds for the characters it portrays, the labors it describes, and the grand, rich, lonesome landscape it inhabits are extraordinary. Everything here is genuine, down to the black lunchbox and the motes of hayfield dust. What Darin Cozzens has seen and known he delivers to the page with earnest vividness. This volume is as honest and hearty as a fresh-baked wheat loaf."

> — Fred Chappell, novelist and poet laureate
> of North Carolina from 1997 to 2002

"These stories rise from the dust of the Wyoming landscape. In them, Cozzens gives us real people, worthy of our admiration. They work, socialize, and worship together; they know one another's weaknesses. Their mettle is tested in the ordinary moments, when it can't be faked by outward trappings. But there are secrets here too. Motives lie hidden. Longing and resentment nag at even the most stalwart characters. In a land like this, there's no use wasting words. With Darin Cozzens's stories it's the same: Every word counts."

—Jack Harrell,
author of *Vernal Promises*,
English professor at BYU–Idaho

"The voices in *Light of the New Day* are completely believable, the prose spare and precise, the setting utterly simple. For any who appreciate fine writing, Cozzens's stories are like rivulets of irrigation water to parched earth—a theme that goes through several of his pieces. Within this volume are unexpectedly beautiful or surprising moments in the most unadorned places. Cozzens presents rural life, which he clearly knows well, in a way that reveals something we hadn't realized we needed to know about humanity. We come away understanding that we did need that drink of good Wyoming water. We just hadn't realized it was available, or that we were so thirsty."

—Margaret Blair Young,
coauthor of the *Standing on the Promises* trilogy

To my father,
Matthew Cozzens
(1932–2006)

# Contents

# No Say in the Matter

ONLY ME AND CRISWALL KNOW the whole story behind the District firing Quin last fall. Far as I'm concerned, with fifty-eight days until my retirement plaque and full county benefits, that's the way it's going to stay. Quin's gone—just moved to Billings—and with all the snow this winter, nobody wants to bring up the drought or Darl Sebright's five acres of dead beans anyway.

Except maybe Vanderfisk. Caught me off guard, him calling me at home like that on a Sunday night. Mill Vanderfisk is a big man around Balford—stake president and irrigation commissioner both. And it was no secretary on the phone. It was Millard P. himself. "Eb, can you spare a few minutes next Thursday night?" He wants to see me, in his office at the stake center. Do you know how long it's been since I stepped foot in a Mormon church building?

I'm not what you'd call an active member, which Criswall the vice-commissioner never lets me forget. "Finally got your fill of snake oil, Eb?" It's not a joke, either. I'm not sure what religion he goes by, but whatever it is, the main doctrine must be to save the world from Mormons. Ravening wolves in fleecy wool. I heard him say that one time, though nowhere close to Vanderfisk. No, around Mill Vanderfisk, he's the picture of get-along Christian brotherhood.

But something tells me this meeting with Vanderfisk isn't about church. I heard Quin came back to talk to him the other day, and this was quite a while *after* he got the new ditch riding job in Billings, thanks to Mill Vanderfisk and his many connections. The point is, he was well past needing a reference. Who knows what he might have said? And why Mill Vanderfisk is worried about talking at work, I don't know either—unless he doesn't want Criswall to see us. But see what? There's nothing so unusual about the big boss—not this one—sticking his head in the shop to say how goes it to the one ditch rider they keep on winter payroll. Somebody's got to service the fleet and sweep a clean floor.

After him and Quin talked, Vanderfisk's bound to know there's more to the story than he thought. And after last fall, he'd probably like to hear it firsthand, and make sure the newspaper doesn't. Truth is, some days I wish I could tell somebody. It's been a long time since I talked to a bishop or stake president one on one. But no matter what Quin might have said, nobody needs to worry about me talking to the paper. With fifty-eight days left? No, come April, I'm through with cracked head gates and dead beans and all the rest. Just give me a fishing pole and a tall, cold one, and I'll ride into the sunset, no questions asked.

The stakes are maybe higher for a commissioner and vice-commissioner, at least in their way of thinking. Vanderfisk's contract is up this summer. Depending on a lot of things—a full reservoir won't hurt—the Board may or may not offer him another five years. And if they do, will he take it? If he doesn't, they'll likely pick a replacement on his recommendation. So neither guy can afford a fight right now. Believe me, it doesn't take much to start one around here. Ralston and Garland aren't pioneer Mormon towns like Balford, but they are part of the same irrigation district. With a Mormon in charge of the water in a dry year, you can see the problem.

Who else knows anything? Just Darl and those two kids on the District's weed crew. The older one, the one driving the spraying rig—he's gone off to college somewhere—he claimed it was an honest mistake. And after everything that went on last summer, everybody was more than glad to let it go at that. But maybe now, sitting by his fireplace on a stormy night, Mill Vanderfisk gets to wondering why that kid *really* flushed his tank right where he did and why the District got off so easy, why Darl Sebright didn't ask for what those five acres were worth. That's when Vanderfisk asks can I spare a few minutes next Thursday night.

If I was going to say anything to anybody, I'd say Quin dug his own grave. And I'd say that even if he was of my religion. He had a good dozen years in—was halfway to retirement benefits himself, which are pretty darned good for ditch riding—so allotments were nothing new to him. If the allotment doesn't stretch in a dry year, who can you blame? We're not rainmakers. That's one place I agree with Criswall.

It *was* dry. We'd had almost zero snowpack in the Absarokas and no runoff to speak of up North- or Southfork, either one. And no rain for planting anything. The main canal and all the laterals coming off it were brim-full the end of April, almost a month earlier than usual, draining a reservoir that didn't have it to spare. The paper kept quoting Vanderfisk. All spring he urged everybody to stay calm and keep a positive attitude. He said with foresight and prudence, everybody could get through the crisis together.

Quin said foresight and prudence had nothing to do with this valley's water problems. He said it was way worse than anybody wanted to admit, especially on his line. He was in charge of a lateral just below Balford, dug in the old days with teams and slip-shovels and lots of faith. In sacrament meeting, Mormons still tell the story of Prayer Rock. After all kinds of dynamite and trying to go around it, it one day split in a lightning storm, right down the middle, right where the surveyors said the channel had to go. There's a lot of people swear by it. Nowadays, this lateral loops around to catch maybe half a dozen smaller Mormon farmers, then ties back into the main canal. Not so far downstream, that canal feeds some pretty big farmers—who, by the way, are *not* Mormon. You get the picture.

If they'd had their way, the big boys would have shut down the Balford Loop altogether. They say the water rights claimed way back when by the Mormon homesteaders were never properly recorded. Even in a good year, the big boys complain the Loop gets more water than it's due just because of where the farmers over there go to church. Everybody thinks that's why the District put Quin on that line in the first place—he had no stake in the matter. No religious stake, maybe. But it sure wound up mattering to him for some reason, which I don't think anybody figured on.

Everybody knew it was bad when Vanderfisk called a meeting early last June for all water users. They brought in folding chairs, set them up on my clean floor in the District shop, had a couple a big fans for the heat, a portable podium and microphone, the whole bit. Just before the meeting, Vanderfisk talked to the ditch riders in the board room. With the Board's approval, he and Criswall had decided on some policies in light of the drought. Vanderfisk said if everything was made clear, if we were positive and supportive, we wouldn't have any problems. "We want to be fair and aboveboard about this." That's how he put it.

Of course Criswall pipes up, like he always does. When they're together in any kind of meeting, you get the feeling he doesn't think Vanderfisk has put enough spine into whatever he's said. So Criswall takes it on himself to clarify: "Every land owner gets so many acre-feet, according to his water right, and when it's gone, it's gone."

Quin's the only one of us said anything. And anything he said was going to rub Criswall wrong. They don't much care for each other. Criswall tried one time to get him to take his side against Mormons, and Quin didn't bite. He said he'd fry in hell before he joined the Mormon church, thought their doctrine was the biggest pile of hooey he'd ever heard, but Mormon farmers had as much right to water as anybody.

At the meeting he naturally wanted to know about the Balford Loop. Would it be guaranteed enough acre-feet to cover the farmers over there? The place went dead quiet. Ditch riders are a pretty loyal bunch. A lot of them felt the same way the downstream farmers felt toward the Balford water rights. But what could they say with Mill Vanderfisk standing there? Me, I work a lateral that feeds all kinds. Just tell me which head gate to open or shut, and I'll do it. With fifty-eight days left, I keep my loyalties to myself.

Vanderfisk was patient with Quin's question. For a man with his kind of clout, he's a nice guy and pretty well liked. The Board would never have hired him otherwise, let alone keep him on for ten years. He said conservation was the one thing would save us in a dry year. And prayer. He said it in such a way that everybody smiled or laughed. Everybody knows he's religious and got some political power around here, but he gets along okay with regular guys, too.

Quin wouldn't let it go. He says, "If the Loop gets less water, everybody else gets the same amount of less?"

"We're going to be as fair as we can about it. We don't want any panic."

The whole time, Criswall keeps checking his watch. Finally he asks Vanderfisk should they mention the padlocks. Vanderfisk tried to keep up the lighter mood. He says, "I didn't line up any riot police, Tom."

We all laughed at that, too. Except Quin. He said we'd never actually locked anybody's gate before. Criswall said other summers maybe not. He says, "But you got to get used to the idea this one is different."

Then Vanderfisk says, "Any way I say it, it's going to sound bad. I'm in a no-win situation here."

"Sooner or later they got to know the policy. No exceptions." That was Criswall putting plenty of spine in his last word on the subject.

Mill Vanderfisk was nodding his Vanderfisk nod. By that I

mean if you're around him much, you know that's his polite way of saying no. He says, "No need to make anybody sore today, so let's hold off with this padlock thing."

Right then, if Quin had just kept his mouth shut, he would've been okay. But, no, he had to get in his two cents' worth. He comes right out and says he's still waiting for a straight answer. Then Vice-Commissioner Criswall, who wants to be Head Commissioner Criswall so bad he can taste it, he says, "I don't appreciate your tone, mister." That's when Vanderfisk puts up both hands, like to stop them if they go at each other, and he promises Quin they're going to do the best they can. And just from the way he says it, we all know the meeting's over.

That's all you can do is the best you can—when you got no real say in the matter. Quin used to be the golden boy. Even Criswall liked him, until he wouldn't take sides against the Mormons. He was a hero even. Four or five years back, a car blows a tire on the highway, plows into the main canal. Lucky for the driver, Quin sees it and knows how to swim. The paper took a picture of everybody, quoted Vanderfisk saying how glad he was nobody got hurt and what an outstanding employee Quin was.

Truth be known, the farmers over on the Loop liked him better than anybody they'd ever had, including a few duds of their own faith. He always opened their head gates on time, and he kept his trash traps clean, which is no easy job out there. The Loop's got some of the last cement head gate boxes and open-ditch laterals in the valley. So he's still fighting the same stuff we all used to fight—weeds, moss, driftwood, road trash, and such. Sometimes a gunnysack full of rocks and dead pups or kittens. Quin said he'd like to get his hands on the low-life who could do something like that. None of that will be a problem anymore when the District gets around to laying pipe out there like they have everywhere else. Quin thinks they're dragging their feet on purpose, doing everybody else first. But they couldn't very well *start* with the Loop, could they? Their phone would have rung off the hook. You playing favorites, Brother Mill? So Vanderfisk just keeps telling whoever wants to quote him that the upgrade schedule will include the Balford Loop sometime in the very near future.

I liked Quin. I really did. We used to park our pickups right there where the Loop comes off the main canal and shoot the bull before rounds, real early in the morning. He was always asking me this and that about how to do things, how things work. I sort of took him under my wing. But you can only push so hard before a guy like Criswall starts pushing back.

That's more or less what I told Quin the first time he came to me about Darl Sebright's leaky head gate. That was a week or so after the meeting. Darl and his brother farm the last places along the Loop, get their water from three or four head gates each. I said, "Quin, they'll lay pipe out there when they're good and ready." He said he wasn't talking about pipe this time. It was way simpler than that. One morning, checking in on his radio, he just happens to mention the leak—which he kicked himself for doing—and the District says, Oh, really? Well, that's going to have to be back-counted at least two weeks against Darl's allotment. But Darl hadn't ordered the water, and he wasn't using it. Weird as it sounds talking about everything bone-dry, he didn't *need* the water right then. The leaky head gate fed a big hayfield, and, right then, Darl Sebright's first cutting was down. He didn't *want* that ground wet, not until the hay was cured and baled and put up. And all that time this water being charged against him would just run into a waste ditch.

I warned Quin against getting on Criswall's bad side. He said he was already there, but thanks for the heads-up. He said it like I was supposed to go along with him. Over a leak! You want to have a pretty good reason before you go marching into the District office in your irrigating boots asking to see the gentlemen behind the doors. But that didn't stop Quin. He wondered who'd come up with the idea to count leaks against the farmer. Criswall says, "Yours truly." He says, "You got a problem with that?" Quin says nobody knew things were going to work that way; it wasn't fair. And he had a point. Naturally Criswall has to get his dig in, says maybe the Mormon pioneers could pray giant rocks in half but weren't so good at mixing cement; maybe the cracks were their own fault. Quin says maybe so, but when the District was set up all those years back, it took responsibility for *all* head gate boxes, no matter what religion they were. And he wanted this one fixed before another drop was counted against Darl Sebright's allotment. Criswall says why should the District lay out all that money on labor and concrete for one crumbly old head gate when it was going to get torn out anyway soon as the pipe was laid.

And when was *that* going to happen?

In the very near future. Criswall must have loved saying that.

Quin says we're just talking a patch-job, so why not authorize a few bags of ready-mix off the pallet in the storage shed and he'll fix the head gate himself. No dice, mister. As far as the leak, it was use it or lose it.

So Darl stops in the middle of baling hay, hitches up his ditcher, and digs a ditch from the leaky head gate, right across the hay stubble, smack through the middle of his field, all the way down to twenty acres of beans that got their water from a different head gate. Use the leak water on the beans, and send *their* ration somewhere else. Or add to it. That Darl is no dummy. Truth is, the leak didn't amount to all that much extra, not at first. But it was too much to have counted against you in a dry year. I can see that.

The thing is, the leak didn't even matter during July. Darl and everybody else on the Loop was drawing all the water they had coming just to try to make a crop before their allotments ran out. And hot and dry like you wouldn't believe. *Pray For Rain* signs started popping up all over the place. I heard, in stake conference right after the Fourth, President Millard P. Vanderfisk asked everybody to fast and pray for a tempering of the elements. Dry as it was and edgy as the farmers were getting, I thought about doing it myself. Couldn't hurt. I even went to priesthood meeting one Sunday. First time in who knows how long. Almost thirty years doing this, and this drought was as bad as I've ever seen. I know the Mormons weren't the only ones talking about it in church, as a sign of the times, as a consequence of sin and all, and I'm not being partial here. But it *was* on the night of their pioneer celebration, the twenty-fourth of July, that we had the only soaking rain we got all summer.

Next day or so, the whole District Board took a trip to the reservoir, got their picture in the paper, with a quote from Vanderfisk saying the rain had lifted spirits and maybe broken the drought to boot. He said he was optimistic. Quin said there was nothing to be optimistic about. His farmers were hurting, were maybe not getting the allotment they had coming. He wanted to measure the flow where the Loop came off the big canal, double-check the hash marks, maybe raise the big gate just a hair.

No dice again. Criswall tells him to leave the measuring to the Board and if the gate on the canal flume is tampered with in any way, he'll personally see him thrown in jail. Quin asks is everybody else in the valley getting cut back. Criswall says other allotments are none of his business. Quin said maybe the commissioner would feel different, which at least got him in to see Vanderfisk. But all Vanderfisk could say was how sorry he was, but the day-to-day managing of allotments came under the duties of the vice-commissioner.

I told Quin he ought to back off, for his own good. That's when he asked me—and he was a little short about it—did my farmers have enough water. Apples and oranges. My laterals are all pipe now. With pipe, you don't lose any water to evaporation and ditch bank vegetation. That's what I told him. Same thing Vanderfisk has said all along. It was a bad summer to be getting your water from an open lateral and head gates fifty years old.

By the first of August the main canal was way down. Every issue of the *Balford Clarion* ran articles about the water level up at the reservoir. Beets, corn, beans—all at the crucial stage in their development. Vanderfisk said some belt-tightening was inevitable in a year like this, but he estimated that seventy or eighty percent of the crops would still be okay. He said cooperation had pulled the valley through hard times before, and it would do it again.

That was just before Darl Sebright's allotment ran out, which was on August third. I remember that. I know Mill Vanderfisk good enough to know he would've given Darl another week or ten days, but the whole valley was watching was he going to bend the rule, and for who? For Criswall, big as he was on showing spine, it was the chance of a career. August third he calls me in real early to the District office, before anybody else gets there. He says he knows I'm tight with Quin, despite our differing religious beliefs, but sure hopes I won't let that cloud my judgment. So I say, What judgment? He says if he was in my shoes, looking at retirement with a clean record, he sure wouldn't want to be anywhere close to anybody pulling a dumb stunt. I said I didn't think there was any dumb stunt going to be pulled. And if there was, I didn't know anything about it. He says he's sure glad to hear that.

That same morning Criswall issued Quin three padlocks for three head gates, said if he wanted a sheriff along, all he had to do was say so. Quin said why, did somebody expect gunplay? Nobody could've thought that was very funny. These farmers get pretty crazy watching their crops shrivel. You never know. Even a nice guy like Darl Sebright might grab a rifle and see just how rough the District was going to play.

Lucky for everybody, it didn't come to that. Quin drove to each head gate and locked it shut. Then he shook Darl's hand, said he was sorry as could be, which I'd say too, and that was that. No quotes or pictures in the newspaper. The water just quit running. The paper did ask Vanderfisk if any allotments had expired and what was the District's response. He said everything was being done according to District policy. What else are you going to say? It wasn't like Darl was ruined. He harvested *some* winter wheat, green-chopped the barley for silage, and he had the hay. And I heard he had some crop insurance.

After my huddle with Criswall, I was grateful Quin saw fit to do his job and leave it at that. But I'd be lying to say it didn't surprise me, him putting on the padlocks and suddenly clamming up, even to me. Just like that, not another word about how he hated us having to pass a death sentence on a farmer's crops, how the big bosses ought to be doing their own dirty work. It wasn't like him. So I started wondering was this whole deal as shipshape as it looked. It took me a few days, but I finally figured it out.

It was the leak. In six weeks' time, with all the praying and predictions and looking for rain clouds, everybody forgot the leak. Everybody, I imagine, except Quin and Darl. And a funny thing happened. The leak got a lot bigger. I know because when everybody was in sacrament meeting the next Sunday, I drove over to the Loop and saw for myself. From the road, even with the burned-up second cutting of alfalfa only up about knee-high, somebody just driving by couldn't hardly make out that little ditch across Darl's field, let alone how much water was in it. Pretty clever, really. And even if you could see the water, how would you know, without an eye for such things, how much ground it could keep wet? How about enough for a field of pintos way down below the road and out of sight—the pods just starting to fill out and stripe? The leak wouldn't have been near big enough to start with, but with a little coaxing? How hard would it be to wedge a digging bar in a crack in the bottom of an old head gate box? And who's going to see any sign of such as long as water's running through that box just fine, on back to the main canal?

Whoever did it, it's hard to blame him. Even if it wasn't Quin, he had to know about it. And knowing about it could look just as bad as doing it. If I'd just stayed away from the Loop that morning, maybe gone to church myself, I would've been okay. But there I was. And I know a quarter foot of water when I see it. Quin had to figure, as much as Criswall stays holed up by the air-conditioner this time of year, it would be weeks maybe, maybe never, before he found out.

Unless somebody told him.

Thirty years! Who's going to risk that over a field of beans covered by good insurance? And I didn't say a word about the *size* of the leak or my idea how it got to be that way. And nobody ever questioned it. To do what he did later, Criswall must've found out. But he didn't find out from me. Not that part, anyway.

On that particular morning, just the using of the leak was enough. Criswall blew a gasket, which sort of surprised me there, too. I got to tell you, I was half-expecting a pat on the back. Good job, Eb. You sure know which side you're bread is buttered on. But instead he acts half-miffed, like maybe I've been holding out on him. We're sitting there in his office, before anybody else has showed up on Monday morning, and he grabs the phone, calls around until he finds someplace open to send out a truck with a yard of concrete. Then he calls the yard foreman and orders a crew and equipment out to the Loop ASAP to plug a leak in a head gate box. And he tells me to get out there myself and show them which box, that he'll be along in a while. That's Criswall for you. And I'm just leaving his office, just had opened the door, when he says, "We'll pour the whole damn box full if we have to."

And there's Mill Vanderfisk standing right around the corner. He says, "Full of what, Tom?"

If you want the man's job someday, you about got to tell him. Then Vanderfisk says it's one thing to enforce a shut-down on an official allotment; it's another to waste water just to go by the book. He says as long as he's still commissioner, Darl Sebright can use whatever's leaking from a District head gate. And he reminds Criswall whose idea it was not to spend money fixing that very one. He says, "So you can call off the cavalry, Tom." He had all kinds of spine that morning. He says if people think he's favoring a fellow Mormon, so be it.

But they couldn't hardly say that with Quin in the picture. If anybody had done any favoring of Mormon farmers on the Loop, it was him. Vanderfisk had Criswall on this one. With the head gate already locked, you could be pretty sure nobody was going to give the District much flak over that leak. Unless the big boys downstream were feeling some pinch—which they weren't—it wouldn't have mattered how much that leak was letting by. Not when it meant the District could enforce policy and have a heart at the same time.

And you can bet Quin had figured on all this.

And that was the whole story until Darl goes out early to move the water on his rescued beans a couple of weeks later. It's just getting light, and he thinks maybe his eyes are playing tricks because it looks like a big patch of his field is turning brown. He doesn't know what else to do but call Quin. Quin right away knows it's something in the water, but nobody else on the Loop or below is reporting anything wrong. So he starts making calls, six o'clock on a Sunday morning, catches Vanderfisk just before he leaves for another long day of meetings at the stake center. And he gets on his truck radio and calls me. In an hour he's got Millard P. in his suit and tie, Criswall in a tee shirt and pajama bottoms, and the eighteen-year-old driver of the sprayer rig hiking a third of a mile through grass and thistle to get to the top of Darl's field. There we are, staring at five acres of crop that Napalm couldn't have killed any deader.

Criswall says, "And this couldn't have waited until tomorrow?"

Vanderfisk's nodding that nod of his, and he says, "Not by the looks of it, Tom."

Then Mill Vanderfisk asks the kid was he working over this way last evening. The kid starts to sweat, takes a long time to say, yeah, but he wasn't the only one. Vanderfisk says he understands that. He says, "I'm just after some straight answers, son." Then he says he's got one real important question for him. He says he needs to know where did they flush their tank.

That was some moment of silence. You should've seen that kid's face. And Criswall's was even better. They were looking back and forth at each other, back and forth. Finally the kid points back to the road, and off we go across Darl's hay field, suit and pajamas, hiking back to the head gate. If he'd just flushed in the main lateral, which was the easiest place, the spray would've probably got diluted long before it made it down to the big farmers. So if he's wanting to be done and get home, why hop the head gate and drag that hose an extra twenty feet, just to let it drain into Darl's little ditch? He said he thought it was a waste ditch and harmless. He says, "It was an honest mistake, I swear it."

Then Vanderfisk faces Darl, says he's sorry as he's ever been in ten years in this job. Then he asks does he have insurance on the beans. Darl says, yeah, some. Vanderfisk says to let him know how it goes with the adjuster because he wants to make this mistake one hundred percent right with him. That's how they left it. Then for a little while we all just stood there by the head gate listening to water leak out of the box. A quarter foot makes a pretty good sucking noise, and Vanderfisk heard it just like the rest of us.

By September most farmers had survived the drought and were worried now about harvest and an early frost. Meantime the newspaper had got wind of the leak and the killed beans. Criswall told us ditch riders not to say anything, to refer all inquiries to the District front office. Mill Vanderfisk told the paper his goal was open communication and cooperation. But this time it was going to take more than a quote to smooth things over. There started to be some pretty loud demands for somebody to pay up for the District's mistake. And I don't mean in money. People get in a certain mood, it doesn't matter if they know pintos from potatoes. They want somebody fired. And it's a heck of a trick how that somebody is decided on.

Vanderfisk would've made good on his offer to Darl. I'm sure of it. But Darl let it go, and not just because he's a good guy.

I'm pretty sure our friend Criswall had a chat with him about how stealing water is a felony and using it is no better. Just like the chat with Vanderfisk when the paper's snooping made it a whole lot easier to hear how that leak probably got to be so big. All Quin would say was how maybe somebody prayed it bigger. Criswall said whoever was responsible had a lot more important things to pray about now.

Mill Vanderfisk was in another one of his no-win situations. Since he didn't want to see the law involved in an allotment violation, he had to feed the paper the only angle he had, which was negligence on Quin's part in regard to the killed beans. Ditch riders do take an oath, by the way—to safeguard the natural resource in their charge and the interests of those it is intended to benefit. The funny thing is, Quin actually took it serious, and he's the one they fired. All I can say is I hope they have pipe laterals up around Billings. He deserves them.

And come Thursday night, I guess I'll head over to the stake center to see what President Mill Vanderfisk wants. I'll be brotherly, but I don't plan any confession, no baring of *this* soul. Yes, sir. No, sir. I'm not sure on that one, sir. It's one of those deals where you can't say much without digging yourself in deeper, and with fifty-eight days left, I'm already in about as deep as I want to go.

# The Darlington Girls

Exactly when—and why—the neighbor boys stopped coming by, which Sunday afternoon they didn't show for Chinese checkers and popcorn, Flynn Darlington could not have said.

"Where's Russell these days?" he asked Marcene, the oldest of his four daughters, one afternoon in late September of her eighteenth year. "I haven't seen him in a while."

She didn't answer. With a book in one hand, she half-sat, half-lay on the sofa in the living room, a bare foot resting on one of its arms. In fact, Russell had slipped away from a tug-of-war on the Sunday evening before school started, a month earlier, and hadn't been back since.

"Where's Bart and that cousin of his?" asked Flynn, who had taught social studies at Balford Junior High School for almost twenty years. "Where's old Ruth-less?"

"Nobody calls her that anymore," Marcene said.

"*I* do. Why don't you holler at Gayla and Dee—they're around here somewhere—and get up a game of kick-the-can? Susie's got half a dozen kids out back right now. You can have a weenie roast in the orchard afterward. I'll make fudge."

"Susie's seven years old, Daddy. Gayla and DeeBeth don't *want* to play kick-the-can with her friends. And neither do I."

"Bart might take a little coaxing—he's more a chess man—

but Russell will come running if you promise him fudge." Flynn ran a finger up the sole of the bare foot. "*Call* them. The day's wasting."

"Let it go, Flynn," his wife said from the other room.

"We've got a neighborhood gang breaking apart here, Artelle. I can't give up without a fight."

Flynn looked at Marcene. The ticking of the mantle clock punctuated the sound of children playing in the yard behind the old house, between the garden and orchard on one side and five acres of pasture on the other—all that was left of his father's homestead just outside Balford, Wyoming.

"I make awful good fudge," said the only son of an only son.

• • •

No classmate or adult in the little town could have disputed the merits of the Darlington girls. In preparation for bright futures—whose promise of marriage and motherhood they never doubted—the girls refined their minds and hands. They read constantly, studied hard, earned high marks; they cooked and canned, sewed and scrubbed, planted and weeded and picked. They were kind and chaste. On top of all that, they were musically gifted. Many a sacrament service featured Flynn and his daughters singing as a group, and Artelle's piano accompaniment was often supplemented by one of the girls on her flute or viola. Hardly a week passed without an invitation to perform at someone's wedding reception. Flynn often joked, as he announced yet another special musical number, that he got a little tired of his tenor being so far outnumbered.

Yet, for all their merits, his daughters lacked the one that mattered most to boys. Not once during high school did a male caller wish to do anything more than verify the starting time of the Mutual cookout or ask for homemade brownies for the next French Club meeting. When Susie answered the phone on such occasions, she yelled, "Marcie, it's Prince Charming!" or "Gayla, it's your true love!"

"Who is it? What does he want?"

"I couldn't catch all of it," Susie liked to say with solemn pauses, "but I think he wants your hand in holy matrimony."

Only Flynn found this as funny as freckle-faced Sue Ellen Darlington, the youngest, the one born after he thought his quiver was full, the one he expected to sweeten his old age.

"My teeth are straight enough," Susie said once when her two oldest sisters were wearing braces. "And I don't have a hairy mole on my face."

"Costly cosmetics or no," Flynn said, "it's what's inside that counts."

After seeing what a dermatologist in Billings could do to a facial mole, DeeBeth began to brood about several others located well below the modest necklines her parents enforced.

"That's just *not* something you need to be worrying about," Artelle said.

"At least not until your honeymoon," Gayla said.

"Shush," Artelle said.

"Your husband will love you, moles and all," Flynn said. "That's part of the deal."

On her sixteenth birthday, DeeBeth, like her two older sisters before her, received a book entitled *Dating—An Eternal Perspective*. And, like her two older sisters, she left for BYU two years later without ever having a chance to act on the author's two hundred pages of advice. During residence in the dorm and the first two or three college apartments, her book, like theirs, went from nightstand to unpacked milk crate to closet. Then her book, like theirs, stopped making the trip to Provo altogether and ended up in a box in Flynn's garage. That's where it was when Marcene took a job as a pharmacist in Ogden. That's where it was when Gayla left for her mission in New Zealand. And that's where it was when DeeBeth, home just after graduation, mentioned that a guy from her student ward might stop by the next Friday evening on his way to a family reunion in Sheridan.

"His name's *Blair*, Daddy, not Blake."

"I like Blake better," Susie said. "It sounds more masculine."

"A name has nothing to do with masculinity," Flynn said.

"He *is* a boy, isn't he?" Susie asked.

On Friday evening, the Darlingtons delayed their dinner. For the tenth time, Artelle looked in the oven. "This roast has about had it," she said, prodding with a long fork. She pulled off her oven mitt and tossed it beside the saucepan full of shriveled green beans.

"He's not coming," DeeBeth said.

"Old Blair-Blake may surprise us yet."

"I'll be surprised if I don't die of starvation," Susie said.

"He would've called."

Artelle sighed and said, "That was going to be such a lovely roast."

"I really am going to die if we don't eat *something*."

"We can save him a plate."

"He's not coming, Daddy."

• • •

During Susie's last two years of high school, the Darlingtons still sang in sacrament meetings whenever they were all together. During that period, Flynn grew less and less comfortable in front of the congregation, more and more conscious of the boyfriends and fiancés and husbands his three oldest daughters didn't have. More than once he said, "We really do need some more male voices in this choir." In time, he passed on his announcing duties to Artelle or Gayla or whoever would agree to the arrangement, and stood behind the rest. Gradually he stopped joining them altogether and retreated to a back pew, where he was easily distracted by couples holding hands, the light caress of slender fingers across wide shoulders, young mothers cradling infants.

By the time Susie got to BYU, with her copy of *Dating—An Eternal Perspective*, Flynn was facing facts. Unlike her older sisters, she had been on one date in high school, albeit an arranged dinner with her cousin's brother-in-law. But otherwise, the wit and cheer and sociability Flynn cherished in her had, like her sisters' virtues, gone uncherished by young men.

"What's the matter with them?" he had asked his wife when another prom season came and went with no invitation. "Are they just plain blind?"

"No," Artelle said, "they're boys."

Just before they said good-bye to Susie outside her dormitory, Flynn felt to speak in a way he hadn't spoken to her sisters at this threshold into a world of student wards and lovesick roommates and an endless round of pairing off and engagement and marriage. "At college," he said, "things are different. People are a lot more likely to see you for who you are." He hugged her to him, kept his eyes closed tight against tears. "But you've got to let yourself be known, Sweetie. I want you to get out and meet people . . . some nice boys, go on a few dates."

"I'm eighteen, Dad. You're making me sound like an old maid."

Artelle patted her husband's arm, tried to ease the soberness of his tone with the artificial playfulness of hers. "For heaven's sake, Flynn, let her get settled first. There'll be plenty of time for all that."

Eight semesters, in fact. But hardly any dates. At home for the summer before her first year teaching high school chorus in Springville, Utah, Susie endured a brief frenzy of interest from a guy named Kip, just back from his mission in Tonga. Although some at church felt a Darlington girl had better take what she could get, this Kip had little to recommend him besides a frankness about his libido. Susie didn't particularly like him, and even Flynn had to admit the boy was a poor gamble. As it turned out, though, all related concern was unfounded. Two weeks after Kip tried to kiss Susie on the collarbone, he proposed marriage to an eighteen-year-old from Cowley.

She accepted.

• • •

In early October of Susie's second year of teaching high school chorus, an unseasonably heavy rain found a leak in the roof of the Darlingtons' old house. Reasoning as a man facing retirement with four unmarried daughters, Flynn convinced himself that a leaky roof might somehow deter suitors. So fixing that leak became an obsession that tar-patching wasn't going to satisfy. The whole thing needed to be re-shingled at the first opportunity. Fall break fell on Thursday and Friday. Those two days, supplemented by three from his huge surplus of personal leave, would give him that whole week. With a week and some hired help, he wouldn't have to bother with a contractor. He was sixty-four, but, he assured Artelle, he could still swing a hammer.

"So where you going to get this help?" she asked one morning at breakfast.

"I've got former students all over the valley," Flynn said. "I'll find somebody." He paused. "And maybe Susie can help some. She's off that same Friday, said she's coming home."

"Maybe Sue has other plans."

"Like what?" Flynn asked. "Tell me what Susie's got planned. I'd like to know."

They sat at the old table, eating toast with cocoa. One wall of the dining room served as a gallery for photographs of progenitors, cousins, nieces and nephews with their spouses and ever-multiplying numbers of children, and, above them all, large single portraits of their four daughters.

"Listen to me, Flynn. A lot of girls—married and changing diapers—would trade places with her in a minute, would *love* to have the chances she's had. Studying in Europe, master's degree by age twenty-three, has a good job in a good place, a principal singing her praises all the time, drives a nice car, flew to Hawaii last summer . . ."

He nodded listlessly.

"Life is full for her."

"Well, we say that," Flynn said, "because what else *can* we say?"

"She can't be holding her breath, Flynn Darlington, for something that'll happen in its own sweet course. You can't pressure these things."

"Maybe not, but I *know* the Lord wants Susie married. Her patriarchal blessing says so."

"And he wants our others single? Their blessings say the same thing."

"No, no. That's not what I mean. I mean, if he wants her married, there must be a guy out there for her. No more Blakes and Blairs. No more Kips. I mean a *good* returned missionary— somebody who deserves her and will take her to the temple. And there's got to be a way to find him."

"Hadn't you better leave such a way to Sue?"

Although, outwardly, Flynn went along with his wife, he was already persuaded that a new roof was some kind of helpful first step toward the blessings still awaiting his youngest daughter. Taking that step, however, presented an obstacle he hadn't figure on. Ordering a load of shingles was easy enough, but finding somebody to help get them on the roof wasn't. Every likely hand was either in school or busy in the beet harvest. So Flynn ran an ad in the *Balford Clarion: Roofing help needed, week of Oct. 14.* As of the Sunday before the scheduled week, only one person had responded: a disabled war veteran who wondered if there was any part of the job that could be done without climbing on a roof.

"No, it can't wait until spring," Flynn told Artelle. "Somebody will show."

Monday morning dawned clear and, more important to roof walking, frostless. Already wearing a nail apron, as if to will that Somebody into the yard, Flynn circled the house, studying the roof from many angles. Then he re-counted the rolls of tar paper and bundles of shingles waiting in the garage.

Just as he stepped back in the house to start down the telephone list of roofing contractors, a faded white van pulled into the drive carrying an extension ladder on its cargo rack. The driver sat for a long time, then got out. He surveyed the orchard, the barn and corral, the old house; he adjusted and readjusted the cap on his head. Standing on the porch, Flynn waited for the gaze to sweep his way.

Finally, the young man strode forward, approached the bottom porch step, and swallowed hard. He was lanky and sober-faced, with a pointed Adam's apple.

"I'm Lyle Brimhall—here about the ad."

Even that much disclosure seemed to tax him. His face and throat contorted when he spoke, as if utterance pained him.

"The roof? You bet!" Flynn hurried down the steps, shook the young man's hand, then held it as he mused. "Brimhall, Brimhall, Brimhall. You must be Mormon."

Lyle Brimhall's eyes grew wide, and he pulled his hand free. "I suppose so," he said. "I ain't been to church in a coon's age."

Flynn snapped his fingers. "Over by Star Valley. Sure. A whole clan of Brimhalls."

"I don't know anything about that," Lyle Brimhall said. "I'm from Garland."

"Garland will do. I'd about given up on anybody from anywhere." Flynn patted Lyle Brimhall's shoulder, an action the young man watched with the eyes of a flighty horse. "You're hired."

On the roof, holding a hammer, square shovel, and pry bar, Lyle Brimhall surveyed the expanse of weathered asbestos shingles, the hips and valleys, the sparrow droppings clotted in a gable recess. It occurred to Flynn that the recess was formed over thirty years earlier, with the add-on of the utility room.

"Maybe go at it one section at a time?" Flynn said. "I'd hate to get the top off and have a storm come up."

In boots that looked too big for his body, Lyle Brimhall

climbed to the main ridge, straddled it, and stepped solidly along its length, as if testing the collective strength of the rafters. He reached the end of the ridge and started down the east slope.

"But it's up to you," Flynn said to the back of his head just as it dropped out of sight.

By the time Flynn toed his way up to the ridge, Lyle Brimhall was already clawing up shingles around the chimney to expose tar paper and tongue-and-groove sheathing. After a few minutes with the hammer, he grabbed his shovel. With short thrusts, he wedged the blade between shingles and tongue-and-groove, and levered upward. Old roofing tacks popped loose half a dozen at a thrust.

"Looks like your folks raised a worker," Flynn said. He paused long enough to tear a scrap of tar paper from a missed tack, then sidled toward a clarification on which much suddenly rested. "Your wife's a lucky woman."

The handyman didn't say anything.

"A guy as handy as you—shoot, he's bound to be married."

In its thrusting and wedging, the shovel broke rhythm only this one time. Lyle Brimhall's face showed a hybrid of grimace and smile.

"Not hardly," he said with a snort.

• • •

By noon Lyle Brimhall had shed a jacket and two sweatshirts, and the roof's east slope was laid bare. In four hours Flynn had developed a deep admiration for the boy, for the fluidity of his movements, the doggedness of his shovel, the sureness of his footing on tongue-and-groove now strewn with shingle grit. Often Flynn found himself distracted from his own work—pulling missed tacks, sweeping, channeling old shingles to the roof's edge. Though Lyle Brimhall never ventured conversation and more or less ignored everything but the work before him, he seemed even-tempered. Though he was not handsome, he was healthy and vigorous. Though apparently he had not been on a mission, he seemed decent enough.

When the handyman refused Artelle's invitation to eat his lunch in the house, Flynn hurried down the ladder and carried his own food back up so he could catch Lyle Brimhall in a rare moment of relaxation, eating crackers and Vienna Sausages. The day was brilliant. From his perch on the roof, Flynn could make out the topography of the whole Shoshone River valley, could place the Darlington homestead among all the other pioneer homesteads along the river. Sitting atop the roof with a meatloaf sandwich in one hand and a can of orange pop in the other, Flynn felt exuberant. "Whoee!" he blurted. "What a day to be alive. It's hard to beat an Indian summer in Wyoming."

The only acknowledgment the handyman granted was to quicken the pace of his chewing. He was looking in the direction of Jersey Teague's shiny silos and milking parlor across the river and at the Binghams' vast beet fields and at Rowe Sloan's pastureland. From his own angle, Flynn could see all that and the oldest residential section of the little town, including the very house in which the now deceased J. Guyman LeGrand had given the Darlington girls their patriarchal blessings.

"Does wiriness run in your genes?" Flynn asked.

Lyle Brimhall's pointed Adam's apple bobbed deeply with a labored swallow. "I suppose."

"It's funny how heredity works," Flynn said, taking another bite of sandwich.

"Take my Susie, for instance—she's the baby, teaches school down in Utah. Not an ounce of fat on her, could always work and play most boys right into the ground. But a fellow wouldn't want to be fooled by that. She's a lady, too, if you know what I mean—just like her mother. Heredity's a powerful thing."

Chewing the last sausage, Lyle Brimhall held the little aluminum can to his lips, tapped it to dislodge every last bit of packing jelly, every drop of yellowish broth. Then he reached into his cooler and brought out something wrapped in wax paper.

"Say," Flynn said, "somebody sure knows how to make a cake."

Lyle Brimhall actually nodded as he took a first big bite.

"It's a rare woman who'll tackle one from scratch anymore. That's one thing my wife has taught our girls. They can cook, every one of them." Flynn ventured a sidelong glance at the handyman. "Though I have to say, Susie's the best—hardly had to be taught at all. It's heredity, I tell you."

• • •

At dusk on the third day, the autumn twilight shone handsomely on bright flashing, on course after course of new shingle tabs. In three days, they had nearly finished the entire roof. Even on the steepest slope over the utility room, despite having to rent scaffolding, the work went much faster than Flynn had expected.

"You silly man," Artelle had said at breakfast that morning. "Here your roof is all but done, and you're acting half mopey."

He wanted to tell her, to share this glorious new possibility—and his worry that it was going to slip away unless he acted. But he couldn't say anything yet, not after so many such hopes for his daughters had come to nothing. These three days working side by side with Lyle Brimhall had been wonderful, especially the afternoon they drove to the rental place for scaffolding. Standing before the press-wood counter, savoring the gum of tar paper on blisters, Flynn sensed the eyes on him, noted the second glances, the subtle curiosity as the other customers sized up the young and able Lyle Brimhall. So what if he wasn't a churchgoer? Many a man had come back under the influence of a good wife.

And now after crowning the final ridges, after returning the scaffolding and hauling the old shingles to the dump, after three full days to do all this, Flynn was oppressed by only one thought: even figuring for every last touch, he and Lyle Brimhall would finish the job the next morning—Thursday—and Susie wasn't due home until Friday afternoon.

So he took measures.

Long ago, on the far side of the orchard, his father had built a shed—half barn, half orchard storage. Though it had served thirty years without so much as a coat of paint, though the leaks in its cedar shake roof did no harm to the buckets and ladders and apple butter cauldron stored inside, its condition had begun, in the past twenty-four hours, to bother Flynn. So at quitting time on Wednesday, he summoned his courage and said, "I've been thinking about these leftover shingles."

In answer to the proposal of another job, the handyman nodded slowly and said, "I suppose."

"I've tried to keep it to myself," Flynn told his wife that night. "But this is more than happenstance, Artelle. He's going to be here, and Susie's going to be here—same day, same time, same everything. Can you call that happenstance?"

Artelle bit her lower lip, appeared skeptical and encouraged at the same time. "Shouldn't we call Sue and let her in on this happenstance?"

"No, no," Flynn said, waving his hands in protest. "She's likely to stay down in Utah, avoid the whole deal." He paused a long moment. "No, the less we say, the better. If this is meant to be, all we need to do is let nature take its course."

• • •

By quitting time on Friday the orchard shed featured new shingles *and* a fresh coat of paint.

"It looks grand," Flynn said. "You've done marvels for me, Mr. Lyle Brimhall."

The handyman shrugged. Although he was as reticent as ever and his smiles scarce, Flynn sensed a growing bond. Though Lyle Brimhall had thus far refused to join them at the table for breakfast or lunch, he had accepted a fresh cinnamon roll yesterday. And this morning, after some coaxing, he had come onto the porch to eat one of Artelle's bacon and egg sandwiches.

The five o'clock whistle blew at the sugar beet plant in Ralston, its shrillness muted by distance.

The moment was upon them.

"Listen," Flynn said, trying to look and sound and *feel* nonchalant, "why don't you stay for supper? We can settle up after a good meal. I talked to my wife. She put a nice roast in right after lunch. Mashed potatoes and gravy, fruit salad, green beans—the whole works."

The invitation floated, came to rest, incubated a full minute against the drone of beet diggers in distant fields.

Finally—finally—the sober-faced Lyle Brimhall said, "I guess. If it's no bother."

If not for considerable restraint, Flynn Darlington would have flung himself at the handyman and hugged him. "Bother!" he said in a tone of mock chastisement. "You better know we'd love to have you."

Dusk came with a chill breeze. As he drove the orchard road back toward the house in company with this young man of such promise, Flynn was assailed by memories—apple picking, hayrides, capture-the-flag played between pasture dikes, softball with bucket-lid bases, bonfires of windfall branches, the innocent play of girls and boys. Once upon a day and night, once upon a spring and summer, it all had happened here on the Darlington homestead.

"A hot meal will taste good," Flynn said, wiping his eyes and nose on a sleeve as they cleared the orchard, skirted the barn, headed toward the house. Lyle Brimhall shifted in his seat and braced his hands against his knees.

Rounding the pump house, they both saw Susie's car.

Artelle had warned him: *Don't make a big deal out of this, Flynn. Don't get your hopes up.*

"That's my daughter's car," he said, pointing as he coasted his old truck to a stop. "Susie—the one I told you about. Did I mention she was coming home for a couple of days? If we're lucky, she'll have us a cobbler or pie. Or maybe," he said, winking, "a chocolate cake."

Except for flexing his jaw muscle, Lyle Brimhall showed no reaction. He glanced at Flynn, then got out, leaned over the truck's bed, and made as if to gather tools.

"Leave them," Flynn said, hopping out and moving toward the porch. "I'll put them up tomorrow. Let's go eat!"

"I always put my tools away."

"Ah, let them go," Flynn said, beckoning from the base of the porch steps. "It's getting chilly out here, and supper's calling." A new and strange excitement flowed through him. In his haste climbing the steps, he stumbled several times, grasped the worn banister when he reached the top, stood for a moment as if anchoring himself.

Lyle Brimhall approached the steps.

"Come right on," Flynn said, beckoning for the fourth or fifth time, gazing at the porch swing, the dying garden, the aged trees of the orchard, Susie's nice car parked portentously close to the van. The breeze carried a whiff of overripe Winesaps. He said, "Come on in."

Lyle Brimhall reached the porch deck, stepped across it in his boots just as he had stepped along the roof ridge that first morning. As Flynn pushed open the door, the sound of an electric mixer flooded from the kitchen. Again and again the beaters raked the thick glass of the mixing bowl, raked and raked, round and round.

Then stopped. The whole house smelled good.

"We've got hungry men here," Flynn yelled, holding the door wide. "Come on," he said to Lyle Brimhall. "Come on in."

"Come in and wash your hands," Artelle said. "I've fixed us a little bite." Flynn caught her eye and in one conspiratorial instant knew everything had gone as planned—the unobtrusive announcement of the repaired roof, her father out working on the orchard shed with *some guy* he hired, and no mention of the dinner invitation. If Susie asked about the little bite of supper, Artelle was to say they were celebrating her homecoming.

"Sue will be down in a minute," Artelle said, "and then we can eat."

At the utility room sink, Flynn lathered and rinsed his hands, offered the wafer of soap to Lyle Brimhall.

While moving about the kitchen to stir, dab, season, mash, ladle, and pour, Artelle kept up a constant chatter. Among other things, she said, "Sue made one of her cakes."

Flynn dried and re-dried his hands with the clean towel waiting atop the washing machine. Contentment stung his heart, and he could not resist winking again at Lyle Brimhall, tossing the towel to him with a little flourish of familiarity. Lyle Brimhall caught the towel clumsily, his Adam's apple twitching.

"Take off your hat and relax," Flynn said. "Just put it anywhere."

"Let's eat," Artelle said. She stepped lightly into the dining room and back, in and back, loading the table with a cloth-lined basket of hot rolls, a gravy boat, a clear glass pitcher of water with lemon slices floating among the ice cubes.

Flynn reached toward his guest to guide him through the kitchen doorway. "Let's eat, son." The young man's fingers gripped, in passing, the door frame, counter and sink edge, refrigerator handle, the padded back of a stool. And then the two of them were standing in the dining room and photo gallery featuring the Darlington girls.

"Are you about ready, Sweetie?" Flynn yelled up the stairway. "Come and get it while it's hot."

When the muffled reply came, he beamed at their guest. "A week to remember—huh, Mr. Brimhall?"

Steam curled upward from half a dozen different platters and servers on the table, gave the light in the dining room an odd liquid quality. Before Lyle Brimhall could flex a throat or jaw muscle this time, the door of an upstairs bedroom opened, and she was coming down the stairs. Flynn smiled so widely his face ached.

Then they saw each other, Sue Darlington and Lyle Brimhall, and they knew the dinner for what it was. And in the moment of their realization, a peculiar and awful awkwardness settled in the room like a fetidness mingling with the food smells.

Artelle smiled bravely, offered fair warning that the rolls were a little too done, the roast a bit dry, kept gesturing as if to shoo the others to their seats. Even as Flynn smiled, his hands shook. In a fog of timidity and inexperience and wordlessness, they all looked at each other. Finally, it was Lyle Brimhall who spoke.

"I got to go," he said, his gaze ricocheting from face to face, from photo to photo on the wall, as if he couldn't look anywhere without coming under the serene scrutiny of a Darlington girl.

"Just stay and eat a bite," Artelle said, pointing to the food. "At least you have time to eat, don't you?"

"No, ma'am, I don't suppose," Lyle Brimhall said, backing toward the kitchen. "It's nice of you to offer, but I'll be late."

Only gradually did Flynn's smile relax. "Late for what?" he asked.

With just a hint of shortness, Lyle Brimhall said, "I've got a date. I promised my girlfriend I'd take her to a movie."

The change that came over Susie's face then was worse than accusation. Her eyes flashed, just once, in Flynn's direction before she left the room.

"I owe you a week's wages," Flynn said, following Lyle Brimhall through the kitchen. "We can settle up after we eat." He heard Susie's feet on the stairs. "That's what I had in mind."

"Pay him," Artelle said, grabbing her purse from the kitchen counter. She rummaged, handed Flynn the checkbook. "Don't make him late for his date."

Lyle Brimhall stopped in the utility room, snatched up his cap, settled it on his head like a helmet. "It's been nice of you," he said, staring at the checkbook.

"Pay him," Artelle said.

With trembling fingers Flynn wrote the check, folded the rectangle of paper along its perforation, tore it clumsily from the pad. All the while, he kept talking. "You're missing good eats, son," he said. "You really are. That cake is hard to beat."

Lyle Brimhall took the check, mumbled all the same apologies again, and with several long strides, cleared the back door and was gone. At the sound of oversized boots on porch steps and gravel driveway, what could Flynn's wife do but look at the author of another spoiled supper, then go try to make things right with their youngest daughter?

For a long time on this Friday evening in the fall of his sixty-fifth year, Flynn Darlington stood motionless beneath his watertight roof. Long enough to follow the fading shifts of the van's automatic transmission out on the road. Long enough to overhear Artelle upstairs, saying through a closed door, "Sue? Sue, let me explain, Honey. Please." And long enough to synchronize the drip of the old utility room faucet with the tick-tick-tick of the cooling oven.

# Reap in Mercy

On a morning in late July, six months after banker Frett Maxwell Jr. said, "It's no longer a paying proposition, Earl," a big pickup from Bingham Farms pulled into the yard. Through the open kitchen window, Earl Haws watched the driver get out, heard the truck's door latch. For a while the driver, Winn Bingham, stood studying the old log shop, pumphouse, fuel tanks, and the hand-clutch Case tractor and several steel-wheeled implements parked against the long wall of the empty calving shed—the only machinery spared in the auction five months earlier.

The squeak of the screen door against the strange quiet of the yard's workday idleness seemed to catch Winn Bingham off guard, and his greeting came out too exuberant.

"Hey, hey, Earlie. Did I catch you enjoying retirement?"

Earl closed the distance between them so as not to have to match his neighbor's volume. "It's not all it's cracked up to be," he said, hesitating only an instant before extending his hand. Unaided by the setting and habit of priesthood meeting in the Balford Ward of the Garland Wyoming Stake, the gesture felt strange.

There had been no dew. In a field not so far distant, Winn Bingham's wheat combines were cutting their first swaths of the day. Already a haze of dust and chaff rose in the fresh sky.

"You went and rented to somebody else," Winn said with his peculiar smile-frown, "which I wish you'd explain to me sometime. But maybe I can talk you into helping me now."

Earl waited, curious. He knew that, in the house, Ruby also waited—curious.

"The wheat's just starting," Winn said, "and after that, beans. And with the late spring we'll likely be in the beets until November." He looked toward the combines, then back again. "That's a lot of trucking, Earl."

From that day on, Earl never could decide how much that last line was intended as an acknowledgment of Winn's need or a presumption of his own.

"What are you stewing about it for?" Ruby said at supper. "It's a job. That's what you wanted." She set a saucer of pie and ice cream on top of the want ads he was reading, and sat down beside him. "Six-fifty an hour is a whole lot better than nothing. And right now, that's what you *need*."

"Something to buy the grub with," Frett Jr. had said as part of his advice last winter about "securing" off-farm employment.

"In the Marines," Earl said, browsing the ads, "we passed a physical and the job was waiting for us in Korea. But now, sixty years old, I'm stuck selling Avon, assembling products in my home, doing other people's taxes."

"You're sixty-one, and you'd have to learn to do your own first."

Earl took a bite of pie, said absently, "I always figured by this time I'd be helping one of my own kids farm the place. Some sons still come back and do that, you know. Look at Emery Bingham. Him and his old man must be tending three thousand acres."

"You could have rented to them, Earl," she said softly. "Winn offered you a lot more than you're getting."

"Winn Bingham? Farming *my* place?" He shook his head. "I just couldn't find it in me."

Sitting in the same mealtime proximity they had shared for

most of four decades, Ruby placed her hand on his arm, said, "Are you sure that's the only thing you couldn't find in you?"

He set his fork down. "I'll say this for Emery Bingham. At least he didn't go off to college a dozen years more than any normal person needs and outsmart his testimony and dive off the deep end—taking wife and kids with him. And now look at him. A bishop. *My* bishop."

Ruby's hand slid atop his and squeezed. "Lyndon's a grown man, Earl. We did the best we could."

Earl looked into her bright, unblinking gray eyes and said, "Bad as it is, that's not the worst of it—wondering how I went wrong."

Still she didn't blink.

"The worst is trying to figure how Winn went right."

• • •

On leave after boot camp in the fall of 1951, in the last days of stationary threshers, Earl climbed on the bean wagon hitched to his dad's McCormick tractor and hunkered cold all the way to the rocky, sloping acreage Arvy Bingham had homesteaded on the river rim in 1914. By the time the bean wagon crossed the old tile culvert and rolled into the thirty-five-acre field at daybreak, most of the rigs pledged in the last priesthood meeting had arrived.

Two months shy of his twentieth birthday, Earl looked at the overripe beans and at the hayracks and wagons there to help harvest them, and remarked to his dad, "It's comforting to see some things never change."

"He's our neighbor," said Foley Haws. "How about we just lend the hand we can lend and keep our judgments to ourselves?"

In a show of county-fair nostalgia (as opposed to any serious intention to haul beans), stake high councilor A. Frett Maxwell and a drowsy fifteen-year-old Frett Jr. pulled up sitting high on the seat of a bright red wagon drawn by a team of parade mules.

"Sorry I'm late," said Big Frett, whose recent profits from banking and real estate would have filled his parade wagon several times over. "I had a buyer waiting all night in my driveway. War is hell," he added in his booming voice, "but that last one sure was good for business."

Later, with the dew burned off and the thresher receiving the morning's loads one by one, Earl stayed with Winn Bingham out in the field piling beans. On this particular day in the fall of 1951, Winn was especially conscious of his piling skill and kept kidding Earl. "You're rusty, boy. You maybe can handle an M-1—maybe—but you've sure forgot how to work a pitchfork."

Throughout the long morning, he came behind Earl, scrutinized every pile, offered little bits of advice. "Just go with the fork, Earl. Don't fight it." All this amid profane comments on boot-camp haircuts, on the effects of saltpeter on beard growth and libido, on his own enviable sexual exploits over the past three months. And all *this* around a cud of wintergreen snuff tucked deep along his jaw, unnoticeable until he spat.

By mid-afternoon, Earl had suffered all the coaching and competition and digs he cared to suffer. "So what about you?" he asked finally. Winn was twenty-four and never had served a day in the military, not even the Reserves.

Winn nudged the toe of his boot with one of the pitchfork tines. "Flat feet," he said. "The mighty military doesn't want me." Then his restless fork stopped. They were standing at the far end of the field, the distant thresher hardly audible. Still, he looked around as if for eavesdroppers before he whispered, "But if the Lord will have me, I'm going on a mission pretty soon."

During Earl Haws's long winter in Korea, that was a centerpiece of the news from home, Winn and the mission he was going on pretty soon. Every letter reported reformed habits, increased conviction. Beer, tobacco, promiscuity—all behind him now. While Earl froze behind the steering wheel, running resupply through the Suipchon Valley, Winn prepared to serve the Lord. He bought a suit and set of scriptures with his name—*Winn P. Bingham*—embossed on the front covers, impressed sacrament meeting and fireside audiences with his testimony, attended two or three going-away parties held in his honor.

But all the build-up and preparation ended one February morning in 1953 when, at his wife's bidding, Arvy Bingham left a plate of hot scrambled eggs to take the full swill bucket out to the pigs. The eggs grew cold, then hard. That's when Winn went out and found his father slumped over the long trough.

Weeks later, across an ocean, mail call brought news of Arv's heart attack and funeral. According to the letter from Earl's mother, Etha Bingham blamed herself and told anyone who would listen that the swill could have waited. Her only comfort was having Winn home. Keeping him home, Sister Bingham claimed, was God's compensation for this great loss in their lives. And, she said, in its own way, fulfilling his obligations at home was as much a mission as any he might have gone on. So, in answer to a thousand well-meant queries, twenty-five-year-old Winn bravely said he planned to work the farm and carry on.

• • •

When Earl got out of the service in late May of 1954, the nightmare of Bunker Hill was almost two years behind him, and worries closer to home soon supplanted it.

Earlier that spring, Foley Haws had forgotten to take a water bag when he went back to burning weeds after dinner, and worked in the heat and smoke all afternoon without a drink. It was a very minor stroke, the doctor said—if there was such a thing for a man of sixty-two. The episodes of garbled speech would come less and less frequently; the headaches would ease. But he couldn't stay in the sun, couldn't ride a tractor for any length of time. And hand work was out of the question.

"Why didn't you tell me?" Earl asked twenty minutes after he climbed off the bus in Garland to meet a mother whose purse hung from her wrist like a weight and a father who had aged ten years in three.

It was late in the planting season. But Earl drove tractor until after dark every night, followed his furrow or disc markings with one murky lamp mounted on the McCormick's fender. Aside from church, he didn't go anywhere, didn't socialize, certainly didn't play guest of honor at firesides. In just seven days he had the beans in and was all set to cut the alfalfa before it turned rank.

But, as he was soon to find out, his parents weren't the only ones who had lived through a hard spring.

On the morning Earl planned to start mowing, the very moment he was riveting the last new cutter section onto the sickle bar, Winn Bingham chugged into the yard in a battered pickup, rolled to a stop, and sat a long time behind the wheel. When finally he shouldered open the badly dented door, he had one message:

"I'm in a bind, Earl. I'm in a terrible bind."

• • •

The frequency of that refrain over the next three years made it no easier to hear—with reference to tardy plowing, planting, haying, cultivating.

"How can I ever thank you?" Winn said over and over, season after season. "I'll get my feet under me one of these days."

It was right to help a neighbor. Still, Earl would have preferred to be somewhere else when the other men turned to him on Sunday mornings, wondering what could be done for Brother Bingham. In those meetings, Winn was cast as the lone son, still grieving, and now bound to look after his widowed mother and the farm—soldiering on gamely, courageously, admirably.

The brethren in the quorum didn't know the whole story. As a farmer, Arv Bingham had been forever behind, but at least he worked at his livelihood. And he lived his religion. Not Winn. Even in summer, he seldom got out before ten o'clock, devoted his meager labors to ill-timed, soon-forgotten projects. In several years he managed to dig one hole for a pair of clothesline posts, paint two sides of a barn, reinforce three legs of a weather-ruined picnic table.

And it wasn't grief and obligation weighing him down, but drinking and tom-catting—the same entertainments he had enjoyed in high school and most likely never abandoned even during the time he talked of going on a mission. Only now, Winn was pushing thirty, and the consequences of his choices went beyond tearful confessions in the occasional testimony meeting. Aside from Widow Bingham and the hired hand Eugenio, Earl was the only other person living with those consequences between Sundays. And his charity began to fail.

• • •

Ten days of rain in the middle of bean harvest, September 1957, persuaded Earl and Ruby to go ahead and get married instead of waiting until November.

"Wise move," the stake president said when he signed Earl's temple recommend. "You're what—twenty-six? Why risk improprieties at this point?"

When they got home on Sunday evening from their one-day honeymoon in Jackson Hole, his parents' house was dark. Tentatively opening the front door, they were met with the smells of fresh paint and bleach cleanser. Earl flipped on a light. Other than essentials—ice box, cookstove, table and chairs, couch, rocker—the place was empty; forty years' worth of orderly clutter and accumulation, gone. Every surface, every cupboard and corner had been scrubbed. There was food in the refrigerator, kindling and split wood in the fireplace, and, in what had been his parents' room, a made-up bed covered with a new quilt. On their first night beneath that quilt, with the glow of the fireplace reflecting off the bed's brass headboard, they drifted to sleep to the sound of rain on window panes.

Early Monday afternoon, in a weakening drizzle, a truck from the implement dealer rolled into the yard towing a brand new International 80 Bean Special pull-behind combine. Up high in the cab, beside the driver, sat Foley Haws.

"You didn't have to go and move into town in a rush," Earl said. "And we can't afford a new combine."

"You'n't the one 'fording it," said Foley Haws with his laborious, stroke-afflicted manner of speech. "*I* am. And if you and this nice girl are going t' farm this place, you going t' have the house. And you going t' start with a new combine."

Eager to impress his wife of three days, Earl lost no time hitching the new machine to the McCormick and greasing every joint and bushing. By dusk, the sky had cleared, and the radio weather report promised sun and warmth for the next week. With two thirds of his crop left—fifty acres of beans that had lain in windrows since early September—he was eager to get started.

At just a little past dawn on Tuesday, Earl was aroused from his third night of conjugal sleep by a vague, familiar chugging somewhere in a far-off land of rivers, canal roads, cattle pastures. Whatever it was, it needed a muffler badly, gurgled closer and closer until it threatened to come straight through the bedroom window.

Then he was awake. In a cold panic, he flung back his half of the honeymoon quilt, bolted up and stood dumbly on the wood floor, goose flesh overspreading thighs, loins, belly, chest. Blinking like a stunned hen, he fumbled for underwear and pants and shirt, fumbled in his mind to close doors, latch shutters and screens, pull blinds, throw down timbers and sandbags—anything to keep that chugging engine out of their newlywed chamber. He half-expected to hear a rapping on the bedroom window, to see a face peering through the glass. *What you doing in there, Earl?*

Just as Earl got to the kitchen, the chugging died. At the sink he splashed water on his face, dried off with a straining cloth and finger-combed his hair, all the while watching through the window. Behind him, he heard the bathroom door close. Presently he heard the toilet flush and the squeak of faucets. Three days married and already he knew how fast Ruby could dress.

Out in the yard, in the first sunny glow of a fine day, Winn Bingham hesitated for a moment against the dented pickup door before making his way to the front step. It was just past six-thirty, too early in the day for combining. But, with the dew, it was just right for cutting and raking dead-ripe beans, which is what Winn should have been doing.

Earl met him at the porch door. "You're out early," he said, conscious of Ruby in the kitchen, the sound of a frying pan on a burner, the door of the ice box. "Have you had your breakfast?" Just by looking, he knew Winn hadn't eaten a proper meal—or attended in any other way to the care of his person—in a week. His hair and clothes were disheveled, forehead oily, eyes bloodshot, lips dry. A rash of acne along his neck and jaw gave his whiskers the look of mange. When he stepped across the threshold, he paused and tried to tuck in the tail of his shirt.

"I'll have toast and eggs in a jiffy," Ruby said as the two men stepped from porch to kitchen. Winn Bingham turned his head robotically, stared as if confused by her presence.

"Winn, this is my wife, Ruby."

Winn kept staring, made no response when she offered her hand. "You—married?" he muttered, amazed that this passage in life should be made by Earl Haws before it was made by him.

Gradually he recovered, swallowed hard, scrubbed his face with a dry palm. "Pay him all this time," he began, with no preface, no transition, no move toward the chair Earl offered, "a full two bits better than labor wages—give him a house, garden spot, truck to drive, all the apples he wants from my trees, and he up and quits me, just like that." He reached a trembling hand, laid it on Earl's shoulder, gripped a handful of shirt. "Left me in the lurch, I'm telling you. Said he wouldn't wait no more for his money. Said he was going back to Texas."

"It's not the end of the world," Earl said, prying the hand from his shoulder, only now realizing that the traitorous ingrate in the story was Eugenio, the hired hand.

"I would've paid him," Winn said. "Soon as I got my beans out." He moaned at the very mention of beans. "Fifteen or twenty acres to thresh, and the weather ain't going to hold." This time he placed a hand on Earl's upper arm, said, "I'm in a awful bind, Earl. God knows I'm in a awful bind."

•  •  •

For the next three decades Earl remembered the morning he pulled the wedding-gift combine away from Foley Haws's cedar-log shop in the fall of 1957, away from the beans waiting in his own field. He remembered the McCormick humming in fourth gear down the gravel canal road, then fifth gear on the paved county road, the combine trailing smoothly behind, remembered coming finally to the rocky field on the river rim.

When Earl eased through the gate and over the narrow tile culvert, he felt a kind of despair. Fifteen or twenty acres? Though Eugenio had cut and raked into windrows every pod and vine, there were still a full thirty-five acres to combine. And rocks were only part of the miseries of those acres. With enough water, the cobble yielded surprisingly good pintos—and astounding weeds.

Showing more loyalty than Winn gave him credit for, Eugenio had made a good start cleaning the windrows, disentangling ragweed and pigweed and corn-tall sunflowers from clinging beans, casting thick stalks into rake-swept spaces beyond the reach of combine teeth. But as was soon enough evident, he left for Texas before getting through even a tenth of the field.

Then what a breaking in for the new machine. Again and again, root clods hit the threshing cylinder like two-by-fours, clouded the air around the combine with powdery dirt that sifted into Earl's hair, eyebrows, lashes, and dulled the shine of brand new paint. Woody as timber, tensile as cable, weed stalks were forever wrapping around and choking shafts and drums, defiant to pocketknife blades, screwdrivers, hammer claws. Before long, overcautious of both weeds and rocks, Earl combined at a crawl, clutching every inch of every run up and down the slope. Time and again he stopped completely, set the tractor's brake against the hill's slope, chocked the big tires with rocks, and climbed over the pick-up carriage to clear weeds from the combine's parts. The tearing and unwrapping dyed yellow gloves green and strained finger joints until they ached. And though the weather had held thus far, every passing hour compounded the awareness that it wouldn't hold forever.

"Poor guy," Ruby said that night, holding Earl close. And, misconstruing the object of that compassion, Earl took comfort—until she added, drowsily, innocently, "His mother must really appreciate him."

Bad as they were, the big weeds proved a far lesser curse than the short, seemingly harmless berry weed. At first contact with vibrating machinery, the plant's pea-sized berries shook loose and amassed in the lowest point of housings and chambers. Half broke open between fixed and moving metal, fouled every interior surface of the new combine with bitter, seedy pulp. The other half made it into the hopper intact, the worst possible tare.

When berry pulp finally gummed the auger to a halt, Earl felt something he never had felt before, even in war. Under a nasty sky, the hopper was mounded with beans—beans that had to be unloaded if he was to finish this field and get back to his own crop, which waited ever more vulnerable to frost and wind. Again and again he jammed the long rod lever to engage the auger drive-belt. Again and again the forced idler effected only a shuddering, only a heaving resistance in the tractor's PTO gears. Amid chattering linkage and smoke from the slipping belt, at the considerable risk of impalement, poleaxing, or mangling, he tried a pry bar, then a shovel handle, resorted finally to kicking the pulley spokes until his heel bone felt bruised.

"Damn him!" Earl yelled into the wind. "Damn him to berry weed hell!"

Finally he took pliers and loosened the wing nut latch on the little door at the bottom end of the auger tube, every thread a strain from the weight of beans, let it slam open under the flow. As the beans emptied on the ground, he jumped into Winn Bingham's truck and pulled it close, slid the scoop shovel from behind the strap bracing of the tailgate. Faster and faster he shoveled, his motions almost frenzied, until his shirt was soaked and his mouth dry. Every few strokes he searched the field's border, hoping Winn would show up to find someone else shoveling his tare-thick beans, perhaps shovel some of them himself. The exertion would do him good, sweat some of the pickling out of his system. Or maybe, with any luck, kill him.

"He didn't show up at all?" Ruby asked on another night as she rubbed the ache from Earl's back and shoulders. "Poor guy."

Speaking into his pillow, Earl asked, "What's so poor about him?"

The rubbing stopped.

"That's what everybody in priesthood keeps saying: 'Poor Winn. What can we do to help poor Winn?' Do you see any of them out there fighting poor Winn's berry weed? Let them shovel four hoppers of his filthy beans, and they'd sing a different tune. I have half a mind to pull out and let the sorry beggar stew in his juices."

The bedroom became very quiet. "Earl," she said, "he's had a rough time of it. Lose your dad and not get to go on a mission . . . That's a hard blow. Everybody knew how bad he wanted to serve."

"Right."

"I remember when he came and talked to our class in Mutual." There was fondness in her voice. "We all thought he was so cute."

"How old were you? Twelve? Thirteen?"

"Fourteen and a half. Old enough anyway to know what I was hearing."

"You were hearing bullcrap."

"That's not fair. He was very sincere."

Earl rolled onto his back and looked up at his wife of almost a week. "Prodigal charmer swears off snuff and beer for half an hour, bears testimony with tears in his eyes, and girls melt. I don't get it."

She looked at him as if at a stranger. "Sometimes, Earl Haws, you're not a very nice person."

Not until the shoveling of the third hopper the next afternoon did Winn Bingham finally show. Driving his pickup with the dented door, he roared through the gate, bounced hard over the hump of the tile culvert, bumped across the harvested portion of the field, came on in a cloud of dust. He pulled up at an odd angle between tractor and combine, ran over some of Earl's pile to get close enough to be heard without having to do more than roll down his window.

"Something wrong with your auger?"

Despite an overcast sky and cold wind, Earl felt his face flush, his throat tighten, kept stabbing the wide, flared blade into the mound of beans, again and again, hoisting in steady arcs over the truck's sideboard. "There wasn't," he said, "until I got into your berry weed."

Leaning on the steering wheel, shaking his head in disbelief, Winn said, "Berry weed? In this field?"

"Yep, right here."

"Well, I'll be jiggered," Winn said. Then, after a pause, "And you didn't have a piece of tarp to drop those beans on?"

Earl stopped. One more word and he would have grabbed Winn Bingham by the shirt front, would have dragged him out and ground his nose in green-black berry pulp.

"No, I didn't have a tarp handy, Winn. If you want one, you can go get one. In the meantime," he said, pointing to the loaded truck, "You best run that to the mill, and I'll keep at it here."

Despite the slow nodding, an embarrassed look of confession crept over Winn's unshaven face. "I can't run anything anywhere," he said. "They took my license last week. For six months I ain't even supposed to go for groceries." Then he brightened. "But I can stay and combine, Earl—and let an old Marine trucker run the beans to town."

The tone was more irksome even than the thought of Winn Bingham on his machinery or anywhere close to work he could botch. On the other hand, every windrow of these beans run through the combine put Earl one closer to getting back to his own. So on a chilly afternoon in early October of 1957 he went to town with a load of hand-shoveled pinto beans. And when he got back an hour or so later, he could see, even before he crossed the culvert onto Arvy Bingham's rocky hillside, the brand new combine stalled askew in the middle of the field.

"I don't know what happened," Winn said over and over, poking his head here and there around the silent machine, thumping and wiggling uselessly, his chaotic hair blowing in the cold wind like electrified mop strands. "The dang thing just up and quit me."

As Earl soon discovered, the combine up and quit because of a rock wedged between the threshing cylinder and its sheet metal housing.

And then?

They "had words," as Foley Haws would have said before heat stroke impaired his speech.

*Judas Priest, Winn.*

In fact, the words Earl remembered were mostly his own, accompanied, grotesquely, by finger pointing, arm waving, forehead clapping.

The wedding-gift combine he had coddled through the nastiest beans in the Shoshone Valley, without a breakdown, the machine he needed to finish harvesting his own crop, now stood idle. All because Winn Bingham's bloodshot eyes had missed a rock the size of a melon. And only a ridiculously high RPM could explain the extent of the damage: threshing drum dented and punctured, its shaft warped, bearings burned, chain links on either side of the ladder feeder snapped like candy canes.

*How blind do you have to be?*

The one new piece of machinery in Earl's farming career, and it would never be the same. And a week—at least a week—to get parts in and fix everything that needed fixing. And over all this hung the threat of frost and snow that did indeed end up spotting and marring and making seconds of his own beans before he could get back to them.

But—no abandoning of the field, no breach of promise, no quitting, though the moment was ripe for it.

• • •

What became of two men who farmed season after season on adjoining properties, weaned thirty-five calf crops on bordering pasture, and lived in houses not a mile apart? Two men who went each Sunday of those thirty-five years to the same church meetings, listened to the same talks and lessons, partook of the same sacrament, renewed the same covenants?

Oh, yes, Winn went back to church and changed his life, thanks mostly to his brokered marriage to the pregnant and jilted daughter of Brother A. Frett Maxwell, materially successful banker and owner of well-kept parade mules. The marriage happened in early 1958, just after Etha Bingham asked Earl to farm her husband's place the next season, just before Winn cancelled the deal. After the wedding in the Relief Society room and reception in the cultural hall, Winn and Patricia left for their honeymoon in a brand new Ford Galaxy.

After two weeks in sunny Florida, they came home to a new pickup, new tractor, new sofa and love seat—and eighty foreclosed-on acres across the canal that Earl had had his eye on. All courtesy of Big Frett.

That next August baby Emery was born, just a week before

Lyndon Haws. The two boys were blessed during the same fast and testimony meeting, baptized the same afternoon, ordained deacons on the same Sunday.

"We're so happy for Brother and Sister Bingham," the bishop said when he announced the family's sealing in the Salt Lake Temple.

Through all the years, through the births of other children in each family, Scouts and seminary, periods of home teaching each other, constant association in meetings and classes and quorum projects and potluck dinners, Earl got along with Winn Bingham. Even as Winn was called to preside over him as quorum president, then as counselor in two bishoprics, while Earl found himself clerking or ringing the hall buzzer to dismiss Sunday School classes, he kept his mouth shut and never was pointedly unsupportive.

But he got along by resignation, not reconciliation, a feeling reinforced with every new farming season. As he repaired and reused and went without, Winn bought new. As he fought weeds, rocks, hard irrigation, Winn availed himself of the wonders of modern sprayers, rock pickers, sprinkler systems. Whereas Earl made a living, Winn prospered. Yet fond as Winn Bingham was of telling people about his humble beginnings, he never seemed to recall certain details of those early years, seemed completely to have blotted out the bean harvest of 1957.

In truth, though, when Earl thought back on that time in his life, as he often did, it wasn't so much the harvest that stuck in his memory—not the damaged combine or sacrificed bean crop. What he remembered was the winter evening three months later, when Etha Bingham came to the house all by herself and asked him to farm her husband's homestead the next year. He remembered her standing on the stoop in Arvy's old denim coat, with the hood drawn so tight it constricted her eyes and nose and mouth to a small, cherry-red oval. He remembered her sitting next to the fireplace, clenching and unclenching the hands in her lap. The memory of that action always called to mind Lyndon, sitting in the same place, confiding one night not long after his mission that he didn't want to farm; then, same setting, years later, that he was going to teach philosophy at a university in Illinois and had parted ways with the Church. Then always, always Earl remembered the last words Etha Bingham said to him on that cold January night in 1958, just weeks before she died of a blood clot in her lung. "All my life I have tried to sow in righteousness," she said, staring into the fireplace, clenching and unclenching her hands, "but for the first time in sixty-odd years, the law of the harvest is no comfort."

• • •

In late July 1992, with no other work to buy the grub with, Earl Haws, at age sixty-one, began trucking wheat for Winn Bingham and his successful son Emery. Faulty batteries and radiators, slipping clutches and transmissions, broken door latches, radios, gauges—all were things of the past. As if to remind them both of that fact, Winn assigned him to one of his new tandems, a huge GMC with a diesel engine and two upright, chrome exhaust pipes flanking its cab. "Now that's a lot of truck, Earlito. You can see why I don't let just any old wetback behind the wheel."

The people at church said, "I hear you're helping Brother Winn. How's that going?"

*Ever seen so much wheat, Earlie? How about it, Earlie? Enough to fill the granaries of Egypt, don't you think, Earlie?*

"He does pay every week," Ruby said one night, rubbing lotion on his back to soothe the itch of chaff. "And this isn't forever, Earl."

Wheat, then beans. August, then September. There came the inevitable afternoon when Earl saw the neat windrows stretching away below him on the rocky sloped acreage of the river rim. For an instant a memory stirred so strongly that the leg resting in the cab of the big tandem truck was once again clutching the McCormick ahead of the one new combine he had owned in his life. The old fence was gone, the once overgrown ditch banks scorched clean with a propane torch. Piles of machine-picked rock and bulldozed sagebrush bordered a field twice as big as when Earl had seen it last.

The only thing unchanged about the field was the narrow tile culvert affording passage into it. Earl swung wide to approach the crossing squarely. Why, on a slow morning, couldn't big-farmer Winn Bingham send a few of his many hired men—Leonél, Temo, Hector—to bury a new culvert in a place like this? He had several sitting in his machinery yard. And, in the same yard, a backhoe attachment for any number of big tractors. And loaders with reliable hydraulics. Nothing patched or scabbed or makeshift. With a chain harness and a little shovel work, Leo and the other boys—maybe Leo and *Earlie*—could have this crossing fixed in no time. Then trucks getting in and out of the field wouldn't have to split inches with big tires and great weight.

"Ain't that one heart-stopper of a close fit?" said Winn Bingham, proudly.

"To tell you the truth," Earl said, "it's got me a little spooked."

"Spooked! *You?* That ought to be a piece of cake for an old war-vet Marine like Earl Haws."

"It's got nothing to do with that, Winn." Earl could not keep the edge out of his voice. "The crossing is just plain too narrow."

Something flared in Winn Bingham's eyes, and the affability they had belabored for six weeks—and maybe thirty-five years before that—felt suddenly stretched to its limit.

"If you're uncomfortable with it, Earl, just say so. I'll get one of the others to take your truck across, if that's what we need to do."

"No," Earl said, swallowing the insult. "I'll manage."

On the second day in the field on the hillside, the weather changed. Daylight brought gathering clouds and a rising wind. At noon, Winn Bingham dispatched a second combine, and, spitting straw, the two big machines moved up and down windrows faster than a man could trot. Nothing slowed them—certainly no sunflowers or berry weed. Load after truckload rolled out of the immense field, across a ditchful of water running through the tile culvert.

By three o'clock the job was all but finished—not even two days to do what once had taken Earl more than two weeks. He thought of this, again, as he eased the GMC away from the combine's hopper spout for the last time and aimed toward the narrow crossing. He checked his mirrors. The truck was heaped, overfull, just the way Winn liked to see it. "Fill it up!" he had yelled on the very first day back in July, when Earl started to pull away from the combine, accustomed to the capacity of his own trucks. "That ain't no wheelbarrow you're driving anymore, Earl. Fill it *up!*"

At field's edge, he geared down to a crawl, inched the big tires through the last rough corrugations, across the scar of the border furrow, then up a fairly steep track toward the culvert. He could see only the upstream end of the tile pipe, marked by a tuft of Johnson grass flattened and yellowed under ten-ply tires. He would hug that end and, by so doing, would square with the other.

For an instant, after the cab cleared the deep ditch, when the full weight of the left tandem wheels came to bear on the culvert, and the tile, with the faintest wet popping, began to fracture, he thought the engine was failing. Then the big pipe collapsed, like a casket lid under a covering of long-settled dirt, crumbled beneath the tires, just fell away. The truck shuddered, groaned in its beams, and dropped with a tremendous splash. The wrenching of the frame jolted Earl's neck and jaw, slammed his thigh into the steering wheel, threw him—knee, elbow, and shoulder—against the door, and left him staring upward through a windshield that now framed only sky.

The engine had died. His fingers went blindly to the ignition switch, cranked and cranked until the battery faded. In an agony of urgency and helplessness and shame, he climbed out the passenger door, ran back around the truck. The two pairs of wheels were wedged tight, damming the flow as if cut to fit the contours of the ditch. Already the roiling water threatened the banks. The bed was tilted precariously, the frame beneath it contorted. Besides dumping a good many bushels, the drop had shifted the bulk of the load against a side panel now flexed to the point of splintering.

"You stuck good," said Hector, whose heaped truck stood behind Earl's, waiting to exit the field. He checked the crumbled culvert from several angles, studied the odd position of the tandem tires, the flooding ditch water, then whistled. "Whoo-ee, *pendejo*. You stuck good."

An empty returning truck stopped nose to nose with the GMC. The driver hopped out, curious and gawking, and added his opinion that Earl was stuck.

Then came one of the combine operators on foot. Outside and apart from the high cab of the machine he lived in during harvest season, he seemed disembodied. "I'm full, boys!" he called out. "What's the hang-up?"

Earl slid the scoop shovel from its place in the tailgate and, slogging in the overflow, began trying to flatten the ditch bank ahead of the first pair of wheels. The scoop's aluminum blade, its edge blunt and worn in an uneven concave, was no good for the job. Still, he jabbed and scraped.

From somewhere two or three more hired hands had showed up, stood now with the others in the windy afternoon and watched Earl flounder on the water-slick grass of the ditch bank. They watched him jab and scrape, watched the shovel blade glance off sod, still brick-hard at its root, watched him clumsily check the momentum of each swing and draw back to try again.

Hector said, "Save your energy, man."

A low buzz arose among the others, and along with it, the sound of an engine Earl knew well. A dread settled into his motions, and he jabbed at the sod as if his life depended on haggling out a chunk of it. The chill of ditch water had long since cut through boot leather and socks, and was working its way upward. Then he heard the voice, measured the stride in his mind, and he knew, he *knew*, the instant Winn Bingham arrived and stood looking at his back.

"Well, Earl!" Winn Bingham said. "How did *this* come to pass?" He paused a long time, waited until Earl turned around. The voice was too jovial, too undistressed, even as the eyes took in every particular of the mishap.

"If you're all done sightseeing," Winn said to the other hands, "somebody get up to the flume and turn the water off." Then he squatted on the ditch bank the better to see the truck's undercarriage. He whistled lightly through his teeth, rubbed his eyes, the back of his neck, his clean-shaven jaw, said, "Ho-ly *cow*, Earl." Only now did impatience and authoritativeness strain the tone.

"The culvert caved in. The front got across okay, but—"

"It just up and collapsed?" Despite his smile of forbearance, a challenge crept into the question. "Drive across this thing ten thousand—hell, ten *million*—times, and it picks today to disintegrate?" Winn Bingham looked around at the faces of his crew as if the implausibility of such a thing should be clear even to the likes of them. He pointed to one of the men. "Leo never had any trouble with it." Pointed to another. "Or Temo."

Earl rested the short handle of the scoop shovel against the truck's running board and folded his arms against whatever else was to be said. "I mean, cripes, Earl, the thing must have been here twenty years, people crossing *in*"—he swung his arms in exaggerated crossing motions—"and people crossing *out*, all that time."

"It's older than that," Earl said.

Winn turned to face him.

In that moment the onlooking of the others registered only as a vague periphery.

Then Winn Bingham's eyes fell to the scoop shovel, and his laugh came out like a bark. "I don't know what good you think *that's* going to do," he said, kicking the shovel aside, hard. "As overloaded as you got this truck, it's going to take a crane to winch it free."

• • •

*And you didn't say anything else to him?*

Not a word. Not a wave. Not a greeting or handshake. Not then and not in six and a half years thereafter—through countless sacrament services, Sunday school classes, priesthood meetings, stake conferences. What a feat, such silence! And all the attendant dodging and plotting and maneuvering to move in the same mix of people, to travel the same roads, yet avoid every contact that could be avoided.

"Forgive our debtors," Foley Haws used to say with considerable wryness, "because they need it worse."

It all started at the crumbled culvert, which, despite Ruby's mote-and-beam logic, could not be called a little thing. Through the endless afternoon of Winn's supervision and swelling magnanimity, Earl bit his tongue to ribbons. Only because he was *obliged* to help, only because of that did he stay put, lightening the load onto a huge new tarp—produced upon demand, instantly—fetching blocks and jacks, tow chains, cribbing beams, slipping and flailing in the slick ditch bottom, kneeling in the muck to position and align boards.

*Broad side down, Earlie. Under the axle.*

Oh, how he hustled. How he worked. Solicitous. Submissive. Penitent.

But only until the truck was freed, the accident cleared, the crossing reinforced with ties and planks, the last loads of beans on their way to market.

*We all make mistakes, Earl.*

Only until he trusted his sore tongue to say he wouldn't be back the next day or ever again.

*Dear, I don't think it's just your tongue that's hurting.*

Forty years of resentment—unredressed, unresolved, unrepented of until it was almost too late, until just after the heart surgery that spared Winn, just before the pneumonia that didn't.

It was early August. Lyndon, on one of his long summer vacations from his philosophy professorship at the university in Illinois, had brought his family for a rare visit. Of late, he said, he had felt a strong desire for his children to know something of their grandparents' world—"their heritage, if you will." In the absence of beans to weed and hay to haul for old times' sake, the grandchildren played among the mostly vacant barns, amid their mother's sober warnings of hornets and snakes and rusty nails.

On an afternoon when the children's mother was gone with Ruby to Billings, the oldest grandson found the seatless motor-scooter supporting a pile of gunny sacks in the calving shed. With Lyndon fishing down on the river and Earl taking a nap, the grandson somehow got it running. Using a rectangle of plywood to sit on, he started giving rides around the yard, then around the little pasture, then—opening a gate—around the cattle trails of the Binghams' pasture. The boy's circuit grew until it took in the plank foot bridge above the big irrigation flume. This was the flume that supplied the rocky hillside acreage a young Arv Bingham had grubbed out of sagebrush with a mattock.

With each ride, the boy grew more daring until, with the four-year-old behind him, a too-fast approach and the bump at the plank's unbeveled end threw him off balance. In the spill, both fell clear of the scooter, hit the mossy concrete of the steep flume without breaking a bone, and hurled to the deep pool below as if on greased runners. While Earl's grandson could swim, his granddaughter could not.

As was his habit since unshouldering the management of Bingham Farms, and especially since his surgery, Winn was out riding his property on horseback, heard the trespassing engine, saw the whole thing. A pair of resolute heels in the mare's flanks, and he was there before the boy had time to realize this water was not chlorinated and he had no idea where his sister was.

Despite carrying seventy-two years and a long scar down his

sternum, Winn went directly from saddle to water, within forty seconds had the little girl fished out on the bank, coughing ditch water—and breathing. As soon as Winn verified lung function, he sent the sputtering boy after his dad. Then he wrapped the girl in his shirt, cradled her in front of him on the saddle, and, with the mare running full-out, retraced the scooter's route, which, given the lay of the pasture land, got him to Earl's house before he could have gotten to his own.

On a sofa by the fireplace, Earl traded the wet shirt around his granddaughter for a very old honeymoon quilt, and asked Winn to drive them to the doctor, just to be sure. A cut on her scalp was bleeding, and she had a bad knot. They were about to give her a blessing when Lyndon rushed in, frantic. He was still in his hip waders. After the retelling and explaining, he looked from his father to Winn and back again, removed his fishing hat, then nodded for them to go ahead. For one instant it looked as if he was going to lay his hands with theirs on the little girl's head.

• • •

Word that Winn Bingham is still down with pneumonia comes one Sunday morning in priesthood meeting. The news troubles Earl more than he can say. On the way home from church, listening to Ruby speak of the illness, he feels his eyes welling with tears. For a moment he has all he can do to whisper, "Poor guy."

There is no question now about what he should do and when.

Half an hour later, still in his white shirt and tie, he stands at the threshold of a back room of Winn Bingham's big brick house. When the swinging door clears a certain point, like a stage curtain, Earl suddenly sees what he has only anticipated. On the far side of the room Winn Bingham lies rigidly in the big bed. He looks small. From a table set close by, a vaporizer sends a steady mist in the direction of his face. The spitting hiss of the steam blends with the rasp of breathing. This same table serves as a stand for a folded wet washcloth, hot water bottle, jar of Vicks, wads of tissue scattered around a Kleenex box, a bubble-like bronchial inhaler, bottles of pills and capsules, a glass of water with a straw in it, another of juice—neither much depleted— and a bedpan. It occurs to Earl that Winn and Pat have shared a bedroom just as long as he and Ruby have.

"So," Pat Bingham says, too cheerfully, moving toward the bed, "let's see if we can rouse Sleeping Beauty."

"Let him sleep," Earl says. "I can come back."

She doesn't hesitate. "No, let's let you see him while you're here. He needs to be awake a while anyway. Those pills keep him in the darnedest stupor all the time." She points apologetically to the bedpan. "He fell with me yesterday in the bathroom. When he wasn't getting any better, I wanted him home—in case . . . Well, just in case. I insisted. But I had no idea he'd be so weak. He can't even sit on the toilet, Earl."

Gently she shakes Winn's shoulder, and when at last his eyes flutter open, when she has wiped his mouth and nose after a coughing spasm, she says, loudly, "Winn? Winn, Earl is here to see you. Earl Haws."

For a moment the eyes remain clouded. Then, when the announcement has arrived somewhere deep within him, Winn Bingham turns his head and smiles weakly.

"I'll let you be for a while," Pat Bingham says, tugging and smoothing the bed covers before stepping away. In the doorway, she turns. "He'll be glad you came."

Alone with Winn Bingham in the bedroom, Earl needs no force of habit to take the waxy hand in his own. For the first time he notices, in the V of the open pajama collar, the grizzled stubble of chest hair and the top end of a scar as thick and pink as an earthworm. Winn Bingham blinks, gags on a cough, swallows laboriously. Earl shudders at the imagined ache in his neighbor's chest and at what is not imagined in his own. Thanks to Winn, a grandson has nothing more tragic than a foolish accident to put behind him. Thanks to Winn, a granddaughter will grow to womanhood. How could such ever be repaid?

"Can I do anything for you?" Earl asks.

His words echo oddly off the high ceiling. A gust of wind rattles the bedroom's north window, against the sound of the vaporizer's warm sputtering. He waits, holding the familiar hand, less awkward with each moment, and gradually finds more words. "Looks to be a hard winter. It's a good thing the beans are all in."

But when that hand suddenly clasps his with unexpected strength, Earl is moved to wordlessness. All that passes between them, when their eyes meet now, is a peace and a healing.

# Oasis

The idea to fence the spring came to Rowe as an inspiration. Why let good water run to waste when they got so tight for it every year, February to May, trying to stretch one well between sixty cows and the house? Since he couldn't very practically get the water from such a source to the users, he'd get the users to the water. He planned to build an alley from the corral gate down the gravel hillside and around the spring opening, just fifty yards away. What the spring lacked in flow, it made up for in constancy.

And they could dig a pond. The hillside would make a steep pull for the ones ready to calve, but the walk would get them out of the corral muck. The posts would have to be spaced close, and the gravel would be miserable digging—no way around that. They could drive steels for part of it, but he wanted the thing stout. With cattle against it all day, it had to be. They could use woven wire; he had got a good buy on some at a farm sale when nobody else bid. And two or three strands of barbed over that. With the oldest son helping until he left on his mission to Bolivia and the other boys joining them after school, the job would take four or five days at most.

At breakfast in early March, when the ground had thawed almost enough for postholes, Rowe spoke of his inspiration to Vida. In a little while she could run the clothes washer all she wanted, water her flowers if the weather turned nice, and never worry again about the pump sucking sand and all the faucets belching and popping. The kids could shower whenever they felt like it, a dozen times a day if the water heater held up, and flush the toilet whenever nature called.

"Oh, you and your big plans," Vida said, snuffing the stove flame under bubbling oatmeal.

Rowe said, "I can't think of one serious reason it won't work."

He had calculated the water needs of corral and household. Milk cows and a butcher steer in one pen, two bulls in another, and of course the two hogs and hen house—if he counted their water at all. That was all they would have to hose when the herd started drinking from the spring.

The youngest daughter, an eight-year-old, set bowls, cups, and spoons on the table, kissed Rowe's cheek, and told him he needed a shave. Her older sister, who had turned fourteen on her last birthday, brought a cookie sheet of oven toast and centered it on a quilted pad. Tossing her hair, she said that in four years, five months, and twenty-six days she was leaving for college, and she didn't care what happened to their weird water. Vida carried the pot of oatmeal in one hand, a pan of cocoa in the other, slid them both in front of Rowe.

"Why don't you eat for right now," she said, "and quit bothering yourself with it?" She spooned cereal into a row of bowls. "As if you didn't have plenty to do in the fields without building a silly fence."

Rowe said the job wouldn't take long with four boys—he flourished a hand at each of them—and, in the long run, his idea would free them up sooner for working the barley ground.

The boys chewed toast and looked at him. The one bound for Bolivia said this plan sounded like the idea two summers ago to irrigate the lawn from a ditch running nearby. Trying to channel the water where it needed to go, they had ruined more grass than they saved. And despite all the hand-shoveled corrugations and berms, they still flooded the basement and ruined Vida's hand-braided rug.

The boys laughed at the story.

"Keep dragging that up," Rowe said. "It was for a good cause."

Vida splashed milk on her cereal and didn't say anything.

"The fence will work," Rowe said. "I've got plenty of wire—paid next to nothing for it—and with all those railroad ties, I've got more than enough brace posts"

"You and your railroad ties," Vida said.

"Have some faith."

"I'm about tired of faith."

• • •

The ties had been a good deal, too—at least the first batch. After the railroad maintenance crew had gone over a couple of miles, the foreman offered Rowe the replaced ties just for hauling them off the side of the track. They were still in good shape. He told his boys that moving sound railroad ties—cut from oak and soaked with creosote—might give you piles, but once you planted them, they were there to stay.

Even Vida thought he did all right with that deal. She said, "Every once in a while, Rowe."

So the second time the foreman flagged him down and offered ties for cleaning up another long stretch of track, Rowe agreed without looking at the job.

"But we do want everything hauled away," the foreman said.

On the first cleanup, Rowe and his boys had worked from a utility road beside the track, were never more than ten feet from the ties. This time, there was no road anywhere close. The right-of-way on the south side of the track was a swampy borrow pit choked with thistle and cattails. The north side sloped straight up from the crushed rock of the rail bed and ended at an overgrown canal bank.

In the end, they parked on the highway shoulder, thirty yards away at its closest point. His boys stood looking at the work ahead of them.

"If you got a better suggestion," Rowe said, "I'm all ears."

For five afternoons in early August, they slogged through alkali swamp and wheezed up the highway embankment to haul off the railroad's mess. Down in the cattails, deerflies plagued them. With no hand free for swatting, they could only twitch and shrug, flinch and shudder. This time, for every sound tie, they moved four or five piles of splinters. And many of the full-length pieces were so rotted they weren't worth setting in the ground. It occurred to Rowe that the foreman had not bragged about this second batch.

When they went home for supper at the end of the fifth day, a dead-still evening perfect for cutting barley, Vida asked how many decent ties she would find if she were to peek in the back of the pickup.

"There's four or five," Rowe said, looking at his sons to ensure their complicity in his generous count.

"Probably more like one or two," she said. "And that's hardly worth risking ripe crop to hail." She had just come in from weeding beans. She said she and the girls were making headway, and if he could see his way clear to start cutting barley, he might have that much harvest finished when her pretty beans turned. She threw her straw hat and green-stained gloves on a stool in one corner of the utility room. Her hat band had creased her forehead red. "You guys irrigating night and day," she said, "might pay off if you'd cut the stuff when it's ready."

The boys kicked off their irrigating boots on the stoop, came in with separate slaps of the screen door and stood around the water cooler, which rested on the clothes dryer. Their socks, stuck full of foxtail and brome, had bunched at the toes. Taking turns, they filled cups with ice water and gulped hard. They looked tired. Their tee shirts were soaked through, their Levis powdered with alkali. When he saw the fly bites and creosote welts, Rowe wished he had warned them to wear long sleeves.

"At least we got some cold water," Vida said, draining her cup in smooth swallows. Salt bordered her lips, stood out against her tanned face. "At least we've got that much."

• • •

Both house and corral stood to benefit from the fencing of the spring. But of the two, the house was more important. Twenty years earlier, May of 1959, after the marriage ceremony in the Salt Lake Temple and during the reception in the big Sugarhouse ward building, Rowe had nodded as a hundred Hobarts warned him to take good care of their Vida. After shaking Mr. Hobart's skeptical hand one last time—and more crying than smiling in Sister Hobart's send-off—Rowe had taken his bride from the life of her upbringing and, amid many promises, brought her home to a farm in Wyoming. The promise he emphasized most regarded the digging of their own well.

Meanwhile, living out Mr. Hobart's prediction, they had made do.

To replenish the house's cistern and supply twenty-five head of cattle during the first winter of their marriage, Rowe hauled water from his dad's place in open barrels frozen to the bed of a pickup with no defroster. Every day he made three or four trips, shivering while the barrels filled, gloves iced almost as soon as he put them on. His parents lived only three miles away, but much of the load sloshed out every trip. It was hard to grip the ax handle to chop drinking hollows in the troughs, hard to bucket fast enough to stay ahead of two or three cows drinking at once. Trip after trip, he stumbled through frozen turds, buckets banging his knees and wetting his legs all over again.

On cold nights in December and January, in the last stages of pregnancy, Vida held his hands to her stomach, said their baby wouldn't care where their water came from. She rubbed feeling into his toes, massaged his ankles, and reminded him that the hauling was only for this winter. And she told him how wise he had been to save all those hydraulic oil buckets from last summer. What would he have done without them? She said she was lucky to have married such a brilliant man.

When the baby came, she washed diapers in a metal tub, kept a kettle heating on the coal stove all the time. Her hands stayed chapped. Still, she offered no complaint, said she could get by just fine until the weather warmed enough for well digging.

By the time Rowe had enough cash to hire the job done, fall had come again, the frost was creeping into the ground, and Vida was pregnant with their second child. Against her wishes, he hired a neighbor to witch them a well.

"You're going to rely on this kind of hocus-pocus?" she asked when the neighbor drove into the yard and took his forked willow from a leather sheath. "Why not get somebody who really knows something about water?"

"This guy knows," Rowe said.

While the neighbor held the willow in front of him with both hands and marched here and there, between the haystack and chicken coop and grain bin, very solemn and ritualistic, Vida shook her head.

"This is baloney," she whispered.

"He comes highly recommended," Rowe said.

The witcher finally stopped across the road from the milking barn, in a dry puddle sink. His willow bobbed. "This is sure enough the place," he said, toeing an $X$ in the dust.

"Knowing what you know about prayer and priesthood," Vida whispered, "and you stand for this. It's utter bullcrap!"

"There could be strong water here," the neighbor said, taking the twenty-dollar bill Rowe offered. "But it is late in the season for a proper finding."

Rowe nodded. Vida rolled her eyes.

The neighbor walked to his truck and sheathed his willow. "Even when there is water," he said, "getting to it can be a trick."

The well digger had to go deeper than Rowe could comfortably afford, but finally he hit water. He said he hadn't fought such hard lenses in a long time, and the early frost didn't help. "It's no Niagara," said the well digger, "but it's as good as you're going to get on this place."

Until that moment, Rowe had not known his place was doomed to this kind of want.

"Why do you think the last owner *hauled* water?" the digger asked. "You're living on a mighty dry piece of the planet right here."

Vida said she was just thankful to have enough running water for the added volume of dirty diapers and for drinking. She said, "I've swallowed my last drop from that sour cistern of ours."

To dig trenches for the water lines, Rowe hired a backhoe. From well to corral—six feet deep to stay below the frost line— the digging went fine. But the trench to the house was only half-way along when the operator hit bad gravel and broke a tooth on his bucket. With better work waiting and an early winter loom-ing, he collected his money and pulled off the job. Rowe dug the last thirty feet with a pick and shovel and buried the line on the eve of the season's first heavy snowfall.

Beginning that same fall, he kept back the best heifers to build his herd. In six years he had fifty-five brood cows. He had enough field leavings and hay to support that many through the winter and—now—plenty of well water to see them through until they could go out on summer pasture.

Then, early the next February, a month after he brought the herd in from feeding off bean straw and corralled them for calv-ing, seven years after digging the well, Rowe heard the water pop for the first time. He was holding the hose coupling under a slow stream from the corral hydrant's spout, working his thumb to loosen a gob of frozen manure from the threads. When he lifted the valve handle for more pressure, the hydrant's pipe stem shud-dered, and the stream began to pop in spasms.

Vida told the plumber their water was acting funny. The kitchen faucet coughed now just for a drink, and even a weak stream of bath water set off a straining noise in all the pipes. Sometimes the toilet bubbled instead of flushing.

"And you're lucky if it does that," she said.

The plumber said the water had air in it from the well's low output and they would just have to use less. Vida laughed at the absurdity of such advice. "A mob of growing kids," she said, "and sixty cattle. And we're supposed to use *less*?"

Over the next few years, Rowe tried bringing the herd off the fields later in the winter and turning them out to pasture earlier in the spring. But that schedule still left him nearly three full months of watering. So as not to tax the well too much at any one time, he began to leave the corral hose dribbling through the night while the cows slept. Yet by noon the water disappeared, and by early evening cows again stood by the round aluminum trough tonguing their nostrils, waiting for the hose's meager stream to wet the trough bottom enough to drink. Their fresh need amazed him. Gallons and gallons a day multiplied by sixty animals—water drunk, cycled through stomachs and mammaries and kidneys, left steaming in puddles of green-foamed urine, soaking away into manure.

For the house, Rowe tried rationing—only one flush per four or five emptied bladders, one three-minute shower per person, per day, and as few loads of laundry as possible.

"What am I supposed to do when the hamper's full, Rowe? Go to the river and wash everything on rocks?"

Despite all his measures, the water still popped from January to May. The poor well made a constant quarrel between him and Vida. Why didn't he break down and dig a new one? Because it wouldn't do any good. Could he help it if they just happened to be living on a mighty dry piece of the planet?

Five more years, then six, then nine. On an evening close to the tenth anniversary of the first popping spasm, Rowe sent one of the boys out to start the water. Before long the fourteen-year-old daughter came from the bathroom, clutching her robe at the neck, shampoo in her hair. She said a three-minute limit was bad enough, but most human beings she knew showered with *water*—not sand, not air. She said in case her father was interested, she didn't think farm life was so great and she couldn't wait to leave Balford, Wyoming, behind forever.

All this time the spring had trickled from the base of the gravel hillside, steady as thirst. All these years there was nothing to do but watch it run on the wrong end of gravity and taunt him all the way to the swampy acreage of the river bottom. Until this year.

But no matter how satisfying, his resolve could not undo the other years and the hardships of a sandy well. His oldest son would soon leave home to serve as a missionary in Bolivia, already accustomed to every sort of water deprivation. And how many fourteen-year-old girls looked forward to college just for access to a dormitory shower? And Vida. Winter after winter, she had put up with more than any of them. Thousands upon thousands of loads of laundry, and all she craved was enough water to wash them.

• • •

They started the fence on a Saturday. Every stage of the work went more slowly than Rowe had imagined. Just the marking of the line and the stringing of posts took them until noon— climbing up and down the hillside, fighting willows and briars, slipping on rocks, flailing for balance.

Then came the digging of postholes, more miserable than Rowe had imagined even in his worst moments of doubt. They earned each inch of depth in the gravel only after hard barring and shoveling. At the end of the first day, they had dug only a third of the number needed. They used one day of the boys' spring vacation to finish just that part of the job. With the brace posts finally tamped in, they spent most of the other vacation day driving steel posts, taking turns in pairs on the thick handles of the pounder. The boys said they could have punched posts in concrete faster.

Finishing the fence took another week. By itself, stringing wire took almost two days. Part of the problem was the material. The bargain woven wire, marked with rust spots and breaks, required much splicing and patching. The barbed wire was just as bad. The old rolls came apart in tangled coils and snagged on everything.

"Watch for kinks," Rowe yelled to the boy cranking the come-along at the brace posts. "Watch your eyes."

"That's tight enough," one of the others said.

"Just a little more," Rowe said. "You got to have it tight."

In the stillness, each click of the pawl compounded the risk and dread. Every time a strand snapped, they had to untangle and unsnag and unkink, and fashion a splice that might or might not bear the necessary tension. And the repeated breaks cast a pall over the job. Overcautious, the boys fumbled and tripped at familiar work.

"This wire stinks!" the middle boy said. "This whole fence stinks."

They finished late on a Friday evening, stapling and clipping with daylight all but gone.

"So is your four-day project finally finished?" Vida asked when they all trooped in for supper.

"It was all for the best of causes," Rowe said, throwing his gloves down on the stool in the the utility room. "Water in the desert."

That very evening the fourteen-year-old reported blackish grit in the bathtub.

"Enjoy it like an old friend," Rowe said. "That's the last time you'll see it."

For the second time in the season of the fence's construction, Vida didn't say anything.

The next morning Rowe hurried through breakfast, then trotted to the corral. He laughed in the morning sun when he and the boys wrenched the gate's bottom spar from its manure molding. With their barrier flung wide and the new alley beckoning, the lead cows sniffed that molding, leaned over the threshold, finally stepped from ripe manure onto clean gravel. They waited for rocks or sticks to turn them back.

Rowe said, "They don't even know water's down there."

For a long time he and the boys watched the cows graze their way down the hillside. The new fence funneled them toward a stand of Russian olives and the newly dug collecting pond. At last the lead Angus approached the pool, nuzzled the water's surface, settled into a series of long swallows, her eyes half closed. Others in the herd joined her.

"Hallelujah," Rowe whispered. "They're really drinking from it."

Around the table at noon, Vida looked at Rowe, then at the boys. "Well," she asked her sons, "is it going to work?"

They nodded.

"You got to believe in me once in a while," Rowe said.

She put her arm around his neck, kissed his ear, and said, "I guess so."

· · ·

For three weeks the spring provided for the herd, created abundance for the house, and fulfilled Rowe's dream and inspiration. In his last shower at home before catching a bus for the language training school in Utah, the missionary son reported neither sand nor popping. Meanwhile, the cattle wore a path down the hillside, drank from the pond, and rested often on the return climb. Rowe moved a mineral lick into the alley, slid the empty aluminum trough out of the corral and leaned it against the barn. He spread barley straw over the circle of hoof pocks where it had rested so long relieving thirst. Its ring, pressed into the manure by the weight of innumerable gallons, gradually faded. Cows now congregated elsewhere to chew cud and suckle their calves. Corral muck dried, and the river-bottom pasture renewed itself shade by shade.

The blizzard came in mid-April, the worst snow of the year. Overnight, the world turned cold and white. Cattle huddled in the barn, their hides and faces shaggy with ice. They didn't go for water, didn't approach the hay bunk at feeding time, didn't move at all. The alley leading to the spring drifted full, four and five feet deep.

In winter coats and irrigation boots, Rowe and the boys broke bale after bale of straw into the tromped green soup of the barn. Sickly newborns shivered, bunted weakly at sore udders, couldn't find a purchase on tits swollen too big for their mouths. If the cold and wet didn't kill them, scours would. The back of Rowe's hand grew raw from fingering big medicine tablets down their throats, his thighs sore from straddling their necks. Even weak and sick calves fought the tickle of the big pills along the ribbed roofs of their mouths—slammed their heads into his crotch, clamped their jaws against the intrusion of his hand, then ground young teeth on his knuckles. Saliva chilled Rowe's skin until he couldn't keep his fingers rigid.

But the vigilance paid off. He didn't lose a calf. "Not one," he told Vida.

Three days after the blizzard, the temperature climbed to fifty-eight degrees. Snow melted and disappeared almost as fast as it had accumulated. Rivulets spread from the big drift in front of the barn out toward the hillside. Icicles dripped from the eaves of the house, formed linear puddles around the foundation. Almost overnight, lawn grass and ditch banks turned green. The kids went back to school.

Ground texture was just right for planting the rest of the barley. On the fourth morning after the blizzard, Rowe backed the pickup to an old hen house, one of two watertight storage sheds on his place. Babying the occasional mouse-eaten sack, he loaded seed on the pickup's tailgate and watched Vida hanging clothes on the line.

Suddenly she yelled to him, said they'd have to wash all the windows this year; they were filthy. And the storm door, too, before they put it away for the year. She'd get the kids to help one Saturday, and maybe even him.

Rowe said okay, and he meant it.

With the tractor fueled, the grain drill greased and its seed hopper filled, he moved to a small plot close behind the house. Planting in short rounds, he watched Vida work. After hanging clothes, she pruned raspberry bushes, casting dead stems into a big pile. Slowly she worked beyond the garden, raking twigs from beneath four old cottonwoods. They always shed heavily in winter, especially after a blizzard. How many times had she asked him to prune dead limbs or cut down the trees altogether?

Shortly before noon, on the last lap around the small plot, Rowe noticed the rake leaning beside the yard's front gate. He was hungry. He disengaged the planting mechanism and pulled the drill back to the yard. When he killed the engine and went in the house, he found ham and beans, hot bread, and a plate of sliced cheese waiting on the table.

"It's good to be planting again," Vida said, setting her own bowl on the table, then two glasses and a pitcher of milk.

"It's going to save time," Rowe said, "not worrying day and night about watering those cows."

She dipped a torn slice of bread into her bowl. "I will admit," she said, "it's nice washing a batch of clothes when I need to."

After their meal, Rowe replenished the drill's hopper, loaded more sacks on his tailgate, and, with Vida following in the pickup, towed the drill through the yard, past the grain bins, past the pumphouse, out to the bottom end of the field closest to the corrals. With the twitch of an ear, a cow or two noted the jingle of vibrating seed tubes and planting discs.

"I'll run you back to the house," Rowe offered.

"You go ahead and start," Vida said. "I'll walk; I need the exercise anyway."

"You look good to me."

Their eyes met. She smiled and said, "You're just easy to please."

He filled the hopper three times that afternoon before he saw the school bus. He watched it up the neighbor's lane. The guy was probably witching somebody a dry well right now. The bus returned to the highway, stopped at one trailer house, then turned down Rowe's own road. Given the lay of the road in relation to barns and haystacks and the cottonwoods, the bus disappeared for several minutes. When Rowe saw it next, it was rolling back up to the highway, where it turned toward Ralston, gathered speed, and for several long moments seemed motionless against the horizon before it disappeared.

The sun's brightest afternoon luster was gone. In this particular field, the ratio of completed to uncompleted acreage was always deceptive. Still, Rowe felt sure he could finish by dark. He liked knowing the boys were home—changing clothes, asking where he was, taking crackers spread with peanut butter on their way to do chores. After the work of the day, they would all come together for one of Vida's good suppers. After supper, Vida would fill the kitchen sink with soapy water and supervise the washing of dishes. Later, reading in a chair by the lamp and furnace, he would listen to the clothes washer humming smoothly. Still later, he would shower and shave, maybe put on a little cologne before bed.

As he braked and turned at the top ditch, gripping the knob on the steering wheel, turning as he had turned dozens of times that afternoon, Rowe saw one of the boys running toward him. It was his youngest, Gabe—stumbling every few strides in the tilled ground, regaining his balance, moving steadily closer. In the evening Gabe watered just the pigs and chickens, the bulls and milk cow. Everything else drank its fill at the spring. None of the faucets popped anymore.

The boy's pace never slackened. Rowe clutched and shifted to neutral. He swung out of the seat and walked to meet his son. Away from the hot exhaust of the idling engine, a breeze carried the smell of snow thawing, and buds. From thirty yards Rowe saw the disheveled hair, the grimace from a long, urgent run in oversized boots passed down from a brother. He quickened his own pace.

The boy's breath whistled with strain, and the panting slurred his words.

"Cow's stuck," he said, "in our pond. It's all muddy." He crouched, rested his hands on knees trembling from exertion, sniffed between words. "It's all melted, and she's stuck bad."

Then Rowe ran with him, back across the field, his own strides too slow and laborious. At last he reached the hard, uncultivated bottom border, sprinted through dead weed stalks, scrambled over a gate, then through the corral, toward the edge of the hillside. Cows stood in the alley, their bellies and briskets plastered with dried mud. They shied when Rowe pushed through, then settled back to their cuds.

The other two boys met him and pointed. "She's down there."

Rowe slid down the trail to its abrupt end. Soft with melting snow, the whole slope had caved in, taking a section of the new fence with it, flooding the pond. He turned to the boys. "Get some rope!" he said. "Something to get hold of her with!"

She was a brindle, a big, beautiful animal, and she was mired up to her neck, her eyes quivering. Now and again she thrashed her head from side to side, stuck where, just a day earlier, the spring had flowed so clean from somewhere underground. Rowe waded in up to his thighs, searched in vain for a familiar feature in the new swamp of mud.

They anchored the block and tackle to a scrub cottonwood at the edge of the mud hole, looped a long lariat around the cow's stub horns, then connected the lines. Floundering in mud, the two older boys gripped the pull-rope and leaned backward with all their might while Rowe tried to hoist the cow's flanks. Mud-soaked hemp drew hard through the pulleys. Gabe's job was to hold the cow's nose up, to keep the nostrils clear.

But the brindle wouldn't help them; she was too exhausted to do anything but blow snot and mud with hard breaths. How long had she fought before they found her? Maybe since noon. Stuck worse with every lunge and strain. But if they could get her downstream a little, where she had a solid base under her hooves, maybe she would stand, or at least try.

In time, cold mud coated their arms, soaked shirts and pants and underwear.

"Hold it *higher!*" Rowe yelled at Gabe, who staggered under the weight of the cow's head. "She's drowning just fine on her own; you don't have to help her any." The reprimand brought tears to the boy's eyes.

An hour passed. Then much more than an hour.

Faintly, Rowe heard Vida call for supper. It was too far to answer. Until the fuel tank ran dry, the throb of the tractor's engine would reassure her that he was planting, trying to finish the field before dark. She couldn't know they were where they were, couldn't hear them down the hill.

After straining, pushing, slipping, after a dozen re-riggings of the block and tackle, after dragging the solid weight inch by inch through the mud, at last they had the big brindle positioned to roll onto solid ground. The sun hung low over distant mountains, and the light dimmed fast where they worked in the shade of Russian olives. Beyond the mud, in the rocks where clear water flowed, they could save her.

No serious problem, he could tell Vida. Nothing lost.

With a final, mighty push, they rolled the cow completely over, onto a firm spring bank. Curled at the hocks, her legs hung useless. Silt matted the hair of her swollen udder. The boys stared at the freshening tits. She was due to calve in a day or two.

"Get up, you biddy," Rowe said, hoisting the rear quarters with her tail, hoisting until the tailbone popped. "Get up!"

But she weighed too much and would not help herself. The tail slipped from his gloved hands, and the brindle sagged on the ground. Her head drooped beside a tiny snow drift. With each forced breath, she shuddered. The boys dropped to their knees, pushed and leaned to keep her sitting upright. But they could not counter her bulk. With no good traction, no bracing for legs and backs, their knees slipped against her weight, gouged tracks in the soft bank of the spring.

"Come on, cow, you can get up." Rowe slapped her flat nose with his glove; mud dripped from the cloth fingers. "Get *up*!"

The boys stood and shivered. Rowe's mouth was dry. In the evening air, sweat flushed and chilled his cheeks at the same time. Dusk had been so quiet the past few weeks, the cows no longer milling and restless with thirst. Vida didn't like them coming late for supper. She said if she cooked it, the least they could do was show up to eat it. Pork chops and gravy and apple crisp. At noon she had told him what she planned to fix.

The brindle's tongue lolled from her mouth—rough, scaly, coated with grit. Half-shut, her big eyes stared, dull and un-blinking. The boys watched. They had to be hungry and tired. A soaked jacket lay on the ground at their feet. The next-to-the-oldest son wore short sleeves, folded his arms tight against his belly. His goose pimples looked like hives.

"She could get up," he said.

Between the deepening dusk and last light on the horizon, the fence stood silhouetted. Rowe looked up the hillside at the now indistinct forms of cattle feeding, resting, suckling their calves. With a slow shudder, the cow at his feet strained as if to clear her throat. At last the big brisket heaved, the nostrils distended pink and moist, and, with a final tremendous gasp, her windpipe fell silent. And in the calm of death, somewhere below them, toward the trees and grass of the river swamp, water trick-led between rocks.

# Elk on Chimborazo

ACCORDING TO MISSION GUIDELINES, Elder Myron Haymore's ankle-high, waffle-treaded shoes looked too much like hiking boots. And his suit was too green, his belt too raw-leather brown, and his hair *too* short. Though he had shaved his last morning at the Missionary Training Center in Utah, he stepped off the plane in Guayaquil twenty-seven hours later with a stubble none of the nineteen-year-old elders in his MTC group could have produced in less than a week. And his infractions weren't confined to his person. Instead of the prescribed second suitcase, which would have sailed through Customs with the rest of the group's baggage, Myron had brought a duffel bag. Only President Arnold's diplomacy and fluent Spanish prevented a thorough search of its contents.

"So it belongs to the *infeliz* with the odd haircut?" the man in Customs asked, singling Myron out of eight new missionaries—six elders and two *hermanas*.

"*Sí,*" said President Arnold, who had left a thriving law practice in Sacramento to serve three years as mission president in Ecuador. "With your kind permission, he is *inocente*. Please forgive."

The man in Customs wouldn't have cared about the *Outdoor Life* tucked between two *Ensign* magazines. But among underwear and a dozen pairs of white tube socks, Myron had packed a small tool kit, a roll of baling wire, and, as a harmless stay against missing the mountains of Southeastern Idaho, his war-surplus commando knife.

"Do I even want to know what all's in that bag of yours?" asked Elder Clair Elroy from Pocatello. Though he had been Myron's companion in the MTC, with him every waking hour for the past sixty-five days, not even he had seen the knife.

"What's *infeliz?*" Myron asked.

"It means you boys from Mink Creek are into contraband."

Two hours later, President Arnold looked across his big desk in the mission home and said, since there was no correcting them now, he would just have to overlook the suit and shoes and duffel bag. He said, "I'm more interested in what's on the inside any-way." Then, with piercing eyes, he asked why a farm boy from Mink Creek, Idaho—who needed a shave, by the way—why he would wait to go on a mission until age twenty-five, right at the cut-off. Was there a personal problem? Shyness? Homesickness? Hygiene? Was it worthiness?

No.

Did he have a testimony?

Yes.

After the head shaking and one wordless nod, President Arnold paused a long time, as if concluding that whatever had worked in the first three interviews on his alphabetized list—Abinanti and *Hermana* Bethers and Clair Elroy—wasn't going to work with this one.

"Elder Haymore," he said finally, already looking ahead to Ogleby the reformed hippie surfer, brown-noser Riggs, Sappenfield the crack basketball player, and *Hermana* Yancy, "you're starting this six years later than most, and I'd really like to know why."

• • •

On his first night on a cot in the El Cisne pension, at the slum-edge of Guayaquil, Myron wondered how he was supposed to tell a lawyer with cufflinks that he wasn't from a farm, that his dad and Uncle Dewart built cabins, ran a company called Haymore Scenic Homes; that he liked being by himself in the mountains and had eaten deer liver raw; that even though he dreaded talking to people and wearing Sunday clothes for the next twenty-two months, he wanted a wife just like any other Mormon guy wanted a wife, and it looked like he was going to have to do this to qualify for one.

He wasn't a freak or dimwit. He showered—with soap. And he wasn't a mama's boy like his Uncle Hewell over in Wyoming. Or a pervert. In application interviews with the bishop and stake president at home, he was honest about no nasty methods of getting his own jollies. And he hadn't done anything wrong with a girl—which would have been hard since he had never been on a date. As far as testimony went, he couldn't paint it on like Abinanti or Riggs—*I know without a shadow of a doubt; the Lord has spoken to my heart*—but he believed in the Church. If he didn't, he sure wouldn't be cocooned inside a mosquito net in Ecuador, catching whiffs of a bucket-flush toilet even through the bathroom door, listening to the snoring of his pension mates—Beals and Slocum and his own new companion and trainer, Elder Nathan Ralph from Albuquerque.

So, to get through the interview at the mission home and onto Sister Arnold's good-smelling orientation dinner of sloppy joes and apple cobbler, Myron had said what he *could* say: It was just time to do this. And, with the interview schedule pressing, the president about had to be satisfied with that answer.

After the good orientation dinner, after much talk of surviving thereafter on rice and bananas, after his good-byes to Clair Elroy and the others, he had climbed on a *colectivo* behind Ralph, and they had left the mission home neighborhood of Los Ceibos far behind. During the forty-minute ride, the landscape changed from gated villas and office buildings to dirt side streets and huts stretching as far as the eye could see.

"That's all cane," said Elder Ralph. "Bamboo. They call it

*caña.* Split the stalk, roll it out flat, and presto—poor man's plywood. You know anything about building?"

Finally, just before the end of the pavement on Cisne's main avenue, Ralph yelled something to the driver, and the brakes of the now nearly empty *colectivo* squealed. In a cloud of dust, Myron hopped off behind his companion and stood holding his suitcase and duffel in front of a drab, two-story building with window grilles.

It didn't take long to see all there was to see of the one-room pension. Four cots stuck out perpendicular from the wall, each centered beneath a rolled-up mosquito net hanging from a ceiling joist. A clothesline stretched across the room, from one window grille to the other, and was draped with towels and P-day trunks and tee shirts. In one corner was a bathroom the size of a broom closet.

Between each pair of cots, a low shelf made of poor man's plywood rested on books or bricks. On the half of the shelf closest to Ralph's cot, among stacks of pamphlets, a pad of onion-skin stationery, and rolls of banana stickers, was a small, framed picture.

"She's just a friend," Ralph said. Then, with his chin, he pointed toward Beals's shelf and a much bigger framed picture. "Some of these guys worry too much about their girls at home. That's not a habit you want to get into."

The new companions spent their first night of work hiking into warrens of cane huts built on stilts. No plumbing, except a community privy or the river at high tide. But almost everybody had a TV powered by thin electric lines strung low, from insulators tacked to bamboo posts. During commercials, the lights of the whole *barrio* pulsed. On and on, Myron followed his companion down dusty lanes between cane dwellings, then down a long and rickety and unlighted cane trestle, eight feet above the backwash of the River Guayas.

"It feels flimsier than it is," Elder Ralph said over his shoulder.

During half a dozen visits to meet member families, Myron smiled and nodded at the slurred gibberish of a language nothing like what was practiced in the MTC. Instead of trying to talk, he concentrated at each stop on the hospitable glass of warm pop. Thirsty as he was, even strange flavors were welcome—yellow bubble gum, pink cologne, bitter Orange Crush. At the home of a family named Zambrano, his smiling and nodding got him a plate of *tallarín* spaghetti drenched with chunky sauce, and a steaming glass of something the *hermana* called *qua-ker*.

"Liquid Quaker Oats," Ralph whispered. "Bottoms up."

After the Zambranos and their oatmeal in a glass and noodles that tasted like shredded cardboard, even Elder Ralph was disposed to call it a night. "*Infeliz?*" he explained on the way back to the pension. "It means like poor sucker, out of luck. Like my stomach right now. But you got to eat what they give you. That meal was half a week's wages."

Just before lights-out, kneeling on his own cot, Slocum demonstrated how to let a mosquito net down and tuck the hem under the mattress, all the way around, how to do that tucking from *inside*.

"We'll get you a real pillow next P-day," Elder Ralph said when he saw Myron shaping the duffel as a headrest.

Preparation Day. Until the MTC, Myron had never heard the term. From morning till five o'clock every Monday, as Ralph explained it—writing home, playing basketball or football, going downtown to the post office. And no tie. Now, with eleven hours of Ecuador under his belt, he knew a little better what he would be preparing for.

"Was malaria one of the shots we got?" Beals mumbled before he fell asleep.

Feeling every cross-slat through the cot's mattress, wondering in the dark whether the mosquito drone he heard was coming from inside or outside his net, Myron looked toward Ralph's end of the little shelf. He envied his companion. He envied anybody with only two months left and a girl to go home to.

"Where's your head today?" Uncle Dewart had said one afternoon a couple of summers ago, when Myron kept botching his rafter cuts. "Must be a bad case of hormones."

"Honey," his mother said when another hunting season rolled around, "if you want to meet a girl, you're going to have to go where girls are."

So, at age twenty-three, Myron went to his first Young Adult fireside, listened to some guy just home from a mission in Zimbabwe say five hundred times what an awesome experience it was. Myron watched the girls hang around him during cookies and punch. They were interested in his plans.

"I hear there's lots of girls at BYU," the guy said to his new female fan club. "Any truth to that?"

So, at age twenty-four, to everyone's surprise, Myron got into BYU. There were a lot of girls, but after a few weeks, he was pretty sure not one of them cared in the least whether he could gut a deer or chop a corner notch.

*And where did you go on your mission?*

Long before daylight one morning last October, not even halfway into the semester, he had threaded the sheathed commando knife onto his belt, shouldered his camping backpack, and headed due east into the mountains above Provo. And that's where he stayed until the first heavy snowfall. As he sat his last afternoon on a slope high above the city, flakes falling in the stillness, his gaze was drawn, not to remote peaks and lonely passes, but to the toy buildings of campus and apartment places, where even now girls waited for missionaries to leave or return.

On his first night in the El Cisne pension, burping *tallarín* and *qua-ker*, Myron dreamt of good sandwiches made of heart meat and mustard, of bull elk bugling in morning mist. And he dreamt of admiring young ladies in Sunday dresses encircling him, asking why he had made them wait so long.

• • •

On the morning of a P-day a year into his mission, Myron stood with Elder Clair Elroy in front of the outhouse-sized shop of a *zapatero* in Machala. Reaching into a dark corner beside his little stool, the man produced a pair of shoes that now looked like neither missionary footwear *nor* hiking boots. He pointed to re-soles cut from a truck tire, emphasized the unheard-of shoe size, the laboriousness of the stitching, the toll on his *instrumentos*, all to justify raising the agreed-upon price by a hundred *sucres*.

"A bent awl is your problem," Myron told the man, in much-improved Spanish. "I never asked for no ten-ply."

The *zapatero* looked at Myron, then at Clair Elroy, and tried a different tack. "You *misioneros*—you are permitted to dance . . . with *muchachas?*"

"Not right this instant," said Clair Elroy. "But a year from now? You better believe we'll be dancing with *muchachas.*"

The *zapatero* leaned forward on his little work stool, pointed again to the truck-tire soles, and smiled slyly. "Dancing in these shoes," he said, "you'll easily win the *corazón* of a beauty."

"Pay him," said Clair Elroy.

"I should've just made do," Myron said, lamenting the two curled, smooth-worn waffle soles atop the man's discard pile. "I'm going to look like a dang blowout walking down the street."

In his legs he felt the lanes and sidewalks and rabbit trails of a year, from Cisne to Centenario to Letamendi, then out of Guayaquil and up to Manta, then Ancón on the Peninsula, and finally down here to Machala. Concrete, pavement, dirt, rock. He imagined grains of tread left behind like spoor. In his mind he pictured the gait of each companion: Ralph, Slocum, Gormley, Cousiño, Orquiza the anti-American, and Unsworth. Several of them knew about the raw deer liver, but none had seen the commando knife.

"Time's a-wasting," said Clair Elroy as they stood in front of the *zapatero*'s shop. After an equally circuitous first year, he too had ended up in Machala. Only now he was a district leader and trainer whereas Myron had achieved no rank beyond co-companion.

Begrudgingly Myron handed over three hundred *sucres*, tucked the repaired shoes under his arm, and started with Clair Elroy back up the street. They headed toward an outdoor basketball court, to join Finch and Unsworth, their assigned companions, and the four missionaries from the other district.

"Look at it this way," said Clair Elroy. "They've only got to last you another year. Then it's back to normal work boots and your mountain goat stew—no more *sopa de pollo* with beak and claw floaties." He looked at the re-soled shoes, then at Myron, and said, suggestively, "And that's not all it's back to."

"Yep," Myron said, sensing the usual drift of the conversation, "Targhee is calling."

"Targhee? You got mountains right here. Look at a map, fella. We're in the Andes. That Chimborazo up by Cuenca would dwarf any molehill we got in Idaho.

"Even if I could see it from down here—which I can't—there's no elk on it."

"Haymore, you're pathetic. We're not talking about elk, and you know it; we're talking about *girls*. A year may seem like a long time, but it's *nada*. Piece of cake. Before you know it, you'll be home, with no more excuse for lollygagging. Now," said Clair Elroy, who had been on all of two or three dates himself, "you are a fine twenty-six-year-old specimen of Idaho manliness. But the competition is fierce. If you don't have a strategy, you'll be building cabins for other honeymoon couples the rest of your life. Is that what you want?"

Myron liked listening to him. Clair Elroy always knew a reason the next month would go by faster than all the rest and saluted every time a Braniff roared into the clouds. Early in the mission, he had begun to draw little airplanes in the margins of his Book of Mormon in such a way that now, a year into the project, he could fan the pages and make the plane fly. And he was always optimistic about what he would be flying home to.

"Mink Creek's just up the road from me, Haymore," he said. "We'll get together and go to some Young Adult dances. Whip a little *coma está* on the lovely daughters of Zion. Between that and your new stompers"—he pointed to the truck-tire soles—"you *will* melt hearts. That *zapatero*'s no dummy."

Some guys didn't have to wait to melt hearts. Some got plenty of female attention right there in Ecuador. For guys like Ogleby and Unsworth, the line between brotherly talk and *coquetería* was pretty thin, especially with *muchachas* so easily charmed by anybody from the United States.

Anybody except Elder Myron Haymore. Even around Ecuadorian girls, he felt like a wormy log. Did he have anybody waiting at home? People always asked. It was standard get-acquainted fare for companions, something to talk about as they rode or walked to their first destination. Then faith, hope, and pity: Don't worry; you'll find somebody. There's somebody out there for you.

That was easy enough to say for guys who *had* somebody. Though Elder Ralph never mentioned them, the letters from the "friend" in the bedside picture must have been pretty good because he married her four months after he got home. Gormley didn't bother to play down his girlfriend's devotion. Letters, aerograms, care packages, cards for every conceivable occasion—it took him half of every P-day just to read her many pages of loopy writing, all the *i*'s and *j*'s dotted with hearts. Even the uncongenial Orquiza got letters, from some girl in his home ward in Lima. Myron had peeked at one: *Esteemed Elder, I send you salutations of warmth and fondness.* Even Clair Elroy, who had to stretch quite a bit to call his dating experience "playing the field," even he got mail from somebody besides family.

"They send these to everybody," he said last Christmas at a mission conference when he showed Myron the card from a Young Adult group in Pocatello. *Hope the work is going super for you! Sure miss you in YA. Baptize, Elder!* He said, "It's their Christmas service project. If your name's on the missionary map at church, you get a card."

"It's got female signatures on it," Myron said. "That's better than my nothing."

"I wouldn't call smoked almonds and licorice *nothing*," Clair Elroy said with reference to a recent package from Aunt Lenore and Uncle Dewart. "It's going to be hard to find a girl out there who can make jerky that good."

Out there, over there, up there—always somewhere else. *There's somebody for you.*

After a year in the mission, the variations on that promise came more insistently to mind. Passing through Guayaquil five months earlier on his way out to the Peninsula, Myron was invited to Los Ceibos to meet with President Arnold. "I called you in," the president said, "to give you some insight into your new companion. Have you ever met Elder Orquiza?" President kept saying he was a strong personality, which turned out to mean, among other things, he hated Yankees, especially *infeliz* liver eaters from Idaho. "But if you can at least maintain a working harmony with someone from such a different background, imagine how much easier the give-and-take of marriage will be." Then, as if to fortify against three months' worth of strong personality—in one-horse, two-elder Ancón of all places—President Arnold declared that this, too, would pass and that Myron *would* get married someday. "I make that promise," he said, "without reservation."

At a zone conference last summer, Sister Arnold spoke with conviction, and quite a few tears, about the eternal purpose of missionary work. "Heavenly Father will not let you elders and sisters teach marriage and families during your whole mission only to deprive you of those blessings in your own life." Which sounded a lot like Myron's mother on the day he was set apart as a missionary: "The Lord will reserve one of his sweetest daughters for you." And not so much like Uncle Dewart: "With all the kooks and slimeballs in the world, a returned missionary's bound to look pretty good."

That was the point. From El Cisne to Manta to Ancón. That was the idea. From the year mark through another month in Machala, four in Vinces, then three each in Babahoyo and Jipijapa. And more of everything that made a mission a mission:

Bubble gum pop and *tallarín* and ragweed seasoning. Toe fungus and diarrhea. Coarse crepe toilet paper that couldn't be flushed. Stark absence of root beer and peanut butter and any kind of cracker worth eating. More primer English in the streets—*Hey, meester, what time is your mother? Hey, you, son of a beetch!* Being told over and over to bother somebody who didn't already have a religion. To get lost. To eat *boñiga*, Yankee fag spy.

But to be fair about it, to be truthful, there were good things he never would have seen or known in Mink Creek. Blue-green waves coming into the beach up at Manta. *Siestas* timed to end when the bread came from the oven of the closest *panadería*. Nothing tasted any better than half a dozen hot *pancitos* with a daub of margarine from a tub on the counter. Or oranges, big as softballs, peeled to the white on a little lathe bolted to the fruit cart, opened at one end with a flick of the vendor's knife tip, juiced straight into the tonsils. And decent people in every place who knew way more than most missionaries about being kind and humble and generous. A lot who didn't want to listen to the *charlas* still gave elders a ride or invited them in out of the sun or rain or didn't charge them for food or drink or whatever. And there really were a few who *did* listen, who felt something and got baptized and bore testimony that they had been waiting for the missionaries all their lives.

So in some ways the mission had turned out better than expected. It was the prospects Myron was going home to that weren't inspiring much hope. Somebody. Somewhere. Sometime. You'll find her. As the months of the second year went by— faster than the first year, but still with considerably less speed than Clair Elroy's airplane—it was a promise that got harder and harder to believe.

• • •

With only four P-days left, Sappenfield wrecked his knee playing basketball and had to go home early for surgery. Just like that President Arnold was short a trainer, with a new group coming down mid-week from the MTC. So with only four P-days left, the duffel bag rode one more luggage rack on one more bus, this time back to Guayaquil and a final assignment in El Salado, one district over from Cisne.

On the afternoon Myron met Elder Virlinger at the mission home, right before he got him and his model set of luggage on a *colectivo* bound for the city's far *barrios*, President Arnold came out of his office and said, "Let me shake the hand of my newest senior companion." Nodding toward Virlinger, he said, "You look after this guy. Show him what being a missionary is all about."

After a mission's worth of companions, especially after three months of Orquiza, Myron wasn't picky. But this guy Virlinger didn't look very well suited to Ecuador. Skinny, beardless, pimple-faced, pigeon-toed, helpless without his thick glasses—he'd do fine with the rules against frivolity and rough-housing. But would he survive?

"I don't like rice," Virlinger said on the way from Los Ceibos, "and I've never cared for bananas."

Myron pitied him right off. He hated to see him mince his nice Florsheims the very first night on lanes freshly graveled with crushed shale. Block after block, Virlinger crunched along, sagging under the weight of a fairly light book satchel, mopping sweat from the lenses of his glasses with a monogrammed handkerchief. He was game enough, but when they got back to the pension, he finally broke down and complained of sore feet, said the Lord would have to bless his arches if he was going to be doing so much walking.

Before Myron could show him how to hang and tuck a mosquito net, Virlinger opened one suitcase and laid out ties and slacks and white shirts on his cot. He smoothed and refolded, as if reassured by the inventorying of socks and underwear, everything embroidered with his initials and as yet unstretched and unfaded. Then he opened the other suitcase: scriptures, journal, pocket hymnal, a leather-bound Franklin day planner, box of stationery, pen and pencil set, travel alarm clock, and a book entitled *The Best Two Years and Beyond*—everything monogrammed *GLV* or inscribed *Garth LaDell Virlinger*. He even had a little first aid kit.

"Now then," Virlinger said, straightening up, hands on his hips, "is there a drawer or shelf or something?"

Myron pointed to a fruit crate in the corner and the clothesline. His new companion surveyed everything on the cot and for a moment looked as if he were going to cry. Finally he did what he could with the upended fruit crate and resigned himself, like all new guys, to stowing the rest back in the suitcases. While he stowed, he kept up a brave chatter: piano and trombone since he was five, marching band in high school, member of lots of clubs, math scholarship to BYU. Oh, and he almost forgot— Eagle Scout by age fifteen even though, by his own admission, he managed to get around most of the camping and hiking. "Even *thinking* about the smell of Coleman fuel and raw hotdogs," he said, "makes me nauseous."

In all his disclosure, he never mentioned sports or motorcycles or anything outdoors. Nor did he mention a girlfriend.

"Ever do any hunting?" Myron asked.

"I can't see killing animals for any reason," Virlinger said, "especially for pleasure. As a matter of fact, I've seriously considered becoming a vegetarian."

Just before lights-out, he came from the four-by-four bathroom, eyes wide, mouth foamed with toothpaste. "There's something in the sink," he mumbled.

"Don't swallow," Myron said. "You'll be all right."

Virlinger shook his head. "It's not the water," he mumbled, foam dribbling. "It's some kind of bug—must be three inches long."

"It's just a roach," Myron said, grabbing a flip-flop from beside his cot and stepping toward the bathroom.

"What are you going to do?" Virlinger asked, wide-eyed.

"Kill for pleasure."

Clair Elroy said hell was a toss-up between July parking lot jobs for Bannock County Asphalt and that first week in Ecuador. Though Virlinger wouldn't have approved of the phrasing, he probably would have agreed with the sentiment. There was so much to stare at in pained wonder—the cripples begging along Nueve de Octubre, men urinating on the closest wall, udders and other organs hanging from the yokes of *carne* vendors. The gabbling din of the *mercado* and smell of scalded feathers and over-ripe papaya were bad enough. But he didn't actually blanch until he saw the Indian ladies sitting along a shaded back wall, selling *lotería* tickets and nursing their babies with all South America as audience. Virlinger wore the same expression when thin-bloused *chicas* hissed from doorways or uniformed schoolgirls mashed into them on jammed *colectivos*. At first he would not believe the rat patties on Salado's one paved street were what they were.

"Yeah they are," Myron said. "That's what ten billion tires and a hot sun can do to you."

At the beginning of the second week, shock gave way to indignation.

"It's called crotch rot," Myron explained when the heat and humidity had galled his new companion so badly he could hardly walk. "Everybody gets it."

"Well, I'm not going to call it that," Virlinger said. "That's disgusting." Even so, he took the tube of proffered salve and disappeared into the four-by-four bathroom. He was disgusted, too, to witness the thronging of dogs in heat, to be reminded again and again of all there was to dodge in a place with no leash law. Time after time, sweaty and frustrated, he had to pull up to scrape the sole of a Florsheim.

And a stomach that couldn't handle a raw American hotdog was bound to have a hard go of it in Ecuador. It was one thing to gag at the first sight and smell of coiled tripe broiling on a curbside brazier or half-submerged in a bowl of *mondongo*. But Virlinger was sure every food was a conspiracy. He was so fin-icky he was going to waste away. So when he asked, after two

fairly hearty bites, where a pork sandwich had come from, Myron said a pig, but didn't mention the fly specks thick as pepper
on the vendor's glass case. When handed a glass of Yupi Kool-
Aid or liquid cherry Jell-O or *qua-ker*, the first thing he wanted
to know from Myron was whether the *señora* had boiled the water to make the refreshment. Sister Arnold had urged them to
make sure.

During orientation in the air-conditioned living room of
the Los Ceibos mission home, Sister Arnold also warned new
missionaries against eating or drinking *anything* purchased on the
street. So his new companion disapproved when, several times a
day, Myron stopped for popcorn or pineapple or sliced mango
in sandwich-bag-sized *funditas*. Or deep-fried banana chips or a
frozen banana on a stick or a glass of foamy banana purée. Once,
even before Virlinger spotted block-ice sawdust floating in a tub
of Coke, he turned down Myron's offer to buy. The vendor, who
had no front teeth, multiplied his profits by emptying eight-*su-
cre* quart bottles into the tub, then ladling back into *funditas* and
charging four *sucres* each.

"Who knows what's in that stuff?"

"They do look sort of like bladders," Myron said.

"That's sick," Virlinger said. "That's all I can say—*sick*."

Yet, for all his caution and precaution, it was Virlinger who
was always nursing a condition—sunburn, ringworm, shin
splints, allergies, and, from day one, diarrhea. "How do I know
if I have bugs?" he asked one morning during study time. He had
heard of a missionary who got home from Bolivia with a worm
no prescription could kill, and he was worried.

Myron tossed him an empty film canister, pointed to the
bathroom, and said, "You need a sample. We'll run it downtown
to the lab—give us something to do this morning. Just be sure to
put it in *your* bag."

So much was not mentioned in *The Best Two Years and Beyond*.

Maybe that's what Virlinger was saying in all the letters he wrote. On P-day, while elders from other districts around the city played football or basketball, Virlinger sat in the shade with a pen and pad. He stayed in touch with lots of people besides his folks—his bishop, a religion professor, an old Sunday school teacher. But evidently no girlfriend. He never spoke of one, and there was no picture by the cot. Myron took comfort in not being the only elder without prospects.

The rudest shock of all for Elder Virlinger had to do with the whole object of missionary work. He had to learn the hard way that most people didn't want to convert to anything except color TV. Before he understood what street kids were calling him, he offered them pamphlets. Before Myron could catch him, he approached sidewalk *cantina* tables with his stumbling, pigeon-toed walk and, trying to be heard above the plink of jukebox music, offered pamphlets to two or three *gastados* swilling beer. At night, in what passed for Salado's one park, he walked up to couples necking in the shadows, excused himself, and stuck a pamphlet in the flushed, surprised face of the guy or girl.

"I think they felt something," he always said.

Believing that, Virlinger was bound to cross a line. But he didn't cross it until Myron's last evening in Salado, the end of his last full day before heading home to the States. Walking along a freshly graveled side lane off Portete between good-bye visits, they heard a downshift whine and backfire. They turned to see a taxi taking a shortcut over to Gomez Rendón. In the deep, unsettled shale rock, the little yellow car bumped and rattled, going way too fast. Still, the driver never eased off the gas pedal; gravel pinged against his driveline like buckshot. People up and down the row of cane huts heard the engine and stared out their glassless windows, turned from their conversations. Barefoot kids stopped playing.

Suddenly there was a dull bang. The car pulled hard to the right, rattled on for twenty or thirty yards, then stopped with a jolt just beyond the missionaries. Had it gone five more feet, it would have plowed into a vacant lot piled with smoldering household garbage and the oddments of cane hut construction. The weeds growing up through cans and bottles whispered with scuttling rats.

In a sundown haze of dust, the door on the driver's side creaked open, and the Datsun lurched like an overloaded boat as the shirtless *taxista* climbed out. He was big for an Ecuadorian and peeved. Finger-combing his hair, he checked the front tire on his side, then slowly went to check the other side. As the clearing dust revealed the cause of the mishap—a rock big as a medicine ball, half-buried in like-colored shale—the driver began to kick the mashed tire rubber and bent rim, yelling, "*Ay, Dios santísimo!*"

When he finally tired of kicking and yelling, people turned back to what they were doing before the show.

Only Virlinger still stared.

"Let's go," Myron said.

"Maybe we can help," said the Eagle Scout voice.

"No we can't. Come on."

The *taxista* looked up from where he leaned, arms outspread on the hood of the Datsun. He surveyed the far side of the street, then turned and surveyed his side—the uneven row of cane huts, a Pingüino ice-cream vendor pedaling his three-wheeled rig, the medicine-ball rock, a pig rooting among bamboo stobs and bits of matting, and Virlinger.

"What are you gawking at?" the driver yelled in Spanish. "Eh, *gringo?*"

Myron caught hold of one of Virlinger's skinny arms and said, "Come on. The guy's sore." This was probably the same driver who hunted them after a rain, sliced through the gutter at forty-five miles an hour trying to muddy their white shirts.

Pulling away, Virlinger said, "We have to help people." With his stumbling gait, he closed the distance to the Datsun, fishing in his satchel for a pamphlet. Then he had one in his hand, held it out to the big *taxista*. Both the hand and voice trembled when he said, "*Hola. Co-mo está? Somos misioneros de la iglesia—*"

In response, the *taxista* grabbed his own crotch and said, "Just a little closer, *maricón rubia*. Let's see what size *cojones* you've got."

"Virlinger!" Myron yelled, just as the guy hawked and spat.

Staggering backward, Virlinger tripped and sprawled in the street, let go of the pamphlet and satchel as he went down.

Myron dropped his own things. "Enough!" he yelled, moving between car and garbage, standing suddenly nose to nose with the *taxista*. He had heard of two elders in Mapasingue getting mugged, one of them sliced with a broken bottle. "Leave him alone," he said, pointing to Virlinger. "*Me entiende?*"

It was strangely quiet—not a bark or bray anywhere close, no tinny jukebox music chipping away at the evening. The snuffling pig was gone. Myron could smell the guy's breath and torso. The driver, in turn, studied the haircut, the missionary name tag on the shirt pocket, the raw-leather belt, paused at the tire-rubber soles. Meeting Myron's eyes again, he gritted his teeth and flashed a lot of cheap fillings. From deep in the heavy chest came a low, drawn-out growl. Then he blinked and stomped his foot. And, expecting the next move to be a punch or headlock or beefy *taxista* hands on his throat, Myron flinched and pivoted.

That movement, so close to a lot full of trash, brought one foot down onto something mushy and slick—maybe bananas too ripe to sell, maybe worse—and made him flail for just an instant. In the quick and comic shift, and step, and lunge for balance, the other foot, now bearing more than its share of the weight, encountered a springy resistance, then broke into a cavity. Something scratched the calf and shin, hard, scratched until the pant leg bunched at the knee and stopped sliding. In that instant beside the garbage pile, while rats ingested all things putrid in the undergrowth, Myron felt a bowing of the truck tread on the underside of his foot, felt something stick into the rubber— and stop. The ten-ply had spared him a nail in the foot.

Looking from one missionary to the other, the *taxista* began to chuckle. Every time he inhaled, the sound grew louder, like a motor gaining steam. "*Sí, en-tien-do*," he said with mock deliberateness and gravity. "You speaka *español* very good, meester *gringo*." Then he threw back his head and laughed so long and loud that everybody on the street joined in. Loafers, ladies enjoying the cooler, ninety-degree evening air—*cogiendo fresco*, as they put it—even kids. They all laughed.

Meanwhile, twisting his foot sideways, Myron pried the truck tire off a ten-penny nail, stepped free of the tangle of scrap bamboo, smoothed his pant leg. He gathered his things, retrieved the satchel and pamphlet, and helped his companion up. Virlinger straightened his glasses and, with a monogrammed handkerchief, wiped phlegm from his shirt. Even after they turned down another street, they could hear the *taxista* bragging about how he had bested *los misioneros mormónes*.

A couple of blocks away, Myron found a *tienda* where they could sit down at a table. "You want a pop?" he asked. "No *funditas*, I promise."

"Sure," Virlinger said, slipping off an almost broken-in Florsheim and initialed sock, propping his foot on an empty chair.

Myron paid the *dueño*, slid two bottles of lemon-lime on the table and sat down across from his companion.

"I have weak ankles," Virlinger said, probing his foot with careful fingertips. "There for a minute back there, I thought I had sprained it." He took a bird sip of his lemon-lime and turned from trying not to stare at the calendar nudes on the wall of the *tienda*. "What's *maricón*?"

"They see us, two guys together all the time—they always call us that."

Even when the explanation had sunk in, Virlinger didn't blanch. And he wasn't the one fighting the shakes. He smiled and said, "I don't think I'll tell Melody that part of what happened today."

"She your sister?" Myron asked.

"No."

"Cousin?"

"No-o."

"How many other kinds of female family members are there?" Myron asked, aware for the first time of the soreness in his leg.

"She's not *family*," Virlinger said tentatively, as if risking a handbook impropriety. "She's my *girl*friend, for gosh sakes."

Myron had started to take a drink of his own lemon-lime but now set the bottle on the table. Garth LaDell Virlinger wouldn't last one cold night in a tent on Targhee, and the big *taxista* might have killed him.

"Almost five weeks we've been together. This time tomorrow I'll be on a plane. You never said nothing about having a girlfriend."

"You never asked."

Virlinger was right, and all Myron could think to ask now was whether Melody had sent letters. How had he missed them?

"A couple," Virlinger said. He put his sock and shoe back on, pulled out the handkerchief, and dabbed again at the stain on his shirt. "We promised not to overdo it. No heart-seals. No perfume. No mushy stuff. I'm here to serve, not pine for mail day. She supports me in that." He paused. "Want to see a picture?"

And when the picture came from its plastic sleeve in the wallet, Myron stared as he had never stared before: Virlinger had somebody waiting. Only one girl on earth would care anything at all for him—his queasy stomach, piano fingers, eyes blind as a bat without those glasses. But he had found her.

The leg ached. That broken-edged lath or bamboo or whatever it was in the garbage pile had bit more deeply than Myron thought. Through the fabric of his pants, he pressed the cold lemon-lime bottle to his calf. With the sun down, darkness had come on quickly. Nevertheless, when he pulled up his pant leg to apply the cold glass directly, they both saw the blood.

"Hey!" Virlinger said. "Are you hurt?" He moved around the table fast, knelt and hitched up his glasses to study the long scratches.

"Looks worse than it is," Myron said. "It's just starting to sting a little."

"No wonder," Virlinger said, craning his neck and squinting at the calf with great fascination. "Did you see this trophy of a splinter you scored?"

In fact, out away from the light of the *tienda*, with blood streaking his leg, Myron hadn't seen it until now—a two-inch sliver of bamboo, fat as a matchstick, broken off under the skin.

"Fortunately, it's superficial," Virlinger said, finding his Eagle Scout voice again. "But we really need to get it out. You don't want it to get infected."

For a moment, Myron held the cold bottle to the sorest spot, then tugged his pant leg back down. "It'll be all right," he said, chugging the rest of the lemon-lime. "Let's go."

"Look, Elder Haymore," Virlinger said, leaving half his drink, as usual, "I know you're my trainer, but I really think we need to go by the pension and clean up your leg. Did you notice there were rats in that garbage dump? They carry all sorts of diseases."

Myron tried not to favor his leg as he stepped back into the street and headed somewhere to say good-bye to somebody else on this last night in Ecuador. Virlinger slipped the satchel's carrying strap around his head and shoulder and trotted pigeon-toed to catch up. "And tetanus," he said, "is nothing to toy with. Lockjaw freezes your muscles and joints, the whole body, stiff as a plank. I heard of it happening to a guy over in American Fork. It's like rigor mortis before you're actually dead."

Myron kept walking.

"Okay, I didn't want to mention this," Virlinger said, lowering his voice, "but I've heard, even if you survive it, it can affect the ability to sire children."

Myron stopped. The ache was now disproportionate to the length of the splinter. The throb seemed to radiate up his leg—to the knee, thigh, pelvis. "Where do you get this stuff?" he asked.

Half an hour later he was sitting on his cot back at the pension. While he cleaned his calf with a soapy washcloth, Virlinger cleared off the upended fruit crate and set out a brand new bottle of rubbing alcohol from a *farmacia* up the street and, from his little first aid kit, a tube of antibiotic cream, a couple of cotton balls, and tweezers.

"The only thing I don't have," he said, studying Myron's calf, "is a needle. The end of that splinter is broken off a little deeper than I thought. I'm going to need something sharp to open up the skin just a little."

The day's heat was still trapped in the pension. Only Virlinger's fan, mounted on a brick and stack of books, stirred the air at all. Myron looked at his companion, the future husband of a girl named Melody from Pleasant Grove, the future father of little Virlingers. And the point, the point of everything, was that Virlinger assumed the same future for him. In that moment, in an odd way, taking precautions against the worst effect of tetanus—besides death—inspired a hope that had nothing to do with his leg.

"I got something you can use," Myron said. "Get my duffel bag, would you?"

• • •

Later, after companionship prayer, before lights-out, Virlinger knelt on his mattress, inside the mosquito net, and patched likely breaches with banana stickers. It was a ritual with him. Still, he'd sprawl in his sleep, knees jutted against the net's fabric, wake up with splotches of fresh bites. Sitting on his own cot, the splinter wound salved and bandaged, Myron scrubbed the ten-ply soles with the soapy cloth, then went to work with a shoe-shine kit. He tried to imagine stepping off the plane wearing those shoes. The sheathed commando knife rested atop the duffel.

"That's some blade," Virlinger said. "Is that what you take where the deer and the antelope play?"

"A little overkill for digging out splinters," Myron admitted. "But it's perfect for elk."

Virlinger surveyed his patch job. Satisfied, he sat down on the mattress, stretched his legs out, and leaned back against the cot's headboard. After a moment, he said, "I guess I never asked you, either."

Myron looked up from the tire-tread soles.

"Do *you* have somebody waiting?"

The fan hummed, clicked like a ratchet with every new sweep.

"I was twenty-five when I came out, and I'm twenty-seven now. Nobody's waiting for me."

"Good," Virlinger said, as if relieved and vindicated and gratified all at once. "Because, if you can keep from feeling *too* sorry for yourself, I've got somebody you need to look up when you get home. She's my cousin: her name is Sue Darlington. She's from Balford, Wyoming—didn't you say you have a grandma or somebody up there? But she's teaching down in Utah, in Springville. That's all of ten minutes from Provo." When Myron didn't react, his companion said, "You *are* going back to school, right?"

Even Clair Elroy's irrepressible hope hadn't supplied a real name of a real live girl.

"I quit going to class," Myron said, setting his shoes on the floor. "Wound up withdrawing from everything, except Religion. And I flat-out flunked that."

Virlinger was undeterred. "Talk to Admissions; they'll let you back in. They cut returned missionaries a lot of slack; they figure two years doing this changes a lot of things."

They looked at each other.

"I don't have any idea what I'd take."

"You build cabins," Virlinger said. "So take forestry. Take Elk Hunting 101. Take *something*." He paused. "I'm dead serious. You got to do this, do you understand me? She's maybe twenty-three, twenty-four. Go back to school and look her up. She's no cheerleader, but, next to Melody, she's the best girl on earth. And get a tetanus shot. You got to promise me, Elder Haymore."

Myron found himself nodding.

Virlinger yawned and lay down on the cot, drew the sheet up to his neck and flapped it twice. "I've got her address somewhere. And a phone number." Within two minutes his eyes closed. He seemed already asleep when the drowsy voice added, "I wouldn't recommend her to just anybody."

Myron waited a long time to let his companion settle for the night. He considered writing her a letter, just so it would bear an Ecuadorian postmark, to prove he had done this. Maybe first thing tomorrow. Right now another chore was more pressing. Cautious of floor squeaks, he stepped to the bathroom and soaped the washcloth again. Back at his cot, he reopened a tin of shoe polish and picked up the Florsheims. When he had finished rubbing and buffing, he spread an old issue of *Church News* on the floor next to his companion's cot and set the shoes on it. Only then did he finally take off his shirt and pants and pull the string to the light switch.

For a long while after he stretched out on his well-worn mission mattress, before he draped and tucked his mosquito net, he listened to the fan, to distant salsa music, to Virlinger. Through the window grille, he saw the moon high over El Salado, the same moon shining on snowy slopes all over the world, on magnificent herds of elk. They would never get together for boating or water-skiing or golf—all the things companions promised to do together after the mission. But he thought about what Virlinger had said, what he meant, what he had promised. And on the last night in Ecuador, the last night before he went home to Mink Creek and his world, Myron believed him.

# Vigil

WHEN THE PHONE RANG AT 5:30 one Friday morning, Darl thought his older brother had had another one of his spells. Twice in the past month Eileen had called from the hospital after awakening in the night to gurgling instead of snoring from Roy's side of the bed. Both times she imagined his tongue blocking the throat like a rubber stopper and found his eyes rolled back under their lids, fluttering. And both times, before the paramedics even moved him from their gurney to an emergency room bed, Roy came to, asking, "What's this? What's going on?" In sixty-nine years he had never been a patient in a hospital.

So now, Darl and Avis, who lived only a mile away, on the same side of Balford, lay in bed wondering every time they heard a siren.

"No, we're home," Eileen said on the Friday morning of her latest phone call. "We got back a little early, and he went right to bed. He's sleeping fine." She paused. "That's why I wanted to call."

Even without Avis's urging, Darl would have asked if he could do anything. After the first trip to the emergency room and when subsequent tests and examinations at the hands of specialists required all-day visits to clinics in Cody or Billings, he had offered to help. Half a dozen times he had offered to feed their animals—a few cows, a pair of pigs, the dog—lay in more firewood, go for groceries, mind their water pipes on extra cold days.

But he had not volunteered to cover for them driving the mail truck's night route.

And so far, since Eileen had declined all help anyway, that one gap in his willingness went untested. She always thanked him, said they were managing.

Until this Friday morning in early February, when she said, "There is one thing."

"Whatever I can do," Darl said, imagining black ice on unfamiliar highway curves, bolting deer, weak night vision, heavy-headed sleepiness.

"He doesn't like not being able to drive," Eileen said. "Says he feels worthless just riding. But it still scares me to let him behind the wheel. The doctors can't find anything really wrong; the diabetes and blood pressure are under control. Then they turn around and tell me to be careful because this sort of thing happens without any warning. I already knew that—three thousand dollars ago!"

For a moment their laughter eased what Darl thought was the inevitable direction of the conversation.

"What if he has one of those apnea spells—or whatever it is—out in the badlands between Worland and Thermopolis, forty or fifty miles from a hospital?"

"Does she need somebody to drive for her?" whispered Avis, who well knew her husband's feeling toward that particular duty.

Darl held up his hand, concentrated hard on the telephone receiver. He wanted to tell Avis to go back to sleep, that he knew what he was doing, had everything under control.

After forty-odd years of marriage to him, she wasn't likely to believe that. But she was likely to relish what she saw as a better-late-than-never role reversal—a chance for Darl, the younger of the two youngest brothers in the family, finally to assume a little say-so in the relationship and for Roy to try *his* hand at deferring and acquiescing and putting up with and keeping quiet to preserve harmony. Despite the peace she had made with Darl's limitations, her old ambition still flared occasionally.

"Seizures or not," Avis had said just yesterday, "he shouldn't be driving truck at his age—especially at night. It's good money but not *that* good."

"I've got him an appointment Monday at a sleep clinic in Billings," Eileen was saying over the telephone. "We've got two nights off, so that's when I scheduled it. They're going to wire him up and watch him sleep. Between now and then, though—"

"Tell her you can drive," Avis whispered. "As many nights as they need."

Only on guard duty in the Army, only for a two-week rotation at the sugar factory one winter thirty years ago had Darl ever *had* to stay awake through the night. With little effort, he could still summon a profound fear of falling asleep when alertness was an obligation.

"Listen, Eileen," Darl heard himself say, strangely aware of his own breath reflected off the plastic of the telephone receiver, "if you need somebody to drive—"

"No," she said. "I can drive it. I'm fine with the driving; I'm used to it. We carry a two-way right in the truck, can radio in to Dispatch if anything happens. No," she said, "what I need is for Roy to stay home and for somebody to stay with him. He's not going to like it, but I think I can talk him into it if you're willing."

. . .

"This is silly," Roy said when Darl showed up on his doorstep at 4:30 in the afternoon with a shaving kit under his arm. "I told her this is silly."

"We've got a sleeping bag somewhere," Darl said. "I could've brought it."

"We raised seven kids," said Eileen, who wore heavy gray

sweats and running shoes Darl had never seen on her. "Bedding is one thing we've got plenty of."

The three of them stood in the kitchen where Eileen was covering a casserole dish with foil. She turned from the counter, slid it into the oven, punched the timer button. "Is stew okay?"

"Sounds good to me," Darl said.

"And there's salad and rolls. Just microwave them when you're ready."

Roy stood staring at the shaving kit. "Is that all you brought?"

"What else do I need?"

"Clothes, pajamas . . . something."

"Oh, pajamas!" Eileen said. "You've never worn pajamas."

"Maybe Darl does. I thought I'd ask."

"I bought you a pair right after we got married, and I don't think you've worn them twice. You said you didn't *need* pajamas—like they were an insult. They're probably still in your drawer."

"I've never needed a baby-sitter, either."

"He's been like this all day," she said, turning to Darl. "I knew he'd fuss."

"I'm not fussing," Roy said. "But I am hungry. When will that stuff be ready?"

"About an hour."

"Will I be okay till then?" Roy asked. This time he looked at Darl, said, "You might end up tending a corpse. I could die of low blood sugar before nightfall."

"Nobody's dying tonight," Eileen said. "You're right on your schedule. You ate half a box of Ritz just two hours ago. You're in no danger." She looked directly at Darl, and for an instant her voice changed. "He's had his shot. You don't need to worry about that."

"Yep, she poked me," Roy said. "My life is in her hands."

She dismissed the comment with a wave. "I've got a fruit cocktail for your dessert, and brownies."

"Sugar-free, I bet."

"What do you think? And don't forget your pills." She hesitated, as if checking off a mental list. "I'll start a load of wash, but you don't have to bother with it."

Her disappearance into the utility room was followed by the ratcheting of the washer knob, the pull-click, the water spilling. When she stepped back into the kitchen, she put on her coat. "I've got your beds made up in my sewing room," she said. In their sweep from brother to brother, her eyes lingered just an instant on Darl. "The light has a dimmer switch. And don't forget there's a phone in there."

Roy reached out and smoothed the fit of her coat on one shoulder, straightened the already-straight collar. "You drive careful," he said sternly. "Those bridges outside Greybull always ice, and being the weekend, they'll have that truck loaded tonight— all the junk mail going out."

"I'll be careful." From a stool beside the counter she gathered a scarf and stocking cap, purse and gloves, and when she turned back toward them, her eyes had misted. "And I won't miss your backseat driving."

"You wouldn't admit it if you did."

She looked straight at Roy, said, "He's crabby and he likes to overdo it on those brownies."

"There's few enough pleasures in my condition."

"You don't have a condition."

• • •

"I sure miss my molars," Roy said. He blew on his second spoonful of stew, slurped, rolled it around in his mouth, chewed with his front teeth. "That dentist in Cody wanted to pull them all—makes a killing off dentures. I told him no thanks, I'm going to use what I got till they're gone."

Almost as a reflex, Darl located each of his own molars with his tongue.

"Eileen's granddad, old J. Guyman, still had his own teeth

when they buried him—ninety-seven years old. You remember J. Guyman."

Darl nodded dutifully.

"Strong teeth run in the LeGrand genes," Roy said. "One of the many virtues of body I've always admired in my wife. By the end, J. Guyman's were pretty mossy looking, but they functioned. And that's more than a lot of us can say about our parts."

It was true. Old friends with bone fractures and crumbling joints, neighbors with various cancers, in-laws undergoing bypass surgery, their older brother Elwin and his encroaching senility, one cousin's defective thyroid, another's prostate—Darl couldn't think of anybody of their generation who was likely to make it to ninety-seven. And aside from some deafness in one ear and occasional gall bladder problems, he was more likely than most.

"I tell you," Roy said, "we're falling apart." He split two rolls and buttered the halves, then looked at Darl. "Does Avis mind you doing this?"

"Are you kidding?" Darl said. "She insisted."

"I know Eileen sure doesn't like being alone in the house."

"She wanted to send food."

"Make a party of Roy's decrepitude?"

"No. Just the good old days working on her. 'You two will be batching it just like you used to.' That's what she said."

"Did you tell her batching isn't all it's cracked up to be? All we talked about when we didn't have a wife was getting one."

"I know. But that's not what she's thinking about. She's thinking about us farming Dad's place together, fifty-fifty. Before I bought my own and right away started needing your help, always borrowing something—"

Roy set his fork down. "Let's get this straight," he said, wagging a finger. "Nobody owes anything here tonight. You always took care of your end."

For a moment they stared at each other over the curling steam of the food.

"I hadn't courted her yet," Darl said, "and she didn't even

know you. She didn't know what it was like—us farming together. But she's made that time into her own memory. It's a fondness to her."

Roy shook his head, said, "Memory's a funny thing."

• • •

The dining room where they sat eating was part of the original house. Their dad bought the place the spring of 1927, and that fall, after his sheep came off pasture in the Beartooths, he built this room and a kitchen and two upstairs bedrooms. Their sister Glenda claimed she remembered standing at the window eating a flapjack when Roy was born the next spring, said the shearers could hear his crying from out in the wool shed. Strong first cry, they said, meant a healthy baby. She couldn't have been more than three years old, but Darl had never thought to question her power of recall.

Nor had he ever questioned people's memories of his own birth—nearly a month early, during the winter's worst blizzard, and breech. By then the house had another bedroom and a kind of parlor built on to the kitchen. Between the cookstove and rock fireplace, the new parlor was the warmest room in the house, so that was where his dad set up the birthing bed. Somehow, their neighbor, Foley Haws, got word of trouble and tramped cross-country, following a fenceline right to their cellar door, to help give a blessing to Darl's mother. Darl's two oldest brothers waited with a team a mile up the lane by the highway turn-off, broke trail for the doctor's car until it got stuck. Then they hitched up and sledded it on the running boards until the last impassable drift, brought him the rest of the way mounted on one of the Belgians. Glenda, always the most pious of Darl's siblings, remembered the horses' appearance in the swirl of blowing snow as a prayer answered and the high-riding, half-frozen doctor as an angel. Because, as she told the story, her six-year-old mind was worried sick about what this labor was doing to her mother, and her six-year-old muscles verged on collapse from hour upon hour of hauling wood and coal to the back porch.

Except for Roy, they all remembered—couldn't seem to forget—the last, extra agony caused by his surprisingly big shoulders, the panic at his wrinkled blueness, his first pitiful cries. Darl knew the story of jaundice and colic, of the apple-crate bed in front of the stove, better than he knew stories of his own daughter's first days.

"We didn't know if your Uncle Darl was going to make it or not," Glenda often told children and grandchildren, nieces and nephews and *their* children. "But thanks to Heavenly Father, he did."

With him liable to spit up and choke at any moment, they had to watch him day and night—no rest for any of them. And he was a sickly thing—prone to thrush or croup or pink eye or fever. This vein of memory always led, in the telling, to Glenda's task that first long winter of tending the apple crate in front of the fireplace. It was her job to watch for sparks popping beyond the screen and to move him, quick as lightning, at the first hint of a smoky downdraft.

His sister's most cherished—and repeated—recollections featured spiritual promptings that had saved Darl's life. In each of these stories, she played the role of the selfless child inexplicably awakened from her forgivable dozing to do something heroic. Once, during an earth tremor, she snatched the apple crate out of the path of the falling mantel clock. "It would have smashed that crate's slats into kindling," she said. Another time she flicked a black widow from the baby blanket into the flames of the fireplace. "It must have come up from the cellar some way," she always said, "attracted to the warmth. It wasn't more than an inch from your Uncle Darl's little chin, some of the most toxic venom on earth—and me scared to death of spiders."

• • •

They finished the stew and started in on the fruit cocktail and Eileen's sugar-free brownies.

"Was it really a black widow?" Darl asked. Avis had always doubted the black widow part of the story, just as she doubted that a six-year-old girl, however prayerful, fully grasped the biology of birth. While she generally got along with Glenda, Avis did not care for her rendering of Darl's early history.

"I don't know how she would've known," Roy said. He chewed apple chunks and grapes one at a time with his front teeth, gummed the banana slices. "I couldn't tell one—not for sure—until I was thirteen." He took another bite of his brownie and winced. "Eileen can say what she wants, but that fake sweetening is nowhere near as good as the real McCoy."

"How about that time in the sleeping bag?" Darl asked. "I'm outside in the yard camping under a tarp tent, and she's upstairs in her room—and she *hears* me suffocating."

"Wasn't that one a prompting?" Roy said.

"No," Darl said, "she claims she heard me, with her own ears." He smiled. "She didn't need God's nudging *every* time she saved my life."

"Either she had awfully good ears, or that was one noisy suffocation."

"You should know. You were in the tent with me."

Brownie crumbs had gathered at one corner of Roy's mouth. "I remember you being turned around and sweating—that sleeping bag had real goose down—but you weren't in danger. You were breathing. So she's got her story a little mixed up." He chewed a last bite of apple and said, "Now me—I've seen you in real danger."

Darl knew instantly what he was talking about.

"It would've been my fault," Roy said, "any way you look at it—any way Mom and Dad would have looked at it. Inner tubes down that stretch of the river! All those rocks and snags. What was I thinking? If one of my own boys had pulled such a stunt, I would've blistered his butt good. If you'd a drowned . . ."

"How did you know to turn around and look?" Darl asked. "When my tube flipped, you were floating twenty yards ahead of me."

"A little prompting of my own," Roy said. "I knew you couldn't swim—which was my fault because I was supposed to teach you. But all of a sudden, I really *knew* it."

"You tried; I just wasn't much of a student."

"That wouldn't have been much of an excuse if you'd a drowned."

Roy began a slow nod, and the eyebrows and lips drew toward his nose, the way they always did when he grew reflective.

"I tell you," he said after a moment, "a thought like that sobers you to the bone."

The fruit was gone, and they stared at the mostly empty brownie pan, then at each other.

"Sugar-free or not," Darl said, "we made short work of those."

"You be sure and tell Eileen you ate your half."

Roy drained his glass, leaned back with his arms stretched above him, and let out a loud belch-hiccup. When the chair rocked back on all four legs, supper was over. While one hand held his plate close beneath the edge of the table, the other brushed crumbs onto it. Then he crisscrossed the knife, fork, and spoon beside a few bits of gristle, added the glass and the wadded paper towel. Then the chair scraped back, and he stood.

Darl had seen his brother end a thousand meals in just this way.

"Wouldn't it be something," Roy said on his way to the sink, "if it was the fake sweetening triggering my spells?"

• • •

Mainly because Glenda had never got hold of it, the near-drowning was not part of the family lore on Darl's close calls. In fact, no one knew of it except Darl and Roy—and Avis. And this particular secret was safe with her.

"I'm glad he saved your life," she said on the morning Roy showed up to help his newlywed brother get the last of his bean seed in the ground on time, "but he doesn't need to save you anymore."

The same thing happened that first harvest, and many thereafter—Darl's predicaments eased because of Roy's watchful generosity.

*Too* watchful, Avis thought. "Tell him we appreciate the gesture," she always said, "but we don't need the help. You can't depend on the man all your life, Darl."

He granted that Roy's charity could be presumptuous and meddling and impetuous, and he granted that dependence on such charity betrayed his own inabilities. But over and over he tried to explain that, like Roy himself, it *could* be depended on. And that was worth a lot.

"Worth you never getting ahead?" she once asked, desperate to believe that Roy's successes came at Darl's expense. "Why don't you get thirty or forty more of your own cattle?" she asked when beef prices were high, "instead of pasturing Roy's for next to nothing?"

"He pays the going rate," Darl said. "Besides, I've got more cows than I can handle now."

"Roy seems able to handle them—at 75 cents a pound."

"Roy can handle a lot of things I can't."

"So I've noticed."

He knew she was sorry, knew she said such things not to demean or even indulge frustration, but to spur in him a fuller ambition. And her ensuing silence and welling eyes seemed to question both the possibility of such ambition and her justification in expecting it.

Yet every time the brothers traded work, shared equipment, exchanged money, whenever Darl forgave Roy's well-intentioned, matter-of-fact criticism or overseeing, Avis was more convinced of inequity. And the harder he tried to explain the intricacies of such dealings, to defend Roy's essential goodness, the less satisfied she was.

"Always sticking up for him," she said. "You're going to go to your grave indebted to the man."

She spoke that way until ten years ago, when the bottom dropped out of their livelihood, when the bank spared his inconsequential operation and more or less told Roy his farming days were over.

"Before this is through," Roy told his younger brother, "it'll get us all."

In the end, Roy was left with the house and barns, eighty acres of their dad's land to rent to whoever was still in business, and a misnamed retirement that required him and Eileen to get what banker Frett Maxwell Jr. called paying jobs. She worked in the cafeteria of Cody Community College, and Roy got on the feedlot's night crew, mixing silage and grain ration for $5.50 an hour.

Yet, when a mail route came open a few years later, it was offered to Darl—$105 per nightly run, better money than a man his age could ever hope to earn as a school custodian, hardware clerk, or gatekeeper at the auction ring. When almost the same day a neighbor came to him willing to rent his place, Darl couldn't help but think seriously about the alignment of opportunity. Since, as Avis reminded him, his monthly social security check at that point would have been chicken feed, he had better do *something* while he was still able. And he would rather drive a mail truck than wear a big key ring and sweep the gym floor during halftime at basketball games. He couldn't see himself prodding cattle while playing straight man for the auctioneer or swapping jokes through the high fence with old cowboys.

Despite the best of reasons, it was anguishing to pass up such a rare boon.

"But why?" Avis pleaded when he finally told her. "Tell me why, Darl."

"I don't expect you'll ever believe me," he said, "but it wasn't the night driving I was thinking of."

In the exquisiteness of her disappointment, Avis could not hear him. "You'd have gotten used to it," she said. "I would have ridden along, kept you awake."

• • •

At 8:30 Avis called—in the middle of a pretty good television movie.

"Is everything okay?" she asked. "I thought I better check."

At first Darl tried short answers to her questions.

"But what *kind* of stew?" she wanted to know.

"Potatoes, carrots, meat—what other kind is there?"

"Oh, you're no help."

For the fifth time he said they were fine, promised to call if anything went wrong.

"Darl," she said, "do you think—if something happens— you'll hear him and wake up? Do you think you'll be able to?"

"I'm going to try."

"I'll call every hour if you want."

"Thanks," he said, "but—"

"Ask Roy if he's got any No Doz."

"I don't need No Doz. You just go to bed. I'll be fine."

"Darl, you know how you get at night."

"I'll be fine."

When he walked back into the living room—Eileen had never called it a parlor—Roy was dozing in his recliner, cradling a box of Ritz crackers.

For an instant, Darl listened closely and cherished, even against the overloud television, the sound of his brother's snoring. If it was clear now, surely he could hear it in the quiet of the night. Surely he would miss it if it stopped.

What if Roy went into shock? Mouth-to-mouth, the Heimlich, CPR—posters and procedures blurred in his mind. When their daughter was still home, Avis had insisted on first aid training. Two evenings of elevating legs, palm thrusts, wool blankets, finger-probing to clear any foreign matter (for example, a mouthful of Ritz), tilting the head, pinching the nostrils and blowing. He remembered the lady at the 4-H building demonstrating on the dummy, spreading a fresh square of plastic wrap over the molded lips, looking at the class and asking, "Who's next?"

He turned the TV down, touched Roy's shoulder. "You ready for bed?"

Roy awoke with a start, rubbed his face all over with one hand. "Is the show over?"

"Not yet, but you were conked out."

"Just dozing a little. I wouldn't call that conked out. Sit down. Let's finish the show." Roy held out the box of Ritz. "Have some crackers."

Darl took a handful and sank into the other recliner, grateful for another hour before bedtime.

"Why did you turn it down? I can't hear it."

"It was blaring. You'd think we're stone deaf."

"We are," Roy said. He stared hard at the television screen, as if his eyes could do what his ears couldn't. "What did Avis want?"

"She wondered what we had for supper."

• • •

Halfway into the ten o'clock news, Roy shook Darl awake.

"Some guardian you are," he said. "Let's hit the hay. The bathroom's all yours. I already brushed my five teeth."

At the bathroom sink, Darl splashed cold water on his face, stretched his eyes wide open, tried to steel himself against drowsiness. When he flushed the toilet, the house's plumbing whined, and a jar of potpourri rattled on the tank lid. At the door, hand poised on the knob, he hesitated, then, at the peak of the toilet tank's whistling refill, turned back to the medicine cabinet's mirrored door. Without a cover sound, Roy's selectively deaf ears would have picked up the squeak of cabinet hinges like radar, would have prompted more questioning.

*Need something, Darl? Got a problem?*

The glass shelves of the medicine cabinet held a shaving mug and razor, Eileen's hair dye and lotion, a mostly empty bag of cotton balls, alcohol, syringes, Crest toothpaste, Listerine, Rolaids, Kaopectate.

And no No Doz.

So there, Avis Louise.

Stepping out of the bathroom, Darl glanced at the closed door of Roy and Eileen's bedroom.

"Ain't it something?" Roy had said the day before his wedding, after Darl helped him carry in Eileen's cedar chest and a new box spring and mattress. "A license and a bed, and I'm a married man. No more sleeping alone."

They had both smiled. Then, as they stood over the clean, unsheeted mattress, the quiet grew awkward.

"If *I* can find somebody," Roy said, "anybody can."

He spoke as if to console, though Darl felt no need for consolation. He was happy for Roy and his mattress.

He remembered their driving off after the wedding in the Idaho Falls Temple and their first night home after the honeymoon in Red Lodge. A mere four months into their marriage, they announced the first of Eileen's many robust pregnancies, gigglingly acknowledged the potency of the alpine breezes off the slopes of the Beartooths.

He and Avis, on the other hand, tried every fertility quackery under the sun, every theory of timing, diet, lunar correlation, and body temperature—and still did not achieve conception until eight years into their marriage. And despite their desire to give their daughter a sibling or two, her birth was a miracle they never could duplicate.

In two steps, Darl crossed the little hall into Eileen's sewing room. On the wall above the sewing machine hung perhaps a dozen old photographs—his parents' unsmiling propriety in front of the Salt Lake Temple on their wedding day, several renderings of the whole family at eight- or ten-year intervals, each brother in military uniform, Glenda's trusting, watchful face in her high school graduation portrait.

"I don't know why Eileen put us in here," Roy said.

Both cots had been turned down, and he was sitting on one of them in his underwear. As Darl sat on his own bed, he tried to remember the last time he had seen his brother undressed. When they were young, Roy was always stronger and faster, arms and legs thick with muscle, barrel chest heaving powerfully under any strain of work or play. And so much stamina. Nobody outlasted Roy.

Now, in the room's light, his legs looked skinny, blue-veined and pallid, the toenails thick and yellow as horn. Patchy, grizzled hair covered the sagging flesh of his chest.

"We could've both fit in that bed of ours," Roy said. "It's queen-size and a heck of a lot more comfortable than one of these cots. I told her we grew up in the same bed, smuggled bread and jam, crackers, read comics with a flashlight. Do you remember that?"

Darl nodded.

"Cracker crumbs! Sounds almost kinky, don't it?"

Roy leaned back once, twice, then, with the momentum, his feet cleared the floor, swung over the mattress's edge, slid between the sheets. He slapped a hollow in his pillow, wormed his hips forward, then lay down and drew the covers to his chin. After a long breath, he exhaled slowly.

"In my condition," he said, "there hasn't been much of anything happening in bed for quite a while. Like a goat my whole life—bothering Eileen the minute we crawled in the sack. And now . . ."

Already his eyes were closing. A minute passed before he mumbled, "Get the light, would you?"

Attentive to the steady puffing through nostrils and lips, Darl lifted his own feet one at a time, grabbed the shin of the bent leg and held it while he untied the shoe and pried it off. The instant the second shoe hit the carpeted floor, Roy's hands let go of the covers and relaxed.

Six hours until Eileen would finish her run.

Six hours.

Darl loosened his belt but took off neither pants nor shirt. Sitting perpendicular on the cot, he stuffed the pillow between his back and the wall, stretched toes and fingers, flexed his neck. With anything in the world to worry about, Avis would sleep poorly, would suffer from a headache all day tomorrow and would ask him tomorrow night to rub her forehead with Vicks. And he would gladly oblige. Heaven only knew how many of his sore spots she had soothed, how many thistles and ticks and splinters she had dug out of him.

From his cot, Darl reached the light's dimmer switch. One last time he looked toward the photos on the far wall, fixed in his mind the location of the telephone on the table beside the sewing machine, the path from cot to doorway, from doorway to driveway, the distance from house to hospital. Then he turned the round switch—dimmer, dimmer—until he could just see Roy's profile, until Glenda's watchful countenance lingered only in his mind, until at last he trusted himself to keep this night's vigil.

# Signs of the Times



*First Seal*

BEFORE THE ASHWURMS MOVED down from Alaska in a converted school bus, Lyndon Haws never gave a thought to the signs of the times. Then, on the first Sunday in August of 1970, one week before Lyndon's twelfth birthday, Brother Orlin Ashwurm stepped to the podium of the Balford chapel for the first time. He cleared his throat ominously. With a bit of tissue fished from the pocket of a maroon sports coat, he swabbed the tip of his tongue, pointed to his seven children and pregnant wife on a front pew, and said, "Brothers and sisters, I have brought my family to Wyoming to prepare for the desolations ahead!"

Had Lyndon been older, and seated somewhere besides the back pew with his own family, he might have noted the adoration on the face of the middle child and oldest boy, a thirteen-year-old named Boon. He might also have noticed the forbearance of Sister Dove Ashwurm, who undoubtedly had heard the same testimony of bleak prospects during seven other pregnancies. As it was, he focused mostly on the wad of tissue—and the worry on the face of the man presiding over this particular fast and testimony meeting, Bishop Frett Maxwell Jr. After such an introduction, there was no telling how far adrift Brother Ashwurm might end up.

Pretty far, as it turned out. Instead of bearing testimony of the Savior and living prophets and the restoration of the gospel and the Book of Mormon, Orlin Ashwurm lectured on the signs of the Second Coming—all things in commotion, love waxing cold, wars and rumors of wars, earthquakes, famine, pestilence. And those were the cheerful elements of his message. He also spoke of flies infesting the earth, flesh peeling from bones, eyes falling from sockets, the sun growing dark and moon turning to blood.

It was rare for a testimony to go over five minutes. It was even rarer for Lyndon to pay attention beyond the first five seconds. But on this day, as the calamities and woes went on and on, he remained rapt. While Brother Ashwurm spoke, clouds gathered over Balford, and the light from the chapel's small side door grew dim. Just as Brother Ashwurm got to the voice of thunderings, a great boom rattled the walls. In the instant before the electric lights and microphone died, he looked heavenward with a weird grimace, as if expecting flames.

A long minute passed. Gazing out over the congregation, the figure at the podium wagged an apocalyptic finger, cleared his throat again, and went fishing in the pocket of the maroon sports coat. Before he could haul out the spent tissue, Bishop Frett Maxwell stood and put a hand on his shoulder. Amid whispers, he guided Orlin Ashwurm away from the pulpit and pointed him back down toward his family. Then the bishop said, "If you'd all bear with me, let's stand and sing 'Scatter Sunshine.'"

In the car on the way home, Lyndon's mother said, "That was some testimony."

"A little doomsday for my taste," his dad said. Leaning over the steering wheel and craning his neck, he peered upward through the windshield.

Sitting in the back seat, next to the window, Lyndon knew why. The storm had not broken up; it was moving south of Balford, out toward their farm. Clouds along the river bluffs hung low and black. Turning off pavement and onto the Hawses' rutted lane at five o'clock on a summer afternoon, the car seemed headed into nightfall.

"These *are* perilous times, Earl."

"Times have always been perilous; you can't quit on life just because of that."

"Seven kids and one on the way—I wouldn't call that quitting on life."

"Before Alaska it was Canada," his dad said. "Before that, California and Nevada. After the meeting, he was talking about his travels."

"Maybe he hasn't found his niche," his mom said.

"His niche is being het up about the millennium."

"Someday he'll say he told us so."

"That someday is for the Lord to decide," said Lyndon's dad, "not Orlin Ashwurm."

The car pulled into their yard and came to a stop no more than thirty feet from shelter and safety. Yet for the first time in his life, Lyndon wondered whether such shelter would suffice.

Twenty minutes later, when stones as big as marbles slanted out of the sky, he remembered Brother Ashwurm's reference to a great hailstorm sent to destroy the crops of the earth. For five minutes, Lyndon's dad cocked his ear to the drumming on the roof of the house, straining to hear a reprieve or abatement. And for the rest of his life, Lyndon would not forget his mother standing at the kitchen sink, staring in ashen despair at the rain-streaked window.

Goosed by a jolt of electricity somewhere up the line, the telephone sounded with one short, frightening jingle. Immediately a clap of thunder rattled the house, and for the second time that day, the lights died.

"This kind of lightning is nothing to mess with!" his dad yelled. "Get down in the basement!"

Downstairs, while the rest crowded in the dark on an old

love seat and spare cot, Lyndon followed his dad to the door between basement and root cellar. Even on the best of days, with a sixty-watt bulb instead of a flashlight for illumination, the cellar was no place to linger. But on this Sabbath afternoon in August, as the flashlight beam probed for leaks around creosoted ceiling timbers, *everything* became a harbinger: hairy onions hung in net sacks, the dead bulb's string-switch dangling like web, sealed buckets of flour stacked against one earthen wall, and a corner potato bin empty at this season except for a mushy cull or two. Plywood shelves built against the other three walls sagged beneath ranks of mason jars. The jars displayed, as in the murk of formaldehyde, stew beef and dill pickles and cherries the size of eyeballs. In the cool darkness, Lyndon waited for the onset of doom.

The pelting on the roof slowed, then stopped. Through a high basement window, the light brightened. With his siblings, Lyndon scrambled up the stairs, eager for fair weather. Then he saw his mom and dad standing at the open screen door, their backs to him. He separated himself from the younger children and, with his parents, stared at hail banked two feet deep against the patio, already melting and slushy in the storm's muggy after-warmth.

On private cue, the three of them stepped outside and wandered separate, aimless courses from garden to orchard to the closest fields.

A great hailstorm.

As concerned the Hawses' farm on the first Sunday in August of 1970, this one qualified. It punched sizable holes in melons and tomatoes and apples. It shredded corn and alfalfa. It made mulch of pinto vines thick with swelling pods. It pounded ripe barley into muddy straw. It stripped every leaf from every stalk.

Lyndon and his parents came together by the flower bed.

"My roses are gone," said Ruby Haws, holding three petals in her cupped palm.

"They'll come back," Lyndon's dad said.

"I really don't care about the squash," she said, "or even the transparents—though they make such good applesauce." Her eyes glistened with tears. "But I do hate to lose my roses."

"They'll come back."

## Second Seal

The roses and apples did come back the next year, and the next. But that regeneration was not enough to persuade Lyndon that the world was going to last long enough for him to grow up in it. During this period, he could not behold the least crimson tint in clouds at dawn or in a rising moon without a deep foreboding. Church leaders and teachers only compounded the feeling. They were forever saying that *this* generation of youth was reserved for the latter days, chosen to usher in the end of times. For Lyndon, at age fourteen, being thus selected was a dubious honor.

His list of harbingers grew. The spring burning-off of fields called to mind the wicked as stubble. On hot June afternoons the action of two belt canvases swathing a sickle-width of alfalfa signified the gathering of scattered Israel. And harvest—load after load of crop bearing a percentage of dirt, stems, weed seed— was one long reminder of the fate of tares.

Then, in September of 1972, in a season when he needed no more reminders of the world's demise, Lyndon and his dad were assigned to home teach the Ashwurms every month.

"I can't get anybody else to go up there," Bishop Frett Maxwell said. "And by the way, Brother Orlin is out of work again."

The Ashwurms lived in the foothills of the McCoulloughs, six miles above Balford, the last five of those miles on dirt road. Since the one time Lyndon had seen the Ashwurms' property, two years earlier during a service project to clear it of sagebrush, the place had grown into a sort of compound. Marking the entrance at the south perimeter was the converted school bus. At the north perimeter sat a double-wide trailer with a built-on shed porch. To the west, perched on jack stands, an aluminum-shelled camp trailer served as the first home of the eighteen-year-old daughter—the oldest—and her nineteen-year-old husband. Inside the perimeter was the motor fleet: a station wagon with cardboard in one side window and sheet plastic in another, an old pickup truck missing a tailgate, a Volkswagen Beetle featuring hood and trunk of different colors, a van with no radiator grill or hubcaps, and an Army jeep resting on four flat tires. The vehicles filled spaces between a work shed clapped together from plywood scraps, a septic tank buried up to the lid and no further, an outhouse, garden plot, clothesline, makeshift hog pen and milk cow stanchion, chicken and rabbit hutches, and several big dog houses, whose tenants converged the instant the home teachers' own pickup rolled to a stop. ("They won't bite!" five Ashwurms yelled.) And right in the middle of everything lay a hole the size and shape of a grave.

"That's my bomb shelter," said Orlin Ashwurm as he ushered his new home teachers through the unscreened porch of the main trailer, past stacked cases of canned food and a haunch hung from a rafter with blood-stained baling twine. The meat was green with aging. In the living room, Brother Ashwurm took the one obvious seat, a big vinyl recliner worn through at the headrest. Sister Ashwurm and the home teachers got kitchen chairs. The bride and groom squeezed onto the one other piece of upholstered furniture, a frayed ottoman. The other kids sat on crates and catalogues, stools and food-storage buckets. Fifteen-year-old Boon sat cross-legged on the floor, at his father's feet.

After listening to a long endorsement of rebar as the key material in designing a shelter against concussion, radiation, and firestorm, Lyndon's dad managed to ask about work.

"Well, if you're referring to the paying kind," Orlin Ashwurm said, "not so good. But I'll tell you straight up, I lose no sleep over material things. With the garden and animals, me and Dovey and the kids get by just fine."

Seated on a rickety chrome-legged chair, little more than arm's length from a sinkful of dirty dishes and an overflowing hamper and laundry basket, Sister Dove Ashwurm smiled forbearingly. She kept her hair in a bun and wore a calf-length work dress made of denim.

"Materialism," said Brother Ashwurm. "That's the problem with this country. And the truth is, I got plenty to keep me busy right here. I need to get the rest of that shelter dug and the concrete poured. When everything falls apart, I'm going to be ready."

"With all the deer around here," said young Boon, "we could live on jerky alone."

Orlin Ashwurm tousled his son's hair. Lyndon imagined the family huddled in a hole, gnawing on greenish strips of jerky.

"I hear the feedlot is hiring," Lyndon's dad said.

So as not to be sidetracked from nuclear holocaust, Orlin Ashwurm waved a hand dismissively and said, "I worked over there most of last year."

"Three and a half months," Sister Ashwurm said.

Her husband cleared his throat, went to patting his pockets, finally found a tiny wad of tissue. "It's no wonder the drug companies are getting rich on cancer and what-not," he said. "Do you have any idea how many chemicals the government pumps into grocery-store beef?"

Twenty minutes stretched into an hour. Instead of Lyndon and his dad sharing a message, they listened as Orlin Ashwurm clued them in to the less well-known signs of the times. His list dwarfed Lyndon's. This Brother Ashwurm had a nose for anything sinister in the offing. The temperature in the Arctic and Sahara, new strains of disease and contagion, bizarre UFO sightings, political intrigue—to him *everything*, big or little, far or near, pointed to the imminence of the world's collapse.

And drugged beef was only one of the conspiracies Orlin Ashwurm was privy to. He read a lot of books. To back up whatever he was saying, he kept pointing a thumb to the overloaded shelves of a bookcase wedged behind the recliner. The titles were all of a kind. *And When That Day Cometh. Sure Signs and Certain Warnings. Great Shall Be the Fall.* From the many books, he knew of assassination plots, tanks and guns massed on distant borders for what would surely escalate into a third world war, huge vaccine shipments, enormous government orders for gas masks, body bags, caskets. He knew where the Ten Tribes were. He spoke authoritatively of food stockpiled in caves above Salt Lake City, of secret, high-level meetings and negotiations, of the Saints being called back to Missouri. He knew things no one else knew. He grasped implications no one else grasped.

"Daddy says there'll be hailstones big as baseballs," said young Boon, sitting proudly at his father's feet.

"Wasn't it golf balls last time?" asked Dove Ashwurm, smiling.

Her husband looked her way for just a moment before he turned back to Earl Haws and said, "You wouldn't happen to have a cement mixer I could borrow?"


*Third Seal*


So went the home teaching visits for the next three years. During the first half of that period, two more Ashwurm daughters got married, the denim of Sister Dove's work dress faded from blue to gray, and Earl Haws's cement mixer sat, unused, in the center of the compound, beside a hole that never got any deeper or broader.

"I can't find the right rebar," Orlin Ashwurm said.

"I don't think he's looking all that hard," Lyndon's dad said on the night they towed the mixer back home.

The perpetually unfinished bomb shelter was the first thing to ease Lyndon's worries about the end of the world. How urgent could it all be if even Brother Ashwurm was taking his sweet time to prepare? Maybe there was some hope for a future after all. This feeling grew when Lyndon turned sixteen and got his patriarchal blessing, which promised everything in due season—work and mission and schooling and marriage. Lyndon reasoned that none of those things could happen with an apocalypse underway.

But the biggest comfort of all was the failed prediction as to the exact timing of the Second Coming. During the Hawses' home teaching tenure, Orlin Ashwurm had already privately disclosed his target date. In fact, he mentioned it during every visit. But then, as if a wider audience would improve his odds, he stood at the town picnic on July 4, 1975, and prefaced his blessing on the food by wagging a finger and declaring, "One year hence!" And when, one year later, the Bicentennial came and went in Balford, Wyoming, without so much as an errant firecracker, people remembered.

*Fourth Seal*

While the failed prediction did not sap the monthly testimonies of their zeal, it pretty much destroyed their credibility. Despite his much reading and expertise, Brother Ashwurm was no longer the featured speaker at emergency preparedness seminars. At best, he was invited to demonstrate water purification techniques or unusual pinto bean recipes.

As an even more unfortunate consequence, the failed prediction, with the attendant whisperings of quackery and nuttiness, divided the family. By the time Lyndon got his call to serve two years as a missionary in and around San Antonio, Texas, twenty-year-old Boon had married a girl from Wolf Point, Montana, and moved up there, a long way from the compound. Three vehicles and several sisters and their husbands went with him. Their departure left the three youngest children and, of course, Sister Dove. Shortly thereafter, Brother Orlin announced that he was moving the other direction, somewhere in Mexico.

"There's aquifers down there that hold ninety percent of the world's fresh water," he said, pointing a thumb behind him at the bookshelf.

In their final interaction as home teachers, Lyndon and his dad helped load the converted school bus for the long trip south. Up and down rickety porch stairs, in and out of the double-wide, they carried the family's belongings—box after box of canned food, buckets of wheat, and, of course, the books. *When Shall These Things Be? The Great and Dreadful Day. As a Thief in the Night.*

"Would you have any use for that?" asked Sister Dove Ashwurm, nodding toward a slab of aging meat. In the late afternoon light, with her worn-out house dress and disheveled hair bun, she looked tired and resigned. Fortunately her husband retracted the offer, and when they gathered for their good-byes, the meat swung from a hook screwed into the bus's ceiling, just inside the emergency door.

"I know you'll be on a mission and all," Orlin Ashwurm said as he shook Lyndon's hand a final time, "but missionaries aren't immune to troubled times."

Good old Brother Ashwurm. Seven years after that first testimony on a stormy Sunday in August, Lyndon had to smile at his own youthful gullibility, at all his groundless worries. Now, with so much of life ahead of him, he actually savored, if only for their charm, the farewell warnings about drug runners and mercenaries tunneling under the Rio Grande and the increasing incidence of killer hurricanes.


*Fifth Seal*


By the time Amelia hit the Texas coast on the last day of July, 1978, it had lost its hurricane potential. Port Isabel got off easy. No shrimp boats smashed. No trees snapped at telephone-pole height. No roofs laid bare. Sitting in an apartment in Medina, three hundred miles north, Lyndon's missionary companion, Elder Ted Cranney, voiced his disappointment.

"Some killer storm," he said. "I was hoping we'd get called down there to sandbag or rescue stranded folks in canoes—get us out of tracting for a couple of days." He said, "Now it's just going to rain."

Sitting at the apartment's little kitchen table a day later, five o'clock on a humid Tuesday evening, Lyndon Haws happened to look up from his macaroni and cheese at the open window above the kitchen sink. A gathering thunderstorm had brought them back to the apartment for an early supper, and several features of that storm now drew his attention—big, splotchy raindrops thumping the pane above the window opening, a hard breeze whistling through a flap of torn screen, and then, all at once, something punching the fine wire mesh.

Before Lyndon could identify the glistening on the screen as slush, before he could shut the window, the slush became ice. Now it was not his mother, but himself, standing at a sink, spellbound at a firmament's quantity of bouncing stones.

"You might want to get away from that window," said Elder Cranney.

Lyndon stepped back, still staring. For sixty seconds, the hail hammered shingles and roof gutters, and pocked aluminum siding. Suddenly, a single hailstone shot through the breach in the window screen, bounced off the kitchen counter, then skidded across linoleum until it came up against Lyndon's well-worn shoe. It was big as a golf ball.

Soon enough, hail gave way to the mere rain Elder Cranney had lamented. Downspouts ran full all night. Early the next morning a neighbor knocked on the door of the missionaries' apartment, which happened to be located on the north end of a road called Stringtown, well away from the river. Others weren't so lucky, the neighbor reported. The Medina was out of its banks, had already flooded Church Street and now threatened the avenues south of Highway 16. Could they come and help?

They got out of tracting for a full week, traded white shirts and ties for P-day jeans and tee shirts. Long after the sandbagging, after the rain stopped and the river crested and the flood waters receded, they helped various groups clean up. Into the fouled homes and apartments of strangers they went with hammers, wrecking bars, garden rakes, square shovels. They pulled up carpet and linoleum, tore out cabinets, stripped stud walls up to the water mark. By the wheelbarrow load, they hauled out soggy insulation and carpet padding. In close spaces, they tried to keep filter masks fitted to sweaty cheeks and noses but ended up breathing mildew anyway.

Everything immersed in the flood waters was ruined—furniture, appliances, rugs, toys, clothing, knickknacks, electric tools and gadgets, bedding, photo albums, books. Curbside piles grew. To keep the streets passable before the dump trucks came, loaders heaped the wreckage in front yards. Sometimes, at the bidding of an owner, even salvageable belongings went into the pile.

"There were snakes in that water," one lady said, as she directed the missionaries to her china cabinet. "I want it all gone."

The destruction was indiscriminate and its clean-up indiscreet. In one apartment, Lyndon shoveled a hundred pairs of women's shoes from the silt in a bedroom closet. In another bedroom, another apartment, the front panel of the top dresser drawer disintegrated with the first tug. Nested in the lingerie was a dead hamster. The most private contents of bureaus and bathroom vanities and medicine cabinets had floated to unlikely resting places—toothbrush in a toilet bowl, perfume bottle in a tackle box, packaged condom in a kitchen sink.

Lyndon had never seen ruin of such scope. Street after street, house after house, room after room. To one who valued stored food, going after the flood into kitchens and pantries and backroom larders was poignant. Every edible in every dwelling was spoiled or made suspect, if not by water, then by the heat and humidity since. Open packages—of anything—hosted maggots and weevil. By the wheelbarrow load, Lyndon and his companion threw away flour, sugar, coffee, cake mix, crackers, cold cereal, oatmeal, pasta, soup and vegetables and fruit. In many places, water had toppled jars and cans. There was broken glass. There were dents and bulges and lots of missing labels.

"If tetanus doesn't get you," said Elder Ted Cranney, "botulism will."

Avoiding such dangers was easy, though. You got a shot. You stayed clear. That's what Lyndon was thinking when, on the seventh morning of the clean-up, he came to the loaded chest freezer in a one-hundred-degree utility room. The normal food and drink left in refrigerators was, by now, unrecognizable for mold and rot and the sealed-in smell. But that smell was honeysuckle compared with what met Lyndon's nostrils when the shovel blade wedged open the freezer lid and flung it back on its hinges.

A week of no electricity and Freon had worked its magic on beef and pork cuts wrapped in freezer paper. Though he was closest to the stink, Lyndon didn't actually retch until he heard his companion's first cough. Then, like his companion, he was on his knees, heaving from the smell and the thought of the smell, wishing for the first time he had been somewhere else in the mission or the country or the world when the rains came to Bandera County.

"Geez-Louise," said Elder Cranney, clapping a hand over his nose and mouth, staggering to open a window, "there's no getting away from it."

Before they could drag the freezer to the pile outside, they had to empty it of several hundred pounds. T-bones and rump roast and chuck. Ribs and loin and chops. The ink had bled and faded on the soaked freezer paper, but the words were still readable. With watering eyes and churning bile, Lyndon rolled a wheelbarrow close. Holding his breath between trips to the window, he worked the soggy packages onto his shovel blade— gingerly. Woe unto him who broke the fragile paper and exposed color and texture. It was bad enough to follow the drips to the black-red juice pooled in the bottom of the chest.

Death and carnage. For the rest of that morning, the phrase kept going through Lyndon's head. They hauled the rotten meat to the front-yard pile, buried it beneath crumbled sheet rock, went on to other apartments and finally got away from the stink. Still, the fetidness lingered in his mouth and nostrils, dulled his appetite for the noontime sandwiches offered at a Red Cross station.

"You better eat," his companion said, holding a bologna sandwich in one hand and grape soda in the other. "I know you'd rather have a steak—aged just right and cooked rare—but this'll have to do."

Lyndon smiled at the joke. And that's when he saw, on a bench in the Red Cross eating tent, a wrinkled copy of the *Kerrville Daily Times*. While Elder Cranney had three doughnuts for dessert, Lyndon read headlines on the aftermath of disaster. An article on an inside page listed the names and ages of the twenty-nine people thus far known to have perished in the flood. Given the way the *Daily Times* article lay on the page, Lyndon started at the bottom and read upward, running the names of strangers over his tongue, along with the names of lots of little Texas towns besides Medina—Ingram and Hunt and Bandera and Pipe Creek and Lakehills.

Except for the few who were hit by floating debris, all the victims drowned—trying, for example, to cross flooded intersections or clinging above the torrent to tree branches until they couldn't cling anymore. In one especially sad case at a riverside campground, three children (ages two, four, and six) and their parents died when their tent was swept away. Lyndon imagined the toasting of marshmallows cut short by the first big rain drops, a hurried brushing of teeth and changing into pajamas, and a father zipping tent flaps shut against all threats of the night. But this father hadn't figured on high water. For that family, and the rest of the twenty-nine—the death toll was expected to rise— the last of the last days had finally come.

But not for anybody Lyndon knew. And of course he himself had survived and could still look forward to a future mostly unmarred by calamity of this kind, and certainly nothing to suggest a pattern culminating in the end of the world. Where this future would happen, he wasn't sure. But he wasn't going to stay any longer than he was assigned in the Hill Country of Texas. Whoever named the towns of Comfort and Utopia missed the mark. After seeing and smelling the effects of fifty inches of rain in a seventy-two-hour period, Elder Lyndon Haws, accustomed to a maximum of eight in a wet year, was bound for somewhere safer.

He smoothed a wrinkle in the newspaper so as to complete his reading of the dead. And that's when he saw Chihuahua, Mexico, listed as city of residence and *school bus camper caught in flash flood*, and knew before knowing that the accompanying name would be Orlin Ashwurm's.


*Sixth Seal*


It was the only name on the list of fatalities for which the article in the *Kerrville Daily Times* gave no location. So in the second half of his mission, and all the years thereafter, Lyndon could only wonder how close he might have been to the place of Orlin Ashwurm's great and dreadful end. More than once he dreamt of the converted school bus parked in a shady camping spot somewhere on low ground. When the dream was especially vivid, he saw water the color of hot chocolate sweeping and uprooting every familiar thing, eddying around tree trunks and bridge piers. Once he dreamt of chocolate water gushing through the bus's windows, soaking canned food and boxes of books, rising fast, and of Brother Ashwurm clinging to the haunch of venison until its tether tore loose from the ceiling hook.

But all this was dream. Lyndon wanted to know what had really happened. At home, right after his mission and then between semesters of BYU, he made inquiries. But no one, including his own parents, knew any more than he did about Brother Ashwurm's death. Nor could anyone tell him what had become of the family. During a visit home in December of 1982, four months before his graduation and marriage, he even drove the long road into the foothills to the site of the Ashwurms' deserted compound. In six years' time, scrub had overgrown the garden plot and reclaimed the cleared spaces. The only trace of the family or their patriarch was the never-completed hole for the bomb shelter, filled now with slough and tumbleweeds, and dusted with snow.

On the evening of that same cold day, Lyndon stood by the fireplace in his parents' home and told his dad he didn't plan, after all, to come back to the farm the next summer—or ever, actually. He wanted to teach philosophy at a university.

"And somebody pays you to do that?" his dad asked.

Lyndon went to more college, first a stretch in California, and still more in Wisconsin. He grew a beard; he grew broadminded. Gradually, the curiosity—and the dreams—about Orlin Ashwurm faded. On another visit home, in another private conversation by the fireplace, Lyndon told his dad that he had long since lost his testimony, that he had been merely going through the motions of religious faith for longer than he cared to admit, that he and his wife and children had formally parted company with the Church.

"How did this come about?" asked his dad, who that very morning had been out home teaching.

Among other things, Lyndon said, he had grown tired of living by fear; he preferred to live by knowledge. It was early January, 1988, and through a pair of sliding glass doors opposite the fireplace, they watched Ruby Haws pruning her resilient rose bushes. She didn't know the topic of their conversation, would cry later that evening when her husband told her. Despite his desire to be forthright with a man he loved and admired, Lyndon kept one important element of his explanation to himself: now that he had dismissed the doctrine behind them, he could happily dismiss the signs of the times and the last days altogether.

While Lyndon settled into teaching philosophy at a university in Carbondale, Illinois, his dad farmed the last years he would farm. One morning in the winter of 1992, his banker and former bishop, Frett Maxwell Jr., said, as kindly as it can be said, that Earl's livelihood was no longer a paying proposition. So, after forty years of farming, Earl Haws sold his machinery and cattle, and rented out his land.

It was to this retired farm of dormant shop, empty corrals, and strange hired men working in the fields that Lyndon finally brought his wife and children for a visit in August of 1999.

"You haven't been back in a long time," Earl Haws said, on a walk from garden to woodpile to orchard, the same path followed after the terrible hailstorm twenty-nine years earlier. Implied in the statement were two questions: Why? And, Why now?

Lyndon stopped under an old apple tree. Its branches sagged with fruit. "I don't know why," he said, "but lately I've felt a real desire to have my kids see what I came from."

"Does what you came from ever include any mention of the Church?"

"Truthfully?" Lyndon said, as much to himself as to his dad. "No more than I can help."

Then came the accident, on the third day of the visit. Lyndon's teenage son was riding his younger siblings around on an old motorcycle, first circling the yard, then the closest pasture, then crossing the plank bridge over the the flume of the irrigation lateral. On the last circuit, going much too fast, he hit the plank at the wrong angle. He and his four-year-old sister pitched onto the concrete flume and, fast as bobsledders, hit the churning pool at the bottom.

Riding his favorite mare nearby, the neighbor, Winn Bingham, saw the whole thing. At the very moment arms and shoulders and heads kissed the mossy concrete, he raked his horse's flanks with spurs which, up until then, had been mostly ornamental. How the mare covered such distance in such time would never be explained. Despite carrying seventy-two years and a scar down his sternum from recent heart surgery, Winn Bingham went directly from saddle to pool, floundering and groping in chest-high water, and in the process made all the moves his doctor had warned against. But without those moves, the little girl would have drowned, and the boy would have lived out a life plagued by guilt.

That night, while the rest of the house slept, Lyndon sat with his dad in front of the cold fireplace. He thought of the heroic rescue. He thought of the priesthood blessing his dad and Winn Bingham had given his daughter, a blessing he didn't put any stock in—but hadn't objected to, either. He thought of that daughter sleeping peacefully now with four stitches in her scalp and a big Band-Aid on her elbow.

"It's strange," Lyndon said. "I don't hold out a lot of hope for this world." He paused, then looked at his dad. "So why am I so glad that little girl still has a chance to grow up in it?"

"Same reason Brother Ashwurm never dug his hole any deeper."

Lyndon almost flinched. He hadn't thought of Orlin Ashwurm and his quackery in many years; he wasn't sure he liked the implied comparison. He said, "You don't think he was just shiftless?"

"That and loony," his dad said. "But he wasn't near as eager-beaver for the end of the world as he let on. His sort never is. He wanted to see life through, for him and his kids, same as any of us." Far away across the river, on the highway toward Cody, a siren sounded. "Close calls have a way of reminding us of that. We all hope for somebody to pull us from the waters."

"Hope, I'll grant," Lyndon said. "I'll give you hope. But not the kind cooked up by religion—especially Mormonism and its fixation on the Second Coming." He chuckled. "That's a hope I just can't swallow."

His dad looked at him and said, "You got a better kind?"

*Seventh Seal*

Less than three months later, Winn Bingham died of pneumonia. Lyndon didn't have to go home to Balford for the funeral, but he went. He could have flown, but he drove. He could have plotted a dozen different routes to get from southern Illinois to Wyoming, but he happened to choose one that took him, on his first day out, westward across the heart of Missouri. And at dusk, in search of gas and a place to eat—after driving three hundred miles without a break—he could have taken any one of several exits off the freeway, but he took a wrong one near a place called Grain Valley, just inside Jackson County.

By the time Lyndon admitted his mistake—no fuel or food anywhere close—he found himself, in the late October twilight, on a remote and narrow road. To leave behind freeway traffic so soon was strangely unsettling. He was hungry, and the needle of his fuel gauge now rested on empty. With each curve and dip in the road, his search for a place to turn around became more insistent.

After another mile, the road forked—pavement in one direction, gravel in the other. Lyndon stopped. Here at last was space enough to turn around—and backtrack how far before his engine sputtered? Perhaps the way to go was forward. In the fading light, both forks were gloomy, overarched by the limbs of huge, leafless trees. He switched on his lights. Farther up the unpaved lane he caught a glint of reflection. He eased his foot off the brake. The crunch of gravel sounded loud through the car's carpeted floorboard.

Until he rolled to within twenty yards, Lyndon didn't make out the rig. A small flatbed trailer stood hitched to an old minivan. The van's hood was propped open. Lyndon pulled behind the trailer and kept his lights trained on it. It was homemade and overloaded—dressers and box springs and mattresses and chairs and a big bookshelf stacked and tied every which way, with only a threadbare quilt to protect against the weather. Its tires were chocked with rocks. Stickers on its fenders heralded the new millennium: *2000 Is Coming and So Is the Lord! Ready or Not—Y2K.* And lashed behind the wheel well was a gas can.

Lyndon waited. He dimmed and undimmed the headlights. No one got out of the van. He killed his engine and climbed out of the car, stiff from his long drive. A chill breeze cut through his clothing. Pulling on a sweatshirt, he approached the trailer.

"Hello, the van!" he called.

For several seconds after his words faded, he heard only the breeze through trees. Then, through those same trees, from somewhere off the road, came a snatch of voice and laughter. Lyndon moved toward the sound. He stumbled through undergrowth and low-hanging branches. Every few steps he stopped to listen. Finally, skirting one big tree and then another, he saw the flicker of a fire.

Ten yards farther, and the woods opened onto a small clearing. Lyndon stopped in the shadow of an oak tree. In the center of the clearing, several adults and children stood around a smoky campfire, roasting something on sticks. Off to one side a woman in a lawn chair kept reaching into a cooler to fill the outstretched hands of the others. A hair bun stuck out beneath her scarf. In the middle of the woods, a long way from anywhere, she was wearing a dress.

And he knew before knowing that this woman was Dove Ashwurm.

"Antifreeze we've got," she was saying to a man standing between her and the fire, "but duct tape's going to be a little harder to come by. You can't hardly patch a radiator hose with chewing gum or Playdough."

Everyone laughed. Then the man cleared his throat, and the sound echoed down the years. For one instant, a maroon sports coat appeared on his shoulders, and a wad of tissue in his hand. It was as if, two decades after death by flood, Orlin Ashwurm had stepped through a curtain of memory and onto the duff of these remote woods in Jackson County, Missouri, a destination he never reached.

The throat clearer, of course, was Boon Ashwurm. The middle-aged woman had to be the wife from Wolf Point. The other? Maybe Boon's daughter. And the children around the fire—progeny of Orlin and Dove—were, like all children, growing up in the only world they had, facing the only future there is to face, one forever beyond the reach of knowledge.

Boon Ashwurm, hunched in a camouflage jacket, gingerly ate something from the end of his roasting stick. Whatever it was—bologna or Spam or overaged jerky—it smelled good. Standing in shadow at the clearing's edge, Lyndon keenly felt his own hunger.

A red moon edged up from the horizon, weirdly overlaid and veined by leafless branches.

"Look," one of the children said, pointing.

"Big as a basketball," Boon said.

"It's really kind of beautiful," his wife said.

"We wouldn't get far with a ruptured hose," Dove Ashwurm said with good humor. "But at least we've got food for the night and a jug of antifreeze."

And a full roll of duct tape in the trunk of a car parked just a short hike away. Stepping into the circle of firelight to make himself known, Lyndon was sure such resources would see them all through the calamities of another thousand years.

# Light of the New Day

*33*

THEY WERE KNEELING AT THEIR CHAIRS, on kitchen linoleum worn especially thin in the region of each kneecap. Arranged on the table top, eye-level between them, were two bowls, two spoons, two glasses, a plate of unbuttered toast and three boiled eggs, a pitcher of milk, jar of jam, and a seldom replenished sugar bowl. In the center of the table, resting on a folded dish towel, was the steaming pot, whose contents he never let himself know until *after* the prayer.

*We bow before thee, Heavenly Father, thankful again for the light of the new day.*

In her seventy-three years' worth of new days, certainly as long as he could remember, there had been no variation in the opening line. Even now, in mid-December, a full three hours prematurely, Edrus Penroy praised the sunrise in prayer. Even early in her widowhood, amid all the dark worries about the farm's fate, she had begun her prayer by invoking the light of a new day.

Nor did its staples vary. The first category of things to pray about was food. Whatever was in the pot, oatmeal or wheat mush or rice flavored with cinnamon, augmented by whatever was on the chipped plate, was blessed to nourish and strengthen them.

Then, after the transition to the hungry and needy, the staples poured forth: grateful for health and strength, mindful of sins and shortcomings, in need of wisdom and guidance. The list was long. She prayed for the sick and afflicted. She prayed for missionaries and soldiers. She prayed for the leaders of nations. She prayed for a troubled world. Finally, hunched for warmth in her lemon-colored housecoat, she prayed for loved ones—for protection and safety on his two sisters, much older than he and settled in places far distant from the farm, and on their good husbands, and on her eleven grandchildren.

The only variation in her prayers lay in the particulars associated with each staple. And these were dictated by the events of the season—military invasions, depressed crop prices, births, deaths, weddings. Ten years ago, for example, when his father died, she included themselves for a month or two among those who needed comfort in their mourning. And just in the last few weeks, her prayer had asked blessings on the forthcoming spring weddings of three of the younger tier of grandchildren, most recently the one named Myron.

He had heard every syllable a million times. But on this morning in December, just as he was ready to say amen and get to his breakfast, she paused, then uttered syllables new to both of them:

*And please bless Hewell . . .*

Only twice in his life had the condition of Edrus Penroy's only son prompted more than a brief particular. At age seven, he almost died from fever and croup. Then, at thirteen, forgetting his dad's caution, he climbed off the tractor without stopping the PTO and banged his shin against the baler's spinning drive-shaft, would have been pulled in and mangled if the leg of his jeans hadn't shredded in the first fraction of a second and torn away clean from leg and boot both. "Thank heavens for worn-out britches," Edrus Penroy had said.

But on this morning in December, with no sickness or accident in recent memory, she went on at such length, in such a peculiar, pleading tone, as to make him a staple all his own. Please bless Hewell and comfort Hewell and guide Hewell. In what way? To what end? Thanks to a sustained vagueness, calculated or otherwise, he could not know until almost the last sentence:

*Inasmuch as Myron has found a helpmeet, in like manner, please remember Hewell.*

Despite the marriages of four or five other grandchildren in the last few years, it was the announcement of Myron's that finally called attention to Hewell's singleness. This was the Myron who left college a month into his first semester to live in the mountains until snowfall, the hunter who ate deer liver raw, the boy who hated suits and ties and crowds and, for those reasons, didn't leave on his mission to Ecuador until he was twenty-five—and then only with considerable coaxing. And this was the returned missionary who never had spoken ten words to a girl, much less dated one. A good boy, but always a little strange, a source of concern for his parents and grandmother. It was going to take a special young lady, everyone agreed. But, not six months after flying out of a place called Guayaquil, with a firm resolve to follow his mission president's counsel and get on with life, he found her. Sue the rescuer. Sue the beloved. And now look at him—engaged and squared away, studying accounting or business or whatever a forward-looking Mormon boy studies, clerking part-time in a department store, serving as Scoutmaster in his church ward, eating his meat cooked. Sue the miracle worker. And *where* did he find her? Nowhere farther than a Young Adult dance.

Even veiled in prayer, Edrus Penroy's logic was easy to figure: first, if Myron could find a wife, anybody could; and second, if his method worked for one hard case, surely it would work for another.

*34*

By the light of a new day in late May, Hewell found himself kneeling but, with last night's wallflowering on his mind, only half attentive as she ran through the day's particulars: bombing in some European country, a beef market that had found yet another bottom, a dead aunt on his father's side, the birth of Myron and Sue's first child, one year to the day after their marriage in the Idaho Falls temple.

Inevitably Edrus Penroy approached her new—and, by now, well-honed—staple. But, on this morning, this staple included a new particular, if you could call it that.

*And please direct Hewell, please bless his . . . efforts.*

They both knew what she meant by the word. As on mornings in his long-ago childhood, Hewell fidgeted—from hunger, from discomfort in his knees, at the memory of a dance he shouldn't have attended in the first place, at her habit of making God the go-between in this conversation.

At the conclusion of the prayer, after some wordless scooting and shifting, the old chrome-legged kitchen chairs supported the one other posture they existed to support, and a quick peek in the steaming pot solved the morning mystery. Wheat mush. He had hoped for rice with cinnamon.

Hewell's mother re-fastened the safety pin where the lemon housecoat had been missing a top button for the better part of a decade. Without looking at him, she unscrewed the seal-band on the mason jar of chokecherry jam, then laid both band and lid, upside-down, beside the sugar bowl.

"Have some jam, Hewell."

"No thanks."

Edrus Penroy nudged the jar toward him. "There's nothing wrong with this jam," she said. "It'd be good on that toast."

"Yes, ma'am," he said, shelling the first of his allotted two eggs. "But I'll just dip it in my mush."

"You say that every morning."

"Because that's what I *do* every morning."

"Suit yourself."

She took up a spoon, very deliberately lowered it through the jar's mouth, and gave it a slow twist. Yet for all that, the amount of jam she dabbed on her slice of toast wouldn't have covered a soup cracker. Still, the reason the jar had lasted since January went beyond frugality. In her kitchen, whatever quantity of sugar a recipe called for was automatically halved.

"Just remember," she said, with a tinge of ominousness, "I've got two dozen jars of this stuff in the cellar."

Using her spoon as a trowel, his mother began spreading the dab of jam toward the bread's edge. Still without looking at him directly, she spoke of the day's work, of the bean planting and harrowing awaiting him.

"Soon as I get myself dressed," said Edrus Penroy, "I'm going to hoe in the garden till Co-Op opens. And then I'll go get you more seed."

Given the "efforts" she had asked God to bless, there was more on her mind than jam and bean seed. Hewell shelled his second egg, sugared his mush sparingly, and awaited the morning's real question.

"So," she asked finally, obliquely, spreading and spreading until the chokecherry jam was more color than flavor, "how was the dance?"

Neither the shrug nor the labored shoveling in of mush put her off.

"You were back fairly early."

"Eleven o'clock don't feel so early," he said around a mouthful, "when there's thirty acres of beans waiting to be planted the next morning."

"Did you have a good time?"

"A dance is a dance, Mom."

"I bet you didn't even ask anybody," she said. "Knowing you, you probably spent all your time at the food table."

She was right. Twelve summers holding a cup and little paper plate or napkin. Twelve summers' worth of chips and dip, brownies and chocolate chip cookies, barrels of punch. What would she do with broccoli and cauliflower *raw* on a serving platter? Or real cheese and something besides bargain-bin soda crackers? Or root beer floats? Or *buttered* popcorn?

She chewed her toast inscrutably, said, "Did you at least *talk* to anybody?"

"Old Newton never showed up. But I did see Gary and that cousin of his—Lon, I think his name is. They're building guard rail over by Gillette, came clear over the mountain just for a dance." He glanced at his mother, said, "That's desperation for you."

"I meant," she said, "did you talk to anybody in a dress."

"I know what you meant," Hewell said. "And I think you probably know the answer."

Now she looked at him, said, "I might have guessed." She tightened the lid back on the jar of chokecherry jam, would have used a pipe wrench had one been close at hand. "You know, Hewell, the Lord helps those who help themselves."

"The Lord isn't the one you gotta ask to dance, Mom."

Her hands fell away from the jar as if they had been slapped. "Well, what a thing to say."

For several moments, the only sound in the room came from his own eating—the spoon in his bowl and the crunch of toast. Yet by the time he dared to look directly across the table, her face showed more grief than anger.

"I'm sorry, Mom—"

"All I know," she said, her eyes welling with tears, "is that, in this life, you have *got* to keep trying. Sometimes trying is all you *can* do." While her wheat mush congealed, she studied him morosely. "Do you have any idea," she asked, "how you come to be here?"

He knew the story.

"Even when the doctor said there wasn't a one-in-a-million chance I'd ever conceive again, your daddy and I *refused* to quit. Twenty *years* after we got your sister! Do you know how long twenty years is, wanting something every night and day of it— neither one of us getting any younger? But we weren't just pray- ing. We were doing our part; we were trying."

In their life together, she had, more than once, ventured into such disclosure—describing, for instance, the history behind his father's hernia operation or her own eventual hysterectomy. But on this morning Hewell was not so much discomfited by her words as he was moved. Resting his forearms on the old eating table, he leaned toward her, said, "I *am* trying."

She snorted. "That's what you call staying home from their outings and giving plumb up on Sunday night firesides? Like a doggone hermit? Looks to me like you're down to dances as your last hope—at your own doing."

"Mom, listen," he said. "Listen to me. Girls young as the ones at these things ain't interested in me."

"Self-pity won't help you none."

"Is it self-pity to tell the truth?"

"You just haven't found the right one."

"Mom, it's ten years of this, and I haven't found *any*body. Not since Gwen."

Abruptly she looked down at her bowl. "I don't really think you had anybody found then," she said.

"Suit yourself, Mom."

"You can't expect it overnight," she declared. "I never have. And you still got plenty of good years to look."

With one last morsel of toast, he wiped his bowl clean. "And where else would you suggest I do all this looking?"

"I didn't say anything about where else," she said. "There's no need for where else—not for a good boy like you, never married, clean in your habits. Not if you'll get off your self-pity and do some asking. There's going to have to be some of that before there'll ever be any courting. That's the way of things, in case you didn't know." She sighed and resolutely patted the table top with both hands. Then she scooted her chair back, stood, began stacking their breakfast dishes—all while looking at him with what could only be called pity.

"It's plenty early in the summer," she said, finally turning toward the sink. "There'll be lots more dances."

## 35

Midmorning of a day in June, after moving irrigation water on the barley and corn, Hewell rode the unpadded dish seat of the old McCormick, monitoring the cultivator assembly bolted to either side of the tractor's front end, keeping each of six rows of fragile new pintos centered between a pair of close-set sweeps. Get the weeds and not the beans, she would say at the slightest evidence of "cultivator's blight."

Already the day was hot, and riding a creeping tractor was tedious, soporific work—leaning first to one side of the steering wheel, then the other, vigilant for a snagged rock or alfalfa root bulldozing the beans. Just yawning or daydreaming, you could take out ten or twenty yards' worth. Keep your eyes open, Hewell. Down the field, then up. Sixty, maybe seventy rods each way, at a crawl.

It was a long time till noon and the big meal of the day. Boiled potatoes, scrambled eggs, Swiss chard stewed until, on the plate, it was little more than a green puddle with stems. Maybe macaroni plain—she didn't believe in melted cheese—maybe beans or peas, *maybe*, if he was lucky, a pan-fried hamburger patty or a pork chop. No ketchup. No apple sauce. No horseradish. Just the flesh of the good beast, cooked like a slab of leather. And let the rest of the world waste their pennies on pop or lemonade. Tap water was good enough for Edrus Penroy. She had never forgotten being newly married during the early years of the Depression. No matter how many meals she had to build around eggs and boiled edibles from field and garden, she was always vehemently grateful to have *something* on the table. To her, even bitter jam was a blessing.

As was refuge from the elements—beneath a roof in dire need of reshingling. And a bed to sleep in—though how she ever had managed to fit a husband on a mattress barely double-cot wide, and how that mattress had accommodated all that trying, was an abiding mystery to Hewell. And wherewith to clothe herself. Home-sewn pants with elastic waistbands (two pairs of polyester, one of light denim), two Sunday dresses (summer and winter), of course the flannel housecoat faded to a dull lemon color, and essential footwear: a pair of rubber snow packs for barn and field boots, white canvas tennis shoes for everyday comings and goings, and lace-up black oxfords for church, for funerals and weddings.

Coming at last to the drain ditch at the end of the field, Hewell clutched, put the tractor in neutral, and hopped off to stretch, jog in place, revive himself for the long run back upfield. Looking at all the ground covered and all the ground left to him, he felt as if he were looking at his life. Forever one direction, an eternity the other. Too short and too long, too. He burped oatmeal and climbed back into the dished seat.

She prayed for health and was inordinately healthy. Skinny and wind-blown, a little arthritis, but healthy. No bowel malfunction, certainly. At a Young Adult fireside a long time ago, Hewell heard a food storage expert warn that an abrupt shift to whole wheat could actually prove dangerous to someone with an unconditioned digestive system. Compared with themes related to dating and romance and conducting your courtship on a spiritual plane—the usual fare at such gatherings—whole wheat didn't seem like much of a topic for a group of red-blooded singles.

*A fireside is a fireside, Mom.*
*What'd they talk about?*
*Surviving on cracked wheat.*
*I could've told you everything you need to know about that.*

In cobble, the click and chink of cultivator tools was a welcome sound. It meant the sweeps and shovels, though rattled loose on their standards every once in a while, were finding their way under and between and *through* the rocks. It was the quiet you had to worry about, when the big ones got stuck in the tools and dragged along for the ride.

Go to dances, do your part. That was her answer. Meanwhile, blink or yawn, and another summer was gone. There was no making her understand, this woman who had married four months before her seventeenth birthday and never knew the joy of even one Young Adult dance, let alone fifteen years' worth. A tank of gas and a long drive to a church house in Lovell or Greybull or Burlington or even as far away as Worland or Thermopolis—just to stand two or three hours at the periphery of a dimly lighted gymnasium, completely detached from the throb of music, studying the dancing couples as if through the glass of an aquarium. She had no way of appreciating the wariness, the banding together, the wide skirting if he happened to be standing between them and a group of new arrivals, guys fresh home from missions or on summer vacation from BYU. If he happened to be standing along their way to the refreshment table, they took another route, spoke to him only if they mistook him for a chaperone or a janitor waiting to sweep.

At nineteen, he had wanted to go on a mission. He could have had his share of dog and humidity stories. At some Sunday evening fireside he could have been the one reporting on his "experiences," fielding the questions of admiring young ladies. *Were the people receptive? Did they have four seasons, like we have?*

Despite what she said to everybody, despite one of her prayer's particulars in that era, she really didn't want him to go. Just wait, she kept saying, until fall, until after the beans are out. Or until after Christmas, when the cattle come in off the fields. Or until the planting's done. Just wait, Hewell. You're my youngest; it took me too long to get you. You have no idea how hard this is.

So he turned twenty, then twenty-one, and the boys his age started coming home. At twenty-two and twenty-three, he would have been old to begin a mission, but he could have gone. There was still a chance. But then, just about the time he was going to tell her—now or never—his dad collapsed right there in the muck of the milk barn, carrying a bucket of rolled oats, and the whole question was settled forever.

*36*

As on numberless other rounds up and down the field, the McCormick came finally to the ditch. Hewell clutched, throttled down, then stared at his hands on the steering wheel. That girl last night had stared. He had just thrown his plate and napkin away in the big trash can beside the refreshment table, still had a mouthful when, not skirting or rerouting either, she walked straight toward him. They all looked young, but she was hardly beyond adolescence.

"Are you here for Heather?" she asked in her helpful, all-business, not-so-adolescent voice.

"Who?"

"You're Heather's dad, right?"

Never again. Even if his weathered face and balding head didn't betray him, the hands would. No missionary or college student fresh home had his hands wrapped around the handle of an irrigating shovel four or five hours a day, silt ground into the callus pad on each thumb and forefinger—impossible to scrub out, May through August.

*Self-pity won't help you none.*

"There's other kinds of missions, Hewell," said Edrus Penroy a week after the funeral. His dad died in late March, just before barley planting, with the spraying and cultivating and irrigating and cutting and baling and harvesting stretching ahead as far as the eye could see. "A mission isn't everything."

And he had listened to her.

"There'll be other girls," his mother had said. "This Gwen is not the only fish in the pond."

In his early twenties, when he should have been on a mission or due home from one, he went out a few times, thanks to the charity of some nice girls. They took pains, however, to let him know that charity was all they felt. But then, at a fireside a couple of summers later, during refreshments and mingling, a girl named Gwen came up to him—and she wasn't looking for anybody's father. After five years in a music room at Ny-man R. Spafford Elementary School in Salt Lake City, she had heard, through relatives, of an opening at a school in Balford, Wyoming. Better pay and a change of scenery. "Does that make sense?" she asked. She was the only girl he had taken out more than one time, the one and only female he had brought to the house.

"A music teacher?" said Edrus Penroy, after waiting up for him that same night.

"What's wrong with that?"

"She's too old for you."

"What's a year or so?"

And too educated. And she's a city girl. And she's hunting marriage.

"You hold *that* against her? Tell me who at those firesides ain't hunting the same thing."

"There'll be other girls."

"Hey, stranger," Gwen said the very last time she called him, "I haven't heard from you for a while."

There would be other girls, his mother said.

And he had listened to her.


## 39


"Hewell?" she asked, pushing the jar of crabapple jelly to-ward him. "You do *like* girls, don't you?"


## 41


Hay dust filled his ears and nostrils; leaves stuck to the sweat of his face and arms. But by four o'clock on an afternoon in mid-August, the knotters had tied a thousand knots—five hun-dred bales in a row—without a miss. Not bad for the old New

Holland, bought the summer before his dad died, used even then.

"Because if you're that . . . *way*, Hewell, it can be cured, you know."

He had said *no thanks*—to the jelly—and she misconstrued. And once persuaded, she was a hard one to disabuse. He had assured her: he liked girls just fine; it was them that didn't seem to like him very much.

"Well, since you stopped going to the dances, I just got to wondering. It's hard to see you so lonely. Sometimes hormones need an injection or something like that."

It was bad enough half the world wondered—nieces and nephews at family get-togethers full of cheerful pity (*How's it going for you, Uncle Hewell?*), all the people at church looking at him, week after week, year after year, wifeless on a back pew, asking themselves what else could possibly keep a red-blooded Mormon man single this long.

Pivoted halfway around in the tractor seat, one leg drawn up, swaying easy to the plunger rhythm of the flywheel, Hewell watched the unbroken flow of the cured windrow—up and off the slightly yellowed stubble and into the burnished, steel mouth of the baler. At that point, the process was a racket of teeth and tongs and blades, so that whatever ended up in that mouth was swept without a handhold into the dark gullet of the plunger chamber.

Halfway down one of the field's last runs, he spotted the bull snake surfing the windrow. The spectacle always fascinated Hewell. A quick, darting slither left or right would carry him off the windrow, between the tires, and out of danger. But by some instinct beyond understanding, a snake surfing for its life couldn't see escape half a body length away, kept coming back to the windrow's center—exactly the position of greatest risk. As always, at the first flagging of an amazing stamina, one of the baler's pick-up teeth caught the tail end and flung the whole body upward; then a boost with another tooth, and inward it went, a writhing loop bounced toward plate steel on which scales would find no purchase, to be swept along with stems and leaves toward plunger knives that could shear a two-by-four without a shudder.

In the summers since his apprenticeship with their first baler, the ancient John Deere that came within a thread of tearing his leg off, Hewell had seen a hundred snakes baled—mostly water snakes and bull snakes, but sometimes rattlers. Sometimes he stopped the baler to go back and see. No matter how carefully he noted the spot, he always had to search four or five bales before he found the loop of scales and skin protruding between compressed leaves of hay—or, on the knife-cut side of the bale, the sheared segments. Often he was lucky to find even a nose or tip of a tail. Once in a while he didn't find anything at all, at least not until January, when the bale, deprived of its twines and broken in a trough, spooked the nearest two or three cows with the scent of something besides cured clover or brome.

Only once in a dozen times did a snake get as far as the pick-up teeth and somehow escape. But on this day in August, with Edrus Penroy's hardest question so clear in Hewell's mind, this one did it. After the first flinging contact with the pickup teeth, its tumbling body, like a boomerang of dog chain, found a current of gravity that drew it back down along the cresting windrow. Though the tips of several other teeth made just enough contact to buffet and disorient, every progress was now down and away from the dark chamber. And suddenly, finding the thatch of sun-cured alfalfa once more beneath its scales, the snake angled sharply from the line of the windrow, skimmed off into the stubble, and was gone.

A thousand sound knots in a row, and the knotter picked that moment, the moment of the snake's escape, the same moment the truck turned down their lane, to miss one. In consequence, the next bale issued untied from the machine's plunger chute and ruptured on the ground. And not at the far end of the field, either. Had her window been rolled down, the driver of the Ralston Light and Power truck probably could have heard Hewell's lamentation as he throttled down and climbed off the tractor. And had he looked up a little sooner from his fiddling with the knotter, he would have realized he had an audience, would have realized, *before* she went by, that the audience was not his eighty-one-year-old mother, who had gone to town after more twine and was due back anytime.

His lamentation gave way to something else when, on the return leg of the meter-reading circuit, the Ralston Light and Power truck slowed, then stopped just across the ditch from where he was still clearing clogged twine from the knotter fingers. The driver rolled her window down, smiled, and hollered something friendly.

Hewell tried to nod a nod worthy of so wonderful a greeting.

With the truck already inching forward, she smiled again, and waved, then was gone ahead of a plume of dust dancing merrily through heat waves.

At supper, chewing unbuttered corn on the cob with teeth unexamined by a dentist in the last fifteen years, Edrus Penroy said, "Did Ralston Power check the meter today? They usually come on the fifteenth."

"Yep," Hewell said, forking, at one time, a half dozen slices of unbuttered, unbreaded, unflavored zucchini, "they sure did."

When the light bill came a week later, Hewell suggested that he pay it in person.

"A stamp's a whole lot cheaper than gas to their office," his mother said. They had prayed—Myron's wife Sue was due any day with her fourth baby—and were now eating breakfast. Thanks to fog and a steady rain, the light of the new day was not impressive. She said, "I don't see why you have to go clear to the far side of town just for that."

He reminded her that she often paid in person.

"I don't make a special trip of it."

Since the patter of the first drops shortly after midnight, he had lain awake thinking. But now, of all times, his reasoning couldn't *seem* calculated.

"It's raining, Mom."

"There's plenty to do right here at home," she said. "You can work in the shop."

Yes, he supposed she was right. He would soon need to start cutting beans, might as well mount the knives on the McCormick while he had a chance.

With great maternal satisfaction, she troweled lime jelly on her toast. Hewell worked cautiously at the shell of a boiled egg.

"The knives!" he said suddenly. "I won't do much mounting without them. And they're at the blacksmith's. I took them to him a week ago, to get them hard-faced."

"Will he have them finished?" asked Edrus Penroy.

Hewell was more than sure he would. He had had all that time. And what better day to take care of such an errand? Then he could stay busy in the shop forever and ever.

He peeled the second egg. And—since Ralston Light and Power was just across the road from the blacksmith's shop . . .

"Now you're talking a little sense," she said. "I may teach you some smarts yet."

At the *Payments* counter of Ralston Light and Power, he asked only whether the change in their meter reader was permanent. But the lady clerk was gabby, and that one question was enough: the new meter reader's name was Benita—Spanish for something like Bernice—just got the job, drove over from Cody every day—that's where she lived—was very religious, didn't party at all—but was the nicest girl, and a *hard* worker—had two or three kids but was divorced from the father—still had his name, Sievers, but hadn't ever remarried. And not because there was a single thing wrong with her.


42


Every month of her first winter as meter reader, on the day her route was to bring her down Road 15A, toward the electric meter of E. Penroy, he found reason to be in the proximity of the field next to the road. Any reason would do. In November, for instance, he carried a hammer and can of staples and walked the fence along the ditch bank—a fence so far gone that the chore was meaningless, like setting out to reshingle a house whose rafters had long since rotted.

"What in the world are you messing with that old fence for?" his mother asked during another supper. "It ought to be torn down."

"You're right," Hewell said, piling his bowl high with stewed cabbage. "I thought I could spruce it up a little, but it's got to go." He assured her he'd get to it in his spare time—which happened to present itself on the same day for each of the next three months. During this same period of his life, he added to his private prayers some particulars of his own:

*Please let the Ralston Light and Power truck break down somewhere nearby. Please let one of its tires go flat.*

In March, with every strand of rusted barbed wire rolled up, every stray staple combed from the undergrowth, every rotted post stump dug from winter-hardened sod—the ditchbank as clean as the dawn of creation—he resorted to burning dead grass in the field's drain ditch. The smoke obscured, but did not discourage, the smile and wave.

"What in the world are you burning down there for?"

In April he hunted all afternoon for wild asparagus among the charred stubble. When the Ralston Light and Power truck passed, he wanted to flag it down and give his findings to the driver. But he could not risk his mother's scrutiny. Not yet. Instead, he settled for the wave and the smile, savored them like water in the desert. Instead, when he went in for supper, he emptied the half-full lard bucket on the kitchen counter.

"Nothing better than fresh asparagus," said Edrus Penroy, setting a pot of water to boil.

He wanted to tell the driver of the truck: You give me hope. I carry your phone number on a card in my wallet. I live thirty days at a time just for your smile and wave. And he wanted to tell his mother: I've met someone, and I'm going to try to see her on some sort of courting basis. Maybe that would convince her—his hormones were A-okay. If only he could explain, make her understand how, one afternoon a month, that ditchbank tilted toward the North Star and became a paradise in waiting.

But he could not afford to spoil this chance.

*She's Mexican, Hewell. You don't even know her. How many kids already and who's their daddy? And I don't suppose she's a Mormon.*

So what was left? Waving and waiting? And if so, waiting for *what?*

### 42 ½

Two more months passed. Another season changed. The electric meter kept turning. And in all that time the Ralston Light and Power truck never broke down and never had a flat.

So first thing in June, when the summer's first crop of hay came off the fields (about a week too early), Hewell made a stack where he had never made a stack before—just beyond their little plot of lawn. It crowded their parking space and looked out of place, but it also blocked any clear view between the house and the big light pole. This was the light pole whose cowled hundred-watt bulb, thirty feet up, provided something to look to on moonless nights. It was also the pole to which the electric meter was bolted.

"But why on earth right *there?*" asked Edrus Penroy after the first run of bales was placed as the stack's foundation. "Sixty years, and we've never put hay there. What were you thinking? I'll have hay dust coming in every time I open a window. And you know it don't take much to give me the cough. One of these days I won't be able to shake it. I'm an old woman, Hewell, but you work and worry me like I was a chore girl." She gave him a hard look. "I swear, I wish you'd said something first."

"Well, do you want me to move it?" he asked, with just the right blend of defensiveness and submission.

"No, I don't want you to move it," she said. "No need to compound the problem by making a wasted effort of it. But you promise me you'll feed this one first between now and next winter."

He promised. A promise that gave him six months at most, six months in which her arthritis and cough and low blood pressure weren't likely to get a lot better—or a lot worse, either.

When the Ralston Light and Power truck rolled into the yard on the fifteenth of June and pulled behind the new haystack, driver side closest to the pole, there was a lard bucket of fresh apricots perched on the meter. Standing behind the shop, between the chicken coop and vacant brooder house, in new pigweed already threading its way through pipe and angle-iron and sucker rod on his dad's scabbed-together metal rack, Hewell watched. She noticed the bucket first thing, the fruit heaped above the rim, and looked around several times before reaching for it. Then she sat for a long time—baffled? worried? scared?—looking down at the seat where she had set the bucket. Another long interval passed before she came back up with the clipboard and pen and read the meter, before he saw the amenable smile.

That night, and many nights thereafter, he imagined her hungry, fatherless children eating good food provided at his hand. He lay awake thinking of all the fruit and produce he could give her. And he thought of other things, too—the curve of her neck, the swell of her blouse. No, he didn't need any injections.

In July there was a lard bucket of tomatoes—and more. Atop a pair of hay bales stacked at the base of the light pole were short boards of various thickness, and atop those, a bucket of cucumbers and a full peck of green beans. Using his own truck window as a guide, he had fashioned the pedestal's height exactly. Thus she could reach the bucket and basket without even opening her door. In August—peaches, more tomatoes, new potatoes, and sweet corn. In September, after just one light frost to help the flavor—a big Hubbard squash and a basket of apples with a note tucked among the fruit. She set the basket on the floorboard of the passenger side, and then she was holding the note, written on the only piece of colored paper to be found in Edrus Penroy's house. From his place behind the shop, among angle iron and ripe pigweed, amid the drowsy afternoon cluck of chickens, he went over every syllable in his mind:

*I'm not trying to bother you or be weird. I just hope you like fruit and such.*

His one regret was the signature: *Yours truly, Hewell Penroy.* It sounded dumb enough even when it wasn't directed at a female. What did it mean, anyway? But then he saw the head tilt and concentration of writing, saw her reach her own folded slip of paper (from a Ralston Light and Power message pad) through the window and wedge it in the meter housing.

Long after the truck was gone, the boards and hay bales back in their regular places, all discoverable evidence of the moment cleared away, he stood behind the shop reading and rereading her words—*I love fresh fruit and vegetables. Thank you so much*—and the telephone number that, until this moment, had been just a number.

He was going to have to tell his mother. This sneaking was no good, this hoping she wouldn't detect his inattention and distraction, praying she wouldn't come around the haystack one afternoon to find him building his monthly altar of hope. Which made him wonder what he could put on that altar next month. It was fall, the nights were colder, the garden mostly down to dying stalks and vines. A few more squash maybe, and the pumpkins. Maybe a little sack of clean pintos. But that was it.

He was going to have to tell her.

*Her name's Benita, Mom. And if you don't like it, that's too bad.*

For three weeks he carried in his wallet the folded slip bearing the Ralston Light and Power logo, studied it two or three times daily. Then, against the urgency of the meter reader's next trip down their lane, he awoke one morning resolved to tell her at breakfast, steeled for what he thought was coming.

On that same morning, October twelfth, Edrus Penroy came from the stove hobbling, holding the handle of the steaming mush pot with both hands. For the first time in Hewell's memory she did not kneel to pray. "I'm a little footsore this morning," she said, lowering herself onto a chair, catching her breath at every movement of her lower leg. "I believe the Lord will make allowance." And in her prayer, after giving thanks for the light of the new day, after petitioning the three thousandth time for Hewell to find happiness, she made a rare reference to a particular of her own physical well being: *Please bless my big toe, Heavenly Father. It's hurting me some.*

Perhaps out of humility or shame for a debility—or both—she was understating. As a matter of fact, the toe was swollen dark purple and oozing pus, and the bright line of fever already had reached her ankle.

"What's this?" he said.

"Oh, it's nothing," she said. "Have some jam, Hewell."

"Why didn't you say something?"

It was no cough or arthritis or low blood pressure that had bested her, but a toenail gone bad. At the first sign of trouble, she had numbed the whole foot in a bowl of ice cubes, then yanked the nail with a pair of pliers. But despite her experience with homemade operations of this kind, the usual week of salt water and vinegar soaks hadn't cured anything.

"Listen, Mom," he said, expecting a fight, "you'd better let me take you to see a doctor."

But she didn't fight; she only mumbled at the pain as he helped her to her room to dress, and again when he handed her a wet washcloth for her face and hair brush for her head, as if any touch anywhere, even at the opposite end of her body, registered in the inflamed toe. She winced when, lifting her like a child, he slid her onto the truck seat, and all the way to town she was pale, her forehead clammy with perspiration. She wore a tube sock on her sore foot, but no shoe.

"You should have come in a lot sooner," the young doctor said. "Infection like this is bad in anybody, but for a lady your age—"

"My age is none of your business," said Edrus Penroy. "I was curing croup and earache before you or your mom and daddy, either one, were even born. I raised three kids with never a broken bone or an overnight in the hospital. And where was all you doctors' good advice when I was trying to get *him?*" The question, accompanied by her pointing to Hewell, meant little to a thirty-two-year-old doctor who was new in town. "None of it worked anyway," she said. "Hot, cold, special schedules—in the middle of the *day* even—we tried everything. What did the doctors know? Nothing. It was a long prayer and a miracle got him here."

The doctor gave Hewell a look of utter bafflement.

"Ma'am," he said, "I'm just saying you've got a staph in a bad place, and it has a pretty good head start on me." He looked again at Hewell, this time with a grave expression.

"I may be stringy as an old hen, but I'll heal just fine, and I'll do it without a lot of overpriced pills and nonsense." Eyes bright, face flushed, she was babbling now. "Just a shot of penicillin's all I need. And while we're here, is there some kind of shot you can give my boy?"

## 43

On the fifteenth of October Edrus Penroy was in the hospital with Hewell at her bedside. After the surgery to drain her leg, she seemed addled, afraid, almost panicky.

"Don't go, Hewell," she muttered. "Don't leave me in this place."

To do the milking and feeding at home over the next ten

days, he had to sneak away, early morning or after dark, and hurry back before the sleeping pills wore off. He had had no time for squash or pumpkins, hadn't even left a note. But one evening, late in the month, passing the light pole on his way to the milk barn, he found the card and flower—still fresh—and tire tracks that did not belong to the Ralston Light and Power truck.

*I heard about your mother, and I want you to know I'm praying for her.*

Several more weeks passed. The electric meter kept turning, the haystack between it and the house went down bale by bale, tier by tier, and, despite a second operation, Edrus Penroy did not recover. Hewell's note, tucked in the meter housing on a stormy afternoon in mid-November, was short:

*Thank you for the flower and card. I'm sorry I don't have anything for you. And I'm sorry I haven't called. My mother has been real sick.*

Sick as she was, her death, two days after her eighty-third birthday, took the doctor by surprise. He had urged against calling Hewell's sisters home, especially during the Thanksgiving holiday, had argued that their mother might linger for a long time, might even get better. Sitting at her bedside on that last night, Hewell knew differently.

"We got you here by a long prayer and miracle," his mother whispered in one of her last lucid moments. "After all that, I don't want you living out your life like a hermit."

"I won't," he said.

She could not hear him, was not really looking at him. "It's no good being alone in this world," she said, blinking long, then gazing into the dimmed light overhead, then blinking again, "no good at all. But one of us was going to *have* to be—that was the problem. And I didn't know if *I* could bear it." Tears flushed the rheum of age and pain from her eyes, then spilled into the furrows of a face soon to be relieved of all its wear and grief. "I'm so sorry, son," she said. "I am so very sorry."

And Hewell Penroy, single and alone in his middle-age, was sorry, too.

In the first few days of December, his sisters arrived, went through their mother's belongings, cleaned the house from top to bottom.

"You really need some new linoleum in this kitchen," the oldest one said. "It's worn through all over the place. And look at that pattern. This is the twentieth century, Hewell."

"I don't see what you two were living on," the other sister said after a trip to the grocery store. "There wasn't one thing in the fridge."

Over the next day or two the old house filled with Edrus Penroy's grandchildren and great-grandchildren, gathered now from places far distant for the funeral of a woman they hardly knew. Hewell gave his bedroom to Myron and Sue and as many of their five children as would fit, and slept on a camp cot in front of the shop's coal stove.

"How goes it, Uncle Hewell?" he was asked at every meeting with a member of the next generation.

By the end of the week it was all over—the viewing, the funeral, the graveside service, the Relief Society lunch at church, the family dinner that night, the distributing of a frugal woman's belongings.

"She'd want you to have this," Hewell said, handing a full case of chokecherry jam to each sister.

"What will you do now?" one of them asked.

What he had always done—eat and sleep and work, one day after the other. That is what he would continue doing, the same schedule he had followed for twenty years, save for one thing. And that one thing wasn't buying the farm, taking care of the legal papers to get it in his name—though, thanks to his sisters' approval, that would happen soon enough. He was thinking of something else.

• • •

On December fifteenth, despite his best efforts to sleep late, Hewell was up at five o'clock. First thing, he went to the switch in the utility room and flipped on the yard light—the first light of this new day, albeit artificial. One more feeding and the stack by the light pole would be gone, six months and a week from the day he had placed the first bales, seven years since the last Young Adult dance, ten since he had stopped attending firesides, twenty since his final resolve to get on a mission. Would she ever have known how long that was?

From the light switch in the utility room he went to the refrigerator in the kitchen and pulled out a carton of eggs, a cake of cheese, a package of link sausage, and a square of butter. From the freezer, orange juice. From the bread box, a full loaf. From the cellar, potatoes. For the next forty minutes he peeled and grated, broke and beat, sliced and cooked. Out of long habit, he started to set the table with two of everything—plates, glasses, utensils—suddenly caught himself. Yet after a moment's thought, he made no changes. With melted cheese dripping from an omelet, from atop a platter of hash browns, he knelt at his kitchen chair and gave thanks for food and shelter, health and strength, for the life of his mother, a person both flawed and decent—and for electricity.

At last, after a long night of darkness, the December sun cleared the horizon. Dishes washed, chores done, Hewell filled out his morning cleaning up the remnants of the haystack, chopping dead pigweed behind the shop and burning it in a big pile by the garden. Then, on a whim, he rummaged through the clutter in the brooder house and found a mostly empty bucket of red paint, another of green—frost-ruined and watery, but with pigment enough for his purpose. Over the shop's stove, he softened the bristles of a brush, then painted alternating rings up the light pole as high as he could reach.

At noon he went in the house, ate two pork chops—one with barbecue sauce, the other with horseradish—then set to work on a fudge recipe clipped from a very old magazine and kept (how many decades?) at the bottom of his mother's cedar chest. Somehow his sisters had missed it, tucked away in an envelope with some family photos and a ticket stub from a 1940 Gold and Green Ball.

The first ingredient Hewell pulled from a shelf of the utility room was sugar—a fifty-pound sack of it. He was careful to use the heaviest pan in the house—the mush pot—on the old stove's fickle burner, careful to stir in exactly the amounts the recipe called for, and a little more, careful to stir the hot candy patiently with a wooden spoon. By the time the chopped walnuts sank into the spoon's swirl, the pot's rich odor had filled his nostrils and the house and the whole world.

Later, with the fudge cooling in its pan, he showered, shaved, put on a new shirt and pair of jeans, combed such hair as was left to him, and waited the last hour he would ever wait for this moment. When the Ralston Light and Power truck finally turned down the lane, he put on his good coat, took the plate of fudge wrapped in bright foil, and stepped outside to meet it coming.

# Alkali Coulee

"I hope that bull got what he was after," said Rowe Sloan, looking down at the wrecked posts and wire at the bottom of a deep coulee. He turned to his son, who stood apart from him on the coulee rim. "Maybe it cheered him up."

"That fence was a joke anyway," the boy said. "It wasn't like he had to hunt a hole."

"Maybe so, Gabe. But if there's a motivation more potent than a heifer in heat, I'd like to see it."

The new sun sent a flush of color through clouds over the Bighorns. It was mid-May, but there was a cold breeze. In the distance a line of Russian olives marked the boundary between the alkali badlands they had just come over and the long, terraced drop-off to swamp and then the river. Now, even with the truck perched on the coulee rim, the close end of the job lay a hundred yards away. And they were rough yards. The slope to the coulee floor was steep and broken. Six-foot sagebrush hid cutbanks and gopher holes and an empty badger den.

"God marks the fall of a sparrow," Rowe said, unlatching the truck's tailgate. "A bull does the same thing with ovum."

"It's *ova*," Gabe said, flipping on the hood of his sweatshirt and tying the drawstring. He said, "If we had a real road down here, like normal people, we wouldn't have to hump all this crap."

The truck bed contained a crowbar and tamping bar, several spools of wire, a come-along and chainsaw, steel posts and a pounder, a wooden level with no middle bubble, and a dozen cedar posts peeled with a draw-knife and still oozing sap.

"Normal people don't go out for breakfast in the middle of the night," Rowe said.

"*I* came home after the movie. The *rest* were going to breakfast. I wish you'd get that straight." From a rear corner of the bed, Gabe lifted a dented Mobil Oil bucket of staples, hammers, fencing pliers and hatchet, and set it on the ground. "It's what seniors do after Senior Awards banquet, Dad. For your information, nobody else had to work on a Saturday."

"I did," Rowe said. He wore a straw hat and a snap-button denim jacket patched at the elbows. The stubble above his lip bore toast crumbs and residue of egg yolk. He grabbed the two shovels lying atop the cedar posts and stuck them upright in the white-powder dirt. "And until you get to college, you're on my clock."

Gabe set the scarred lunch cooler beside the Mobil Oil bucket. "So what's the sudden rush?" he asked. "This fence mess has been down here since last fall—all Thanksgiving, all Christmas, all winter, all spring. But, *no-oo*, it just couldn't wait a couple more hours."

"We're going to need all the daylight we got." Rowe slid the top cedar so he could get a shoulder under it. "If I was you, Mr. Honor Society, I'd be glad your old man let you sleep as long as he did."

"You're not me."

• • •

On the first trip down, the man and boy each packed a cedar post, a shovel, and a spool of wire. All the way to the coulee floor, they slewed and braked and dodged sagebrush branches. On the up-trip, they scrambled and floundered. Back on the rim they both went to the water bag hanging by a rope bail from the truck's side mirror. They took off the jacket and sweatshirt and tossed them in the cab. Already they had sweat a dark ring above their belts.

Gabe pulled the water bag's cork. After a long drink, he said, "There's got to be an easier way."

"When you find it for fencing, you let me know."

"No, really," Gabe said, looking from their gear to the slope and back again. "Maybe we can do this a little smarter—work with our heads instead of our backs for once."

"Is that something else you heard from Ms. V?"

"At least she makes us think about it."

"'Anybody can work on an oil rig or ranch. Don't you want to aim higher?'"

"She only said that one time."

"I should hope so," Rowe said. "I don't care if she is from Chicago; that takes some kind of nerve to say that to a roomful of kids with cows and oil pumpers right out the schoolhouse window. Where does Ms. V think her paycheck comes from?"

"She's from Cincinnati," Gabe said, handing the water bag to his father. "I don't know why she bothers you so bad."

"She's not what bothers me. You don't think your rube old man has heard about hard and smart ten thousand times? Salesmen, bankers, suck-up lieutenants—that's their favorite line."

"To listen to you, you'd think shovel work was something sacred."

The man and his son regarded each other. Over toward the river swamp, a killdeer called.

"Listen, Gabe, you're a good boy, and I was proud of you last night. Anybody who wins a wagonload of awards—that's nothing to sneeze at. And we owe Ms. V for putting you on to that scholarship." With his thumb, Rowe pressed the cork tight into the mouth of the water bag. "But bright future or not, there's some work that's just hard. And there's a whole lot of folks who have to do it every day."

Gabe didn't say anything.

"Run that by Ms. V sometime."

• • •

It took another hour to move the rest of the gear to the coulee floor. In the last load, they carried the cooler and water bag. They drank again, hung the bag from the branch of a sagebrush close to the fence line, then each took up a hammer and pair of pliers.

For another hour, they pulled staples and snipped clips attaching rusty barbed wire to downed and leaning posts. Then, starting with a chest-high loop, they rolled each strand of old wire into a waist-high wreath bulky with kinks and splices.

The sun shone bright in a blue sky. During a breather, Gabe looked at the piles of rusty wire, at posts and props eaten up with alkali, at willow stays bleached bone-white. He said, "We got to haul all this crap up to the truck?"

Rowe eyed the slope. "Two hours ago I would've said you better believe it—if it was you asking. But now," he said, "I can't for the life of me think of a thing this mess is going to disturb if it lays right here through the millennium. Can you?"

"Not me."

"Now then, Ms. V might not like it. This old wire *is* an eyesore on the environment. And there might be an endangered species it's a threat to."

"If she don't like our fencing mess, let *her* hump it up that hill."

"Whose side you on?"

• • •

The alkali of the coulee floor masked veins of rock. Under the edge of crowbar and shovel, the rock defied the shaping of postholes. Still, by noon, a pair of brace posts stood at each end of the fence line. After tamping around the base of the last post, Rowe said, "Let's eat."

They sat in the shade of a lone Russian olive at the base of the slope, where the cooler had rested all morning. From beneath ham and cheese sandwiches, chips, potato salad, cookies, and apples, Gabe pulled two quart jars of lemonade sealed with wax paper. The jars clinked with ice cubes.

"Your mother knows how to pack a lunch." Rowe took off his hat and set it on his knee. The mark of the hat band showed in his forehead. His hair was gray at the temples. "A finer cook and meal maker never walked the earth."

"Does she like farming?"

Rowe swallowed a bite of boiled egg. "Two days home from our honeymoon, we found a heifer trying to calve in a coulee just like this one. The calf had been dead inside her for who knows how long, and she was spent. There was nothing to do but shoot her. Your mother had never been away from home, never hardly been out of Utah. That was our start together in the cattle business. And she's been through every blizzard and branding and lousy market since."

"But does she *like* it?"

"If you put it that way," Rowe said after a long pull at the lemonade, "I don't think it would've been her first choice when we met. Salt Lake is a long way from Balford. And after thirty-odd years, I'm pretty sure it wouldn't be her first choice now. But she's been good about making a life of it."

Bees droned in the blossoms of the Russian olive. Out away from the tree, under the midday sun, the alkali shimmered.

"Did Grandma and Grandpa Hobart ever want you to try anything else?"

Rowe stopped unwrapping a sandwich. "It hasn't been all bad," he said. "We've done okay."

"I didn't say you haven't."

"You or any of your brothers or sisters ever go hungry? Or barefoot?"

"I was just asking."

"Shovel work or not, it's hard to beat the life for raising a family. Even your Grandma Hobart says so. And when you get to pushing sixty, you got something your sons can take over. At least that was the plan."

Gabe held an apple, half-eaten.

"Besides that, dreaming easier or better can get to be its own kind of torment."

"I didn't say better. I was just wondering maybe different."

"I've made a living. You got a better plan than that?"

"I was just asking."

• • •

After lunch they used the saw and hatchet to mortise a cross-piece between each pair of brace posts. To wire the first pair diagonally, Gabe knelt with a tire iron and stuck the tip between separate strands to twist them into one cable.

"Which way you going with that?" Rowe asked.

"I haven't decided."

"That iron gets away from you underhand, and my posterity ends with the fruit of your brothers' and sisters' loins."

"And overhand just cracks my skull open," Gabe said, starting the twist in that direction. "That's not much of a choice."

"I'll do that if you want."

"I'm all right."

The wire twisted and tightened.

"No, really," Rowe said, kneeling on the other side of the brace post, across from his son.

The wire tightened and popped. Reaching, Rowe gripped the elbow of the tire iron and helped with the next two turns.

"I was doing fine," Gabe said. "Your head's no harder than mine."

"Maybe not," Rowe said, working the tire iron through its final turn, "but yours is worth a lot more."

• • •

The afternoon turned warm and still. High in the sky a hawk rode an updraft. They set five cedars at even intervals along the fence line. Then they drove steel posts between those. The pounder was a length of thick-walled pipe capped at one end with plate steel. The heavy rod handles welded to it accommodated two sets of hands.

"You used to run this thing by yourself?" Gabe asked, lugging the pounder from one post to the mark for the next. His face was powdered with alkali.

"That was before I knew so much about working smarter."

Rowe aligned a steel post. Gabe heaved upward and slid the pounder over it. Together they gripped the handles.

"You ready?" Rowe asked.

They started with short strokes, each keeping the toe of one boot against the bottom of the post as a guide. Then, with the post in place, they went all-out for six or eight thumps—and drove it barely halfway to depth.

Leaning on the pounder and post, Rowe breathed hard and said, "And that was before I had piles. So these days I work so dang smart I just fake it and let my son do all the heavy lifting."

Gabe smiled.

They finished driving the post and hoisted the pounder off. Gabe positioned the level. "This rock sure makes it hard to keep them straight," he said, flexing the top of the post toward him.

"The word is *plumb*," Rowe said.

• • •

At quarter to six, the come-along stretched the bottom and final strand of barbed wire. They tied it off, then began working down the line, stapling and clipping. Far off, toward the river, a coyote barked.

At the last post, Rowe straightened from a crouch, stretched, and dropped his hammer in the bucket. A moment later, his son went through the same motions.

"The best part of fencing," Rowe said, sighting down the new line, testing the tension of the barbed wire. "The job all done and one of your mother's suppers waiting—you'll go a long way to find better."

With the heel of his hand, Gabe jarred the top of a cedar post. He didn't say anything. Already the light was fading, the cool of evening coming on. Somewhere a meadowlark called.

"I'm hungry. Maybe we can get these tools in one trip. Your mother will be wondering about us."

Gabe did not reach for the bucket. "Dad," he said, "I want to do other things."

For a moment, Rowe looked at him. He said, "I know that."

"It's nothing against you or the farm."

"I think I know that, too. And come August, I don't want you thinking you've left your old man in the lurch or you're disappointing me, either one."

In the bottom of the coulee, the air was very still. Another lark called.

"But I think you're going to find all this a little harder to put away than you thought," Rowe said.

Gabe looked at him and nodded.

Then they shared the last of the water, and Gabe tucked the empty canvas bag into the cooler. When Rowe tried to grip both the crowbar and tamping bar in one hand, he grunted, dropped them back on the ground with a clang, and said, "Judas, these are heavy. You'd think they're made of steel."

"I'll take one."

"You're darned right you will." When Rowe gave over the

tamping bar, his hand hesitated, then patted his son's shoulder, twice.

Chainsaw, come-along, shovels, bucket.

Loaded with half the gear, Gabe said, "I don't know about doing this in one trip."

Loaded with the other half, Rowe said, "So we'll make two if need be."

Then they started up and out of the coulee while there was yet light enough to see by.

# The Trees in Lyman

IN A FEW WEEKS I'M GOING to Lyman. I've been telling people. Hap's coming for the mill, to set up down there when he gets a good contract. He knows a guy with a skidder and truck. All I need is my chainsaw, sleeping bag, good gloves, some warm boots. Hap said he might cut a few trees himself, to stay out of trouble, but he won't roll until I show. I've been with him too long. He wants me down there, says I'm his best hand. "I need you, my man." That's what he said. We might have us a pile of logging to do after the new year. He's going to let me know when he's ready, told me I might have to live out of my pickup for a while.

That's okay with me. Anything is better than all the questions I get every day. What are you doing, Siler? When you going to Lyman, Siler? I should've kept quiet and just left. I could've left everybody and their nosy questions behind. Now they think I'm full of it, telling my big plans. I wish Hap would call. I wish he'd find something down there.

We talked all fall about it. Things are slow in Balford, nobody building anything. The bars are full of contractors, every gas station and cafe bulletin board in Park County plastered with business cards, homemade three-by-five ads, people wanting work. Even Hap had to go someplace else to keep us busy. He left me finishing portable horse sheds and feeders, went all over Wyoming looking. He knows a lot of people, does business with half the state. He always gets jobs. He'll find something down there and send for me.

My old man says he's known a few Haps in his time, wheeler-dealers, always a thousand irons in the fire. He says the Haps in this world need guys like me. "Hap just starts all these projects," he says. "He won't get you a job till he's got one better." Every night, every night—same thing. My old man sits in his recliner reading his newspaper under the lamp, gets in some crack about Hap. He says a squeeze like this gets to everybody sooner or later. He says, "Hap's an okay guy, don't get me wrong. But he ain't Santa Claus."

Just because Hap's doing what he likes. It bothers people. They don't know what to do with him in their brains. Of course, you're supposed to go on a mission, like my older brother Kemp; then you go to college for an office job. If you don't do either of those things, you're stuck down at Co-Op or the lumber yard. Those are your choices—a real prime career as a blessing of your missionary service or at least something steady, something you can answer questions with. Then people can peg you when they hear your name. Siler Godwin? That younger Godwin boy? Did he serve a mission? No. Is he going to college? No, sure isn't. Oh, he's the one pumps gas and changes flats at the Co-Op. Or he works at the lumber yard maybe. That was him loaded lath for my tomato stakes the other day.

They can't peg Hap, and it bugs them to death. He didn't go on a mission; he's got no *education*, no secure job and benefits. And he's still making it okay. Nobody counsels him.

My Uncle Rector is a cop. Everybody knows Rector Godwin. He gets invited all the time to talk to clubs and youth groups, wedding receptions. Wise advice running out his ears. And a thousand delinquency stories. He tries to work them in every Christmas at the family get-together. He's always pushing good grades, sports, Scouts, missions. Every time, he's one of the first with the golden line: What are your plans, Siler? Same question

I got from the guidance counselor in high school. Same one I get all the time from my mom. Her name's Thelma. Thel-ma. If you're not going to serve a mission, Siler, if that's your decision, have you at least thought about college? It wouldn't hurt to give it a try. What are you going to *do* with your life?

I can't just shrug anymore.

Uncle Rector says college aims kids in a good direction, prepares them to be productive citizens. Boys State, honor roll, Eagle Scout, and you're on your way. Big smile in the yearbook, all your clubs and achievements and impressive plans. To find a cure for all diseases. To donate organs. To serve God and find peace. To drive my truck to the lake and live happily ever after with Marla and my blue heeler. That's the kind of stuff people put in yearbooks.

Everybody thinks it's okay to do hard work when you're young. A little sweat, a few calluses never hurt a kid. Gives you integrity. Makes you responsible. That's what they say. They don't want to do work like that, but it's good for others. Uncle Rector says hard manual labor is invaluable training for life. He says, "You're fortunate, Siler. A lot of these kids today *need* that experience." He says, "I see it all the time in my line of work." I can smell a delinquency story coming every time.

So you're really in a bind when you don't go on a mission or to college *and* you got no job. Things have been real slow here lately, none of the pulling units hiring, welders and roustabouts like my old man working half days.

And then Hap comes up with these horse sheds last September. Just when it looked hopeless. Fencing is his main line, but it dropped way off last year—only one real contract, four miles up in the Bighorns. And it was no gem, either. We hit rock in every posthole. Like Hap told me, "Before this is over, you're going to be intimately acquainted with that crowbar." He said, "You're going to have a *degree* in crowbarring." He was right. It was rough, but it was all we had. We took our sweet time stretching the wire and still ended up with nothing to go to.

After the Bighorns, Hap talked about working me three days a week. He was hurting to have to do that. Then he pulls out this horse shed deal. Some guy from Northfork has a western clothing store in Cody, a half dozen other tourist traps, rifle and pawn shop, ranch in Nevada, cabin in Oregon, breeds horses. He's got money. He wants to run registered Appaloosas up on the Northfork, says the climate is just right for pregnant mares.

So this Appaloosa guy goes elk hunting with one of Hap's friends over in Star Valley, finds out Hap does all kinds of building—fence, corrals, feed bunks, panels, gates. Anything you want, Hap does it all. He sells horse trailers and saddles, trades all kinds of stuff. If one thing goes sour, he's got options. He cuts trees, mills them himself, treats his own timbers and posts. And he pays his help cash—straight out. He says tax paperwork is for lawyers and bureaucrats. I've had to wait a few times, but he's never shorted me a dime. The horse guy finds out what all Hap does and orders five sheds and a feeder just to start with. He told Hap to name his price, and he'd reimburse him for the materials. I've been busy since, up to the last month or so.

My old man thinks the horse guy is a crook, laughs about it. He says, "You guys will be lucky to see one red cent of that man's money." Hap gets burned once in a while, but that's just the business. That's the risk. My old man wishes he had Hap's free schedule. It makes people sore to see guys like Hap coming and going as they please. No boss or punch clock. Hap says he won't live for coffee breaks and five o'clock.

He called me from Lyman right after Thanksgiving. I waited a week or better to hear from him. He said, "I think I got us a contract for mine props—all we can cut." The soda tunnels are still cranking. He's got a friend works in one, thinks they're still buying. Hap said, "I'm going to need you down here for sure." The guy with the truck and skidder has a timber license, so we're set. All we need is a signed contract and some start-up money. Hap's going to call Northfork and collect on these horse sheds when the Appaloosa guy gets back from a stock show in Texas. When that all gets sorted out, he's going to send for me.

I've never been to Lyman, don't know exactly how far it is. Hap says five or six hours. My old man says closer to seven or eight, and more than that if the roads are bad.

He thinks this Lyman idea is crazy—timbering in the middle of winter. And Thelma never likes anything I do. When she was pushing a mission so hard a couple of years ago, even my dad had to tell her to back off. "If he doesn't want to go, Thelma, he doesn't want to go." Then the usual fight. "Just because the Church doesn't mean anything to you, Gurn Godwin." My old man's name is on the roll, but he hasn't stepped foot in the chapel more than half a dozen times that I can remember—a few Christmases and Easters, and when my older brother Kemp gave his missionary farewell talk in sacrament meeting. My dad says he doesn't like forcing things down people's throats.

That's what I feel like with Thelma. She won't just let me have my life. She whines a lot at breakfast. Is this what you really want, Siler? Is it? Is this your idea of a job for your future? Then the college sermon. You could do it, Siler—start your education right here. Go to Cody Community. There's nothing wrong with junior college. You could get in. Just last week she says, "You aggravate me, Siler. You promised you'd think about college after a year working." She says, "High school is long past, and now it's Christmas again. And where are you headed?"

I never answer, just take my last bites, my last swig of juice— one breakfast closer to being gone. Sometimes my old man looks up, sometimes he doesn't. Same round-and-round since he can remember. The funny thing is, sometimes I wish *he'd* push me in some direction, at least give me some idea of a good way to go. It seems strange, I know, but I wouldn't have minded if he'd said something to me about a mission. Anything. All he tells me is not to stack everything on Hap. He says if there was any sweat-and-shovel work to be done, Hap would've called a long time ago. My old man says he's been to Lyman in January and

February, says, "You won't be cutting many trees in that kind of snow."

He should know. He's worked in the oil fields down there and all over. Roustabout for close to thirty years. Once in a while they let him on the backhoe when the operator doesn't show. Sometimes he'll even weld on the machinery when they're desperate. But he'll tell you—most of it's grunt work. Getting up every morning in the dark, Thelma's eggs and cereal, coffee thermos, bologna sandwich, black metal lunchbox.

I've been there to give him a ride when the roustabouts come in from the field, six or seven of them jammed in four-door pickups, bundled up against the cold, choking on each other's smoke. They all wear hard-hats and smell like crude oil. I've watched him drag home from that job a thousand nights. When I was little, it was my job to grab on to his coveralls at the wrist and help pull them off. He'd say, "You set? You gotta get set." Then he'd pull me all around the utility room. "I thought you said you were set." He didn't really need me; he was just playing. But I liked it. Then he'd say, "Why don't you clean that lunch box out for me?" It smelled like oil, too, but inside there was always half a sandwich left or a pudding cup or some canned peaches or a couple of little Dolly Madison doughnuts. "I must have forgot that." That's what he always said. "You better eat it for me." When I was little, I thought he had the best job in the world. I wanted to go with him just to eat lunch out of his lunch box.

But now? If you ask me, Lyman is a better deal. And besides what he's already said, my old man won't fight me on it. Do what you want. Suit yourself. That's what he'll say. Thelma is the one who gets mad. I want to tell her to slack off about this college thing, but it wouldn't do any good. So I just hear it and go on like I did in high school.

She whined bad when she found out my whole day was ag shop, auto shop, work release. She didn't like me forging her signature on my schedule. It took a minute to convince the guidance counselor. "And your parents know what all you're taking here?"

I didn't like lying to the guy, but he's got to have cream-puff answers to everything. I feel sorry for his silly job. You couldn't pay me enough. I didn't *want* brain classes, and I didn't want to go to BYU or Laramie or Cody Community College. But you tell that to Mr. Guidance, and you throw him out of whack.

I laugh about him now, pulling my file, sitting at his desk helping me with my future. Every day in that chair, cooped up in that office, planning classes for all the brown-nosers and burnouts, doing career training. He's always sucking a breath mint, sneaking to the lounge for a smoke between students. What do you want to go into, Siler? What are your interests? We've got pamphlets.

I always said agriculture or forestry. It made him feel valuable. You can't say roustabout or hod carrier. You can't say you're going to tamp posts for the next three years until something better comes up. He doesn't have a pamphlet on any of those. Mr. Guidance looked at my schedule a long time. He said, "Well, I guess if your parents approve."

Guess again, Mr. Guidance. Thelma doesn't approve of anything I do. She didn't like it when I bought Hap's pickup or chainsaw, said I wasn't saving any money for a mission or college education. Hap didn't go on a mission or college, either. He says there's already enough college idiots in the world. "No, my man," he told me once, "that just wasn't my tea bag." He says somebody has to do the real work. That's what Hap thinks. People are afraid of sweat. There is a lot of sweat in fencing. If you want some spiffy uniform or necktie job, you better not go into the fencing profession. I'd like to see Uncle Rector or Mr. Guidance with a crowbar in their hands, busting their hernias lugging posts and wire. Then they could tell you all about Eagle Scouts and career planning.

My first day with Hap, he left me on a two-mile stretch of county road over by Ralston, fence line on both right-of-ways. He said, "This is what you call a fence job, pal," smiled when he said there should be enough holes to keep me busy until he came for me at noon. He said the auger went down on all of them—so they were supposed to be easy cleaning. He took a shovel to one hole to demonstrate, said, "Learn to make a nice pile. You'll get plenty of practice."

When he came for me, it was three o'clock. My back hurt bad. The dirt in the holes had sometime got wet, was all clods now. It was hard going. I was so dry I could hardly swallow. Hap laughed at me trying to talk, said I sounded like a fairy. And I was weak-kneed. I didn't get any breakfast. He came before Thelma had the bacon ready, and he doesn't like waiting around.

We started setting posts after that. Hap lines up and plumbs, kicks my dirt pile in the hole as fast as me and another kid can tamp it with a sucker rod. My hands cramped from curling around that rod, blisters even through gloves. Up and down, up and down. Sometimes my arms went numb at night. I shook them, laid there in bed with my wrists tingling, wondering how many times I lifted that steel rod in a day.

When I got home after dark that first night, my old man said it looked like Hap was going to work me. Thelma watched me pull off my sweatshirts, everything steamy. It was thirty or forty degrees most days working on that fence, and still I went home soaked next to the skin.

Thelma says, "I don't know why you had to go to this Hap guy. There's other jobs, Siler." She says, "You don't have to work to death for this man."

My old man said it looked like Hap was getting his money's worth.

Just because my brother swept somebody's office in high school and ran errands. Tough stuff. Saving for his mission and education, impressing everybody. How determined these college boys are. They can handle a little flunky stuff when they're kids—get a paper route, bag groceries, spray down the lettuce and carrots every night. They impress guys like my uncle. What a nice young man. He'll go far. Work keeps you from turning delinquent.

I know all about college guys and how bad they really want to work. One of Hap's fence jobs was on the road between Laramie and Bosler. A couple of bozos drove out one morning in a dune buggy thing, said they wanted a job through summer vacation. Hap hired them right there to clean holes and tamp. He'll give anybody a chance.

We'd been on that job for almost three weeks, but, with twelve miles of fence, there was plenty left. Really his brother-in-law Percy had the contract. He subbed the posts to Hap because he had the crew—me, a couple of his cousins, and a Mexican kid.

Quick as he could, Hap wanted to turn us loose and go on to Longmont. He had horse trailers to deliver for a guy he knew down there. He said he could make a thousand a trip easy if the buyers lived close to the same place—had it rigged so he could pull two or three at a time behind his pickup. He promised us a bonus if we got the holes cleaned by the Fourth. The college guys said they could sure enough use a bonus.

They took off their tee shirts first thing, said if they had to be outside doing this kind of work, they were at least going to get a tan. Hap took one of them to tamp for him, left the other one with me, cleaning holes.

Before we split up, Hap warned me in private not to work my college boy to death, said he didn't want a lawsuit from the kid's daddy. I could tell we both felt the same about it. We *knew* these two jokers wouldn't cut it. They wore shorts and tennis shoes, never had a real callus in their life. This was a little different stuff than playing tennis or lazing around with girls on a nice lawn.

Before noon, me and my college kid got into a stretch of sand rock. The auger holes were shallow or off the mark, so we had to bar them. And it was hot down in that sagebrush. I watched him work, gritting his teeth every time he heaved his crowbar a little bit. I knew he'd wake up the next day with a sore back, sunburn, blisters stinging him bad when he washed his hands. Whenever he stepped on a cactus, he cussed extra loud.

He said, "This is *truly* sucky." With no gloves, his palms were already red. He kept looking at both hands, wiping them on his shorts. Every few minutes, he took a drink from the water bag, watched the tourists go by in their campers.

He asked me if I did this all summer. I told him this summer *and* last summer. It was good money, better than lifeguarding at a pool or playing counselor at some youth camp. And Hap always had work.

The college kid laughed, said, "Now isn't that a blessing?"

Guys like him piss me off. Half a day on the job, and he was the expert. He kept saying there's better ways to make a buck. Just because he couldn't hack it. Just like that, one day the dune buggy didn't show. Didn't have guts enough to come get their check. They called, asked Hap to mail it. And that college kid's the one giving me advice how to work.

You want to get a job where you use your head, *man*, instead of your back. I've heard other people say the same thing. And if they don't say it, that's what they mean. Do you want to do that all your life? Something about it just isn't good enough for them. Hap says when it comes to work most people are stuck up, stupid, or just plain lazy.

Thelma sure enough thought it was dumb for us to live like we lived down there in Bosler. We stayed right on the job, camped in deer tunnels under the highway—sleeping bags and no shower for a week, Spam, pork and beans, sardines, everything from a can. I know she worried about doctoring the story to answer people's questions. Where's Siler these days? Oh, you know, jobs are tough to find with all the kids home from college. Siler's a worker, though. And it's only for the summer. Come fall, he'll be in Cody Community.

Maybe she really thought I would be. Man, she was sore when she found my application in the garbage. It killed her. She got it for me herself—asked Uncle Rector where to go, made a special trip. I bet she was in heaven walking up the hall of a college building. Nobody in sweaty clothes there.

Thelma says it doesn't take anything special to do what Hap's done, says he's footloose, never grew up. She sees my genius big sister at the University of Wyoming and tells me now *there's* a future. Honor roll girl gets her name in the Balford paper every Christmas and spring. Thelma eats that up. She loves names in the paper.

And she loves my brother in Denver, wearing his tie, doing something in a Woolworth's office. Nobody knows what. It's got a name. Assistant Retail Personnel Director. Thelma spouts it all the time. But nobody knows what it means. When people talk it over with my folks, they decide my brother must boss five or six others. They say, "That must be it." And my old man says, "Something like that."

My old man only knows for sure what people do outside for work. He can see you lifting and digging, pounding, running tools. It's easy to tell. Thelma doesn't care what my brother does, just so he wears a tie and bosses somebody. She always talks about his degree from college, figures out reasons to bring it up—like it gives her a buzz. She tells me that's what education can do for you.

She's just mad because she can't paint it on so thick about me. I'm not even taking classes at Cody Community. She goes to Christmas get-togethers and does her best to brag with her sisters about scholarships, mighty careers. Oh, that's super. I bet you're so proud. If I just signed up, then she could say it took me a while, but praise heaven, Siler's finally on the right road. My college cousins home for vacation always ask me what I'm doing. They've got to be polite. But really they think I'm full of crap, can't figure out a plan. They don't know Hap, don't have a clue what he does. I tell them a few things about fencing or timber, but they don't get it. They think any hard-luck loser can get that kind of job. But at least it's something to say when they ask.

This past get-together I told everybody I'm going to Lyman. They're more impressed when you're leaving for somewhere, something in a different place. It sounds major, and they think your plan is better. Kids go to college in Laramie or Provo, get jobs in Denver and Salt Lake. If it's really big time, they go to California. Thelma won't shut up when somebody goes to California. She reads it in the paper. They've sure done well. They've sure made their folks proud.

Uncle Rector asked me what's in Lyman. I told him I had a job waiting. He said that's what more kids need—worthwhile stuff. He said these delinquents don't have anything to do except loaf in the pool hall and get in trouble. He said getting out on my own will do me good.

And I'm finished with the horse sheds except for the tar paper on one. After that I don't know, if Lyman falls through. Hap still hasn't heard from the guy up at Northfork. All the college kids are gone back, worrying maybe they'll have to get a real job next summer, maybe actually have to hit a lick. Poor kids. But come fall, they've always got somewhere to go. And it's a good answer.

Thelma runs to the mailbox every morning, praying there's a letter from Laramie or Denver. It'll give her something to gab about on the phone with her sisters until the next honor roll comes out in the paper.

And my old man is working a lot of half days now, still leaves at dark, just takes his coffee thermos. He's been eating lunch at home. He's talking about driving a Coke truck, told Thelma he saw an ad. He says I'll run into something, somebody will need help this spring. Sometimes contract roofers will hire early, somebody for the tar pot on big jobs. That's what my old man says. He did that one spring, a long time ago. January is always slow. Even in Balford, things pick up when the weather breaks. The big farmers can always use an extra hired hand.

But the questions will be the same. I'll get them over and over, until I'm so sick of them I could puke. But this time I won't have anything for an answer—not a word, nothing even close. Except Hap went to Lyman. I know he did.

# Handshakes But No Hugs and Kisses

WHEN ROLO CAME BACK from paying November's rent on a Friday night in Provo, Utah, he told Everett their days with three roommates were over. Their landlady, Sister P&Q, said a new guy was moving in. His name was Burton. She knew his folks in Nampa, Idaho, said he was a little different.

"*How* different?" Everett asked.

Not as different as Burton's cousin Myron, who had rented from her a few years earlier. By mid-October, Myron had had enough of college and took a tent, sleeping bag, and commando knife into the mountains to live until snowfall.

"That's pretty different," Everett said.

But then this Myron got straightened out, went on a mission to Ecuador and, according to Sister P&Q, sort of joined the human race. After the mission he had even found somebody to marry him, which was more than either Rolo or Everett could say. So Sister P&Q was a big believer in the life-changing power of a mission. That power explained her willingness to rent to Burton. Unlike ninety percent of her tenants, he wasn't a BYU student, but he had been a missionary in Ventura, California. A married sister out in Orem had already lined up a job for him at a car dealership. He had maintenance and clean-up experience. If he ran into any problems, if things got to be too much for him, he could call this sister or the brother-in-law anytime.

So their other roommate, Tucker, who had had a bedroom to himself since school started, was going to have to get Jeanine's bicycle parts off the vacant bottom bunk. Rolo wadded his rent receipt, tossed it in the general direction of the trash can, and said, "He's been going to fix that bike for her since Labor Day—about the time they started getting chummy. Now that they're engaged, it'll never be in one piece again." He looked at Everett. "Are you and Lois getting chummy?"

At the cramped kitchen table, Everett concentrated on slicing little slabs off a half-round of cheddar cheese and sandwiching them between crackers.

"It's Friday night," Rolo said. "You're here, and she's not."

"She went to Tooele for the weekend with her roommate."

"You got beat out by Tooele?"

"I wouldn't put it quite like that."

"So how would you put it?"

"Look," Everett said, closing the flap on his cracker box. "Would you please not worry about what's going on between me and Lois?"

"That should be easy," Rolo said.

Forty-eight hours later, at quarter to nine on a stormy Sunday night, they heard feet shifting on the mat outside the apartment door, then a key scratching at the lock.

Rolo lay stretched out on the couch, eating cling peaches from the can and watching TV. In response to the shifting and scratching, he tilted his head as if howling to the moon, and yelled, "Come in!"

Everett sat at the kitchen table, close to the phone. He was eating crackers and peanut butter and hoping to hear from Lois when she got back from Tooele. He had told her, "Call me when you get back." She had said, "Maybe." And Rolo, who was betting she hadn't even left town for the weekend, had said, "Fat chance."

The scratching persisted. Everett balanced a fifth cracker sandwich on his stack and yelled, "Door's open!"

Just then the knob clicked, and the latch finally gave, followed by a heavy, clumsy tripping at the threshold. The tripper recovered and stood in the open doorway, snow swirling in the dark behind him. His hair was buzzed short with just enough of a cowlick to comb, the bristles darkened by melting flakes. His ears flared out from his head and, like his knuckles, glowed from the cold. He wore a tape measure clipped to his belt.

Lying on the couch, Rolo drew his knees up and shivered. "Are you Burton?" he asked.

The tripper looked at Rolo in the living room, then at Everett in the kitchen. He said, "Yup." Turning his neck slowly, he surveyed the bowls and glasses on the coffee table, and Tucker's TV in the opposite corner. His eyes came back to the closet door before him and to the outdated and never-honored chore schedule thumb-tacked to it. He stared beyond Everett at three flimsy shelves bracketed to the kitchen wall. They sagged under the weight of cold cereal and potato flakes and macaroni and cheese, dozens of packets of ramen, a gallon can of powdered lemonade, a bunch of bananas freckled with black spots, and a bulk box of saltine crackers. He stared until cold air swallowed the smell of tuna cans in the trash, half a week's dishes in the sink, and a kitchen floor long unmopped.

"I'm Rolo, and that's Everett." Rolo pointed a sock toward the kitchen.

Everett mimed a handshake.

"I'm from Nampa," Burton said. "Up by Boise. In case you need to know." He took his key from the lock and worked it onto a rabbit's foot key chain with two others. Then, as if remembering someone's advice, he thrust the keys deep in his pocket. "I don't want to lose my key right away."

"You sure don't," Rolo said. He drained peach juice into his mouth, licked the spoon, and dropped the can in one of the cereal bowls on the coffee table. He rubbed his arms fast against the chill.

Burton stepped back onto the landing and brought in a duffel bag, a scarred suitcase held together with two bungee cords, and a twine-wrapped shoe box.

"Got everything?" Rolo asked without moving.

"I got my clothes and stuff," Burton said, "and my trophy box." He patted the lid of the shoe box cradled in one arm. Only then, with a backward kick of his foot, did he close the door. "My sister Nona called and said, 'Burton, whatever you do, don't forget your box.' He smiled at Everett and patted the lid again. "Nona don't have to call old Burton. I'll never leave my trophies anywhere I go."

Everett wanted Burton to sit down or unpack or use the bathroom or go to bed. And he wished Lois would call. They could talk, and he could tell her how often he had thought of her over the weekend. And for the first time his words would move her. In a quiet, intimate voice, she would thank him and tell him that it had taken her a while to realize, but out of all the guys she had known—and there were a lot of them—he was the one for her. Sitting behind his stack of peanut-butter crackers, Everett imagined the phone ringing, grabbing it, grabbing Lois, falling together in fluffy snow.

"You get past Point of the Mountain okay?" Rolo asked with a burp. "That can be a bad spot in a storm."

The place name didn't register with Burton. "The worst blizzards in the world are in Idaho," he said. "But my car can go right through the drifts." He made gurgling engine noises in his throat. When he spoke, he used a lot of hand movements, kept shifting his feet, rocking slowly from toe to heel, leaving wet prints on the carpet. "Even four-wheel drives were off the highway. But I made it." He held his chin low and smirked. "I stopped by my sister Nona's house out in Orem. Some girls saw me climbing right up that icy street, and they waved."

Three dates. Three actual dates with Lois since school started—out of how many invitations?

"Girls like Lois just take a lot of wooing," he had told Rolo a few weeks back.

Rolo had said, "You're dreaming, mister."

Everett scooted his chair back and stood.

"There are swarms of girls around here, Burton," he said, moving into the living room and snatching up the scarred suitcase. "Bevies of them. Packs. Herds. This is girl paradise."

"What if they all like me? Ain't that a problem?" The tape measure stuck out above his hip. His jeans and tennis shoes looked new like a six-year-old's on the first day of school, and his dripping cowlick would have tempted a mother's hand. "At home they all liked me," he said. "They wanted to kiss me good-bye. They said, 'Oh Burton, don't leave us.' They probably wanted to *marry* me." Burton laughed as if unable to catch his breath. "I had to get away."

"Why didn't you send a few of them our way?" Rolo asked.

"Nope," Burton said. "They were after *me*." He picked up the duffel bag. "My dad said, 'Burton, you can't let those girls catch you.'" Little bubbles of saliva gathered on his bottom lip and in the corners of his mouth, and sprayed with no embarrassment when he spoke or laughed. "My dad knows a lot of things," he said, unzipping his coat. "He told me to wear this"—he tapped the middle snap of an insulated vest—"told me it's the warmest thing you can find."

Lugging the heavy suitcase, Everett moved toward the bedrooms. In the narrow hall, he remembered Lois in her warm parka, telling him she was going to Tooele for the weekend.

"When will you get back?"

"I really don't know, Everett."

"My dad has me chop wood," he heard Burton say. "I'm the only one can keep the fireplace going. I told him I'd keep doing it over in Utah, and he said, 'Burton, those apartments in Utah probably have gas furnaces.'"

"He's right," Rolo said.

"My sister Nona already got me a job—cleaning up cars, just

like at home. Just like on my mission to Ventura, California. I changed oil on all the elders' and sisters' cars. Kept them vacuumed real nice, too. President Gillespie let me wear a white shirt and tie under my coveralls. He said, 'Elder, this is part of the Lord's work, too.' When it was time for me to go home, none of the sisters wanted me to leave. They said, 'Elder, what will we ever do without you?'"

Standing in Tucker's bedroom, Everett waited for an answer, but none came. He set the suitcase down and called out: "You can bring your stuff in here. And your magic box."

The floor vibrated slightly, and suddenly Burton stood inside the bedroom clenching the throat of his duffel with one big, red-knuckled hand. Under his other arm he held the shoe box.

"It's not magic," he said. "It's just got my trophies in it."

"Sorry," Everett said. He stepped to the closet and pushed Tucker's clothes to one side on the hanger bar. He pointed to the newly made space, several dresser drawers, and a small desk, and said, "All yours." Then he nodded at the bottom bunk cluttered with frame, wheels, handlebars, pedals. "The bike parts belong to your roommate's fiancée. Her name is Jeanine; his name is Tucker. The mattress *under* the parts is yours." He backed toward the door.

Burton turned to the cologne bottles on the dresser, a few high school sports trophies among them, and a framed picture of Tucker and Jeanine kissing in front of a huge tree stump, a snowy landscape spread out behind them. He rubbed his thumb on the picture frame, then on the glass over the photograph. Twice Everett had asked Lois for a picture; twice she had put him off.

For a long time Burton held the duffel bag and didn't blink. Eyes wide, mouth open, he appeared almost grief-stricken. The slightly yellowed top and bottom teeth slanted inward.

"Is that his wife?" he asked.

"Not yet."

"My sister Nona—she lives in Orem with her husband

Phil—she told me, 'Burton, somewhere there's a girl for you.' That's what Grandma Edrus said, too. But first I got to make it on my own. Nona told me, 'Burton, if you need anything, I'm only a phone call away.'"

For the first time, Everett read the address tag on the suitcase, the name *BURTON TIDWELL* skewered crookedly on the top line. The address and phone number were in a different hand. Everett studied the cowlick and teeth, the unattended saliva bubbles and tape measure.

Burton pulled out a pocketknife and, gritting his teeth, cut the twine on his shoe box. He lifted the lid off, then fit it underneath the box. "I told Nona all the girls would probably be after me when they see my trophies." He held the box out with both hands. "You can go ahead and touch them."

The shoe box contained pink and white 4-H ribbons from county fairs dated a decade and a half earlier. It contained laminated newspaper photographs of Burton and three or four others, all of them holding the halter rope of a steer or crouching beside a lamb. It contained a varnished square of cabinet-grade plywood for Best Sport in some fifth-grade contest and a black and white photograph of the class. Almost all the boys had cowlicks. In the bottom of the box lay a plaque and certificate of completion from the Canyon County Vocational Training School and, under it, under everything else, a card.

"You can look at it," Burton said. "Go ahead and read it."

*To Elder Tidwell, who REALLY kept the mission running.*
*We will miss you.*
*From all the sisters in the California Ventura Mission.*
*Handshakes but no hugs and kisses.*

To the right of the last line was a smiley face, then a dozen signatures angled all over the card.

Tears welled in Burton's eyes, and he smiled. "It was against the rules to hug and kiss on my mission."

"Mine too," Everett said.

"They didn't want me to leave," Burton said, blinking fast. He cleared a spot on the corner of the bottom bunk and set his shoe box down. "But I told them. I told them I had to go home and make my life on my own. 'Burton, you're old enough now.' That's what my dad says. That's what my Grandma Edrus says, too. She lives in Balford, Wyoming."

Everett looked at him. "That's where I'm from."

"Edrus Penroy," Burton said. "That's her name."

"I know your grandma," Everett said.

Burton looked directly into his eyes. "Then maybe we got something the same," he said, fingering his tape measure. "Are you a crackerjack worker? My dad says I am." He unclipped his tape and held it like a jewel in his wide palm. Thin crescents of dirt showed beneath the nail of each curled finger. "My dad give it to me last Christmas. It goes to twenty-five. I only had a twelve before, couldn't measure *diddly squat!*" Burton smiled at his recollection of the phrase. He pulled out a foot of yellow tape and let it recoil with a snap. "But my dad says now I can measure anything I want." As the cowlick dried, it stuck up like the bristles of a worn paint brush. "He says I don't leave no sawdust when I sweep. He says, 'I'm proud of you, big man.'" Burton laughed. "And the sister missionaries will be proud of me."

One night, just before they got engaged, Tucker was talking to Jeanine on the telephone. "I'm proud of you," he had whispered into the receiver. Everett could not imagine doing or saying anything to elicit such a response from Lois.

"My mom said I could do lots of things down in Utah," Burton said, touching Everett's arm. "My dad said, 'You know how to drive, Burton. You've got you a license. You know about buying things with money. You can take care of yourself now.'" His voice softened in imitation. "'You've got to give it a try.'"

For a moment the bedroom in Provo, Utah, was quiet except for the snowstorm lashing the window. When the telephone rang, the sound seemed far away. Everett made no move toward the kitchen.

"This could be it!" Rolo yelled. "Time for more wooing!"

Two, three, four rings. Everett stared at the ribbons and plaque and card. At last he heard the couch squeak, heavy steps, the picking up of the receiver, and Rolo's muffled voice.

"False alarm!" Rolo yelled. "It was Tucker. The freeway's closed at Point of the Mountain. He's staying with Jeanine's folks tonight. Separate quarters. No hanky-panky."

Everett looked at Burton. No hanky-panky for him and nothing in the world longer than twenty-five.

"Tell me, Everett," Burton said. "Am I making it? Go ahead and tell me. People are going to ask."

Everett nodded. And as he nodded, the image of Lois in firelight faded irretrievably from his mind, replaced by Burton's suppliant face and a world full of girls all waving good-bye.

# The Treading of Lesser Cattle

In Vida's dream, magpies still pecked mushy tomatoes and squash, deaf to the barking and restless bawling. Plenty of acreage beyond nose range of barn and corrals, and Rowe had to have the garden plot right there. "But it's upwind, Vida. And you got to admit it puts the fertilizer close." In the deep darkness settling over the cutting pens and loading chute, over hay bunks filled one last time, she found the children in a cluster between the two snubbing posts. They were waiting for the trucks.

No, children, it's late April, and your dad says it's time to brand. All night, on opposite sides of a divider fence, cows and calves wore trails, kept thrusting snouts between planks to sniff out the one familiar scent among five dozen others. Your mother married a farmer, and that's how we raised the six of you. Yes, branding hurts a little now, but they'll find their mothers afterward, and by the time they make their way down to riverbottom grass, the pain will be nothing more than a memory.

So where were the boys now? How on earth would Rowe bring the herd off summer pasture this last time without them? The question was a box she couldn't close, and time seemed to fold in on itself. Yet the cattle were already gathered in their pens south of the house, their lowing carried by the wind. The many acres of swamp grass stretching down and away to the river were left to deer and pheasants, and the boys were grown and gone. In their absence, there was a neighbor, a rodeo cowboy with a horse and dogs. And the home teachers—a mortician and an accountant—neither of whom had ever stepped foot in a corral. "I don't know how you got along all these years without horses, Brother Rowe." "Will you need us to help you load tomorrow?" "No thanks. Everything's cut and penned; it's just a matter of running them up the chute." "How's it going to feel, Sister Sloan, when those trucks drive off?"

Then the children waiting between the friction-shined snubbing posts were raised and not raised, at the same time, and the confusion was profound. "Work hard, cowboys, and maybe your mom will bring us a Fudgesicle before lunch." "Daddy! Three of us, counting Mom, are *not* boys." "So you're not, Norene. I stand corrected." It was good to teach children to work, but did he have to expect so much? "For branding, it works out just right, Vida—everybody has a chore. Even Gabe and Marta can be a big help. Even Bern." Despite efforts to imitate his father's deftness, Mitchell strained at the handles of the ear punch. "Down lower, son. Lower! The thin part!" Then their oldest floated into her mind, knelt with the whetted knife, patted the flank of the trussed bull calf with great sympathy. "Ea-sy, Lucas! You're not gutting him."

In the fall we sell all the boy calves and keep back some of the girl calves, and, with the crops, that's how we make our living.

For forty-nine years—ever since she married Rowe in the Salt Lake temple. "You got to admit, that pasture is perfect for a cow-calf operation—grass brisket-deep everywhere you look. I already have my brand registered. In five years, we'll have the place paid off, and then we'll build you a new house."

You see, children, your mother dated a musician, but she married a farmer and ex-Marine. There was such relief on his face when she said yes to his proposal. "You being from the city, I wasn't sure how you'd feel about tying up with me." "My name is Brother Giggons, and I have the privilege of performing your marriage sealing today. Thanks to a divine plan, husbands and wives sealed at this altar can be together forever. Can anyone in this room tell me how long that is?"

In the night-hours before the coming of the trucks, Vida considered opening her eyes. But it seemed vital to first decide whether a consideration of that kind could be made in sleep. If they were branding tomorrow, it *couldn't* be October. All the children would still be young and responsible for a branding chore, and there would be no trucks. At noon they would roast hot dogs and eat chips and pork and beans from the tailgate of the pickup. With the branding fire down to coals for a little while, they could even toast marshmallows. Gabe loved toasted marshmallows. She needed to get up and bake cookies and find a jar of relish in the cellar and make potato salad. They would be hungry.

It couldn't be that late. At age eighteen, your mother met Payton Glassworth and fell in love with a musician. Or she met a musician and fell in love with Payton. Her mind went round and round, and she listened hard for the lowing and treading of cattle. It was so quiet after the herd went down on pasture. And for five months, the corral floor was unbroken by cloven hooves. Crusted under the summer sun, it hardly smelled at all. "It's funny what makes you happy, Vida." Before the corrals emptied completely, Gabe raised his arms high, waving a stick in one hand. "Whoa! Whoa!" "That a boy, Gabe. Don't let 'em past you!"

Everybody has a chore. To stoke the fire, Gabe kept crouching down a nine-year-old with a full head of hair, kept standing up all but bald. Wrapping the shafts in wet gunny sack, he fetched the glowing irons one at a time—the *R*, the *S*, the crown for the latter. "I've already registered my brand." With one foot planted on the ribcage for stability, Rowe bore down, high on the left hip. Then Lucas took his turn. Then Mitchell. Again and again, through layers of seasons, Vida saw the flame, heard the searing hiss and mournful bawling. Calf after calf, layer after layer, the cherry-red iron burned down through hair and hide. "Put some muscle into it, Bern." Bern winced, held his nose every which way to dodge the smoke and smell. "It's called branding for a reason."

To comfort or excuse only called attention to inabilities that didn't matter anywhere except a corral. So Vida let herself be distracted by Gabe, by the finger tracing the crisp, heat-glazed *RŠ*, by his nine-year-old's voice. "Feels sort of like burnt toast." "Yuck." "Gabe, don't tease your sister." "Or maybe the crunchy skin on a turkey drumstick." "Gabe!"

There were so many things to consider before the trucks came. Wasn't *R-Crown-S* just a bit aggrandizing? A bit much? "I know what the word means, Vida." "Momma, why is it bleeding?" "Can you dream with your eyes open, Momma?" Can you cry in your sleep? Vida tried to address all the hard questions, but the chore was tedious and fatiguing. "Do I have the names right? Rowe Sloan and Vida Deanne Hobart? No middle name for the groom? Not even an initial?" "No, sir, that's all there is to me." As opposed to Payton Rutherford Glassworth, III. "It doesn't mean a *real* crown, Vida. That's just what they call it in the branding register. Even if it did, I'm always good and sure exactly where I stand with *you*." "My name is Brother Giggons. If from this moment at this altar you will live faithfully and endure life's trials with patience, the Lord has promised both of you a crown of eternal glory. Can anyone in this room imagine anything sweeter?"

Even before Payton's proposal on a muggy night in August, a year to the day after they met, just before he left for Germany, she had begun practicing the signature.

*Vida Deanne Hobart Glassworth. Vida D. Glassworth. Vida H. Glassworth.*

"I'll never have another opportunity like this to study abroad, Vida. And in the northern part of the country—exactly the same place I served my mission. And the year will fly by. Before you know it, we'll be man and wife."

It's April, children. How did Marta, her youngest, come to

be sitting on a bag of barley seed in the back of the pickup? No matter. Everybody has a chore. With her back to the cab, first-grader Marta held a stub pencil and kept count in the stained ledger. *Nine, ten, eleven* black-white faces and Herefords and Charolais crosses. When Bern tried to help Lucas drag a brindled heifer from the corral at the end of a lariat, at least this one, the last of Vida's six children, was safe from the hooves plowing tracks in the dirt and from other risks in the world. The relief was exquisite. "Watch it—those hind legs pack a wallop." For five weeks Rowe kept a lemon-lime bruise just to the left of his groin from this very thing. "Boys, you can't leave one like that any slack at all. She about had me singing soprano the rest of my days." Just stay there, Marta, and keep count, and you'll be okay; just stay where you are, and you'll all be safe.

But despite her cautions and pleadings, they had scattered to the four corners—Denver, Atlanta, Spokane, Boise. Except Bern. "You are destined for great things, son." Over and over, his piano teacher, Sister Enid Cottrell, mentioned his gifted hands. "You'll go far." He went as far as Cody, was assistant manager in a grocery store. Which was all right. Which was fine. And now he used his gifted hands to make change and stack fruits and vegetables—and to play the piano in priesthood meetings.

*Twelve, thirteen, fourteen.*

At least back then, during branding, Marta stayed put, did exactly as Rowe directed. "Heifers in one column, steers in another—match their ear tags with their mothers' so we know old brood cows from young." He was good at giving directions. "When the trucks come, they want everything cut and counted—by sex, age, weight."

But then her youngest grew up, had two, three, four babies of her own, in just six years. I'm not telling you what to do, Marta—that sort of thing is between you and your husband and the Lord. But if I had it to do over again, if *I* did, if it were me, if life could be lived that way . . .

She should have gone back to the Y for winter quarter. "Honey, the wedding isn't until June, and you're so close to finishing." Straight through, summers and all, since she started at seventeen. "Surely Payton understands that." I'll work while you're in Germany, save money for us to start on. In the mornings she tended the counter at A.C. Drug; in the evenings she gave piano lessons. And there was so much to do to get ready. On Sundays she led the singing in sacrament meeting and repeated her news week after week. "A *musician*? Really? With him playing and you leading, there's no reason you two shouldn't get along perfectly." Had she gone back to school, she could have finished the degree and taught at Starview High School in Murray. She could have traveled somewhere far away or served a mission herself. She could have done so many things. And certainly she would have met others. There were so many nice boys at the Y, boys from neighborhoods right there in Salt Lake, returned missionaries studying to be businessmen and professors and lawyers.

But. Her thoughts kept looping back on themselves. But. How could she have known? She and Payton would have lived in a brick house on a wide city street with croquet wickets stuck in thick lawn grass. Her kitchen floor would have gleamed perpetually. But. She never would have met Rowe—on the last day of February, only a week after Payton's letter. "I know we've only just met and I'm asking you to take an awful chance on me. But half my platoon didn't come home from Chosin Reservoir, and I feel like maybe I was spared so I could meet somebody like you."

"*May*? Honey, it's already mid-March. Aren't you rushing things a little bit? Do you know this guy's family at all or what he plans to do for a living?" "My name's Rowe Sloan, from Balford, Wyoming. Been a member all my life, but, believe it or not, this is my first time to Temple Square. Are you a tour guide?" No. In her coat pocket she clutched the letter with the postmark from Germany. *We'll always share a love of music and for that reason, I hope, can remain good friends.* No. *We had something very precious.* No.

"If you don't mind, I'd like to call you while I'm in town."

Yes.

"I'm not telling you what to do, Honey, but marriage is a big step. At least you knew Payton a while." And look where it got me. "How can you be sure this guy's the right one?" I thought I *was* sure, last August. "But does this guy give you butterflies?" This "guy" has a name, Mother. And you've told me a thousand times: love is a *choice*. "But does he make you *tingle*?"

At every turn, there were hard questions. Had she really been so enamored and silly? So, Mr. Musician, how many kids do you want? "Glassworth offspring are referred to as *children*." "My name is Brother Giggons. The key in most areas of marriage is to distinguish between wants and needs." She wanted six? She *needed* six? To show the world that Rowe was the right one after all? To show herself? Either way, they were sealed forever. "Can anyone here tell me how long that is?" "It's a *long, long* time." "You're smiling; you must be the bride's mother."

In Vida's dream, time was strange. Marta suddenly went from ledger keeper at branding to young bride herself. Then her four babies kept getting mixed up with Vida's six, all of them nursing and teething and learning to walk at the same time. And Marta the wife and mother with her own desires. "He's a good provider, Momma, but I just wish he could be home more." Her own problems. "It's so hard to raise them these days—all the back-and-forth to keep them busy with practices and lessons."

That was one blessing of the farm: always plenty for kids to do right out your back door. One compensation for a muddy lane and hardpan front yard and an old Plymouth with a bird-spattered hood and windshield. Yes, Brother Giggons, marriage requires compromise and sacrifice. Oh, Rowe, you say that every fall. We've got the boys stacked three high in homemade bunks and Norene on a camp cot in the living room. Where are we going to put this baby when it comes? Another bedroom is hardly an extravagance. I'll use my egg and milk money.

Midway through the fiftieth year of Vida Sloan's marriage, morning was a long time coming. The longer, the better. If it didn't come, neither would the trucks. Forty-nine years to be hauled away in rigs coming off a night run from Great Falls to Billings. "Did you know, Vida, that they've had snow up there already?" Mushy tomatoes and squash, maybe, but not snow. Not yet. It was too early. "To tell you the truth, Vida, I'll be glad to see them gone. You got to admit these are the worst fence jumpers and hardest calvers we've ever had—more slinks in this bunch than in the last twenty years put together. Eight of them? Wasn't it eight?"

How does a person put a number to longing? Our children are going to know something besides field work and cows. Bern has a real talent, Rowe. "Even so, I'll not coddle him." But he could do so much with it. "Go ahead and say it, Vida—so much *better.*"

He wasn't the only child who didn't like branding. From the truck's tailgate to the calves trussed between snubbing posts, Norene supplied ear tags, a shaker of flea powder, boluses, vials of vaccine, the big syringe. Back and forth she carried a watering can full of milky disinfectant and the tin of blood-stop thick as tar. "What did you do with my dauber, Sweetie?" "I can't *find* it." "Vida, we need something here; Lucas got a little wild with the horn saw."

How, in that moment of panic, was she supposed to come up with anything to match the milled precision of a stir-stick? There was no time to do it properly, to take a flashlight into the windowless end of the tool shed and search a long shelf of rusted, mostly empty paint cans and old brushes with stiff bristles. She was left with no time. "I need *something,* or this calf's going to have to have a transfusion. Norene, hand me that Fudgesicle stick. Look where I'm pointing." "Yuck." "Just clean it off."

Rowe didn't want to wait until fall. He would have married her after a week. "Too bad you couldn't use those other announcements—just change the groom's name." That's not very funny, Dad. Then she was squatting by the fireplace in her parents' home, crying, feeding announcements into the bleary flames, one by one, until all three hundred were consumed. When they landed just right, they looked like little temples burning up.

Vida!

Mirror, mirror, on the wall, who's the bitterest of them all? Or vainest? Three hundred guests at a wedding reception? Wasn't that just a bit aggrandizing? I know what the word means.

"So what's his hurry?" No, Dad, there's no hidden, sinful *reason*. He's got his rough edges, but not that. Even Payton was more of a hand-holder and kisser. "Has he even courted you?"

*Dear Vida, I'm not much good with letters—or lots of other niceties, as you'll see shortly.*

What a job—to throw a big winter-born bull calf, to get a loop and half-hitch around the hind legs, to bind and snub both ends before the surprise wore off and those hind hooves became bludgeons and maces. When the boys couldn't stretch another half-inch out of the toughest kickers, Rowe stepped in. In one smooth motion, he straddled and grasped the head rope, then leaned hard toward the snubbing post. He pulled until lariat coils squeaked against wood fibers, until the calf's eyes bulged and the stippled tongue hung out of the mouth, until the bowel squirted brown-green at whoever was working that end. "Bull's-eye!" Everything in branding stinks. Won't a hot bath feel good tonight? The big square hand patted snout and forehead victoriously. "How do you like them apples, fella? Try kicking loose now. Once in a while you run into one just doesn't want to change his status very bad."

Corral or concert hall. How is that decided? "Hello, there. My name is Payton R. Glassworth, III, and piano is my life." He used a special lotion for his fingers, since early adolescence had had only three splinters—even counting things like burs and thistle stickers. He had kept track. "My hands are as vital to me as a surgeon's are to him."

"Dad, look! He's not breathing." "Slack off, Mitchell! Slack off!" With one quick, hard tug, he loosened the neck loop, slapped the chops, massaged the windpipe, frantic to revive the calf he had just subdued. It was awful to lose one, especially in front of the children. Such relief showed in his face when the eyes rolled back down and began blinking, when the lungs resumed their work.

"I've seen them die, Bern. You got to get the other leg in the loop to keep the big ones from choking." Don't blame him. If you wouldn't stretch them so tight. "Who's blaming anybody for anything? I can't have them thrashing around, and there's no risk with that second leg in the loop."

No risk? Every choice in life was a risk and a trade-off and a lot of heavy work. But at age twenty she was amenable to so much she couldn't foresee. And forty-nine years later, all of it was to be hauled away in trucks.

"That's all you know about this guy—he's twenty-seven years old and farms somewhere in Wyoming? Has he got any education?" "Your mother's right, Vida. It's awfully soon after Payton to be committing to this. Are you sure you're prepared for that lifestyle?"

Coarse fingernails and toil everlasting.

What I know is this: he's a good man, and he wants kids, and he'll take me to the temple.

"It's noon, cowhands. What do you say we eat?" We're going to need some willow sticks. No, don't use *that* knife. Be sure and wash your hands, everybody. I put a bar of soap on that straw bale by the hose. "That water's too cold." Even so, it will all come off with some scrubbing. "Your Bern is a natural." In thirty years of giving lessons, Sister Enid Cottrell had never seen fingers better suited to the piano. "You might make hymn plunkers out of those other boys, but that one's got real talent; he'll go far."

For a shimmering moment, one hope sustained another: the children were still children, Bern and Gabe hurrying back from the willow tree clutching the roasting sticks while the others cleared the tailgate. Happily, she spread a big towel, laid out the hotdogs and buns, mustard and ketchup, the cooler of lemonade. "Hey. I didn't know you had a bag of potato chips. She hides all the good stuff. And cookies. You can make a picnic out of anything, Vida."

The potato salad could have used more paprika, and she wished again for chives. Norene liked the smell. Of all the odors of branding, the burn salve stunk the worst. Mingled camphor and garlic and sulfur. When to use salve and when to use blood-stop. Vida had forgotten. There was no bleeding when the red-hot edge went through hair and hide both and exposed the quivering white muscle sheath. "Look—wedding satin." Gabe! Such imagination amid a litter of nub horns, scrotum caps, dung, snot, blood. Rowe's hand was red to the wrist.

Such talk while, fifty feet away, the two bulls in their heavy pen went berserk at the scent of the surgery, snorting, groaning, bucking high, dewclaws and fetlocks flashing above the top plank. When the bigger bull dropped to his knees, the ground-shudder ran all the way to the loading chute. "Momma, what's a steer?" Why don't you just keep count, Marta; you'll have to ask your father about that later. What's so funny, Gabe? Where the manure thinned in the far corners of their pen, the bulls rooted and pawed, moaned and gasped. Again and again, they butted the earth with bosses thick as armor and gouged long furrows with down-curved horns. Don't worry, children. "No, sir, that's bridge plank; it could hold an elephant."

Yes, stay where you are. Nothing can get you.

Yet now she couldn't be sure. They had babies of their own and were scattered to the four corners. What was there to hold to?

By December, when she turned twenty, she had saved a thick packet of his letters. They had come so regularly until then.

*Hallo, hallo, Dear Vida, from Hamburg—It would be wonderful to see my beautiful "Freundin" over the holidays, but, alas, a very spartan student budget will keep me here all alone—except for a few other equally pitiful classmates.*

*My Dearest Payton—With all my love forever.*

He called on Christmas eve. "It means *girlfriend.*"

She *was* still his fiancée, wasn't she?

With the world resting on his answer, she bought ten yards of dress fabric and ordered three hundred announcements. "Isn't it just a little early for that, Honey?"

"They don't look like oysters to me." For heaven's sake, Gabe! "Well, she asked." "Daddy, what are they called?"

And tomorrow the corrals would be empty. Everything goes. Yes. Beginning tomorrow, what a sweet eternal relief from the smell and the filthy boots. That will be crown enough. Tromp across my clean kitchen floor, trailing gobs and bits the whole way. I just mopped, Rowe! He lifted one foot, checked the sole, did the same with the other. Then the sheepish scowl and the penitent undoing of laces, right then and there, and the tip-toe-ing back toward the door. A little late for that, isn't it? For a full five minutes he made a show of searching for a rag. "What do you use for cleanser, Vida?" Oh for crying out loud! It's easier to do it myself.

But some things you can't do by yourself.

"Is May too soon for you?" No, no. She was amenable. Of her own free will, she agreed. In one short ceremony, she agreed to all of it. They did not have the place paid off in five years. And the closest she came to a new house was a small bedroom built over a basement he poured one mixer batch of concrete at a time. "I'm sorry about your floor, Vida. I'm a long way from perfect. I don't know what else you want me to say."

Unbidden, Payton Glassworth came up the basement stairs in black concert shoes, buffed to a brilliant luster, and stood above the barn muck. *Mein Freundin* forever.

*When she and I got over here last fall, I assure you we were just friends. But, as we studied together and really got to know each other over the Christmas holiday . . . I'm truly sorry, Vida. I only wish to make this as painless as possible.*

Then he waved good-bye, good-bye, and it was all a long time ago, and everything about him, every possibility associated with him, was hazy and vaporous, untouchable and forever un-knowable.

Rowe was so sure the quiet tomorrow wouldn't be any different than it was in April. "From now on, if we want a steak, we'll get it plastic-wrapped at the store like everybody else in the modern world." No more headaches trying to keep the water trough full against so much thirst. No constant depletion of the well. "For the first time in our married life, we won't be handcuffed to a bunch of cows." No more wondering if the washing machine was *ever* going to fill. No grit in the bathtub. "You've been after me to do this for ten years—maybe more. It's funny what makes you sad."

Riverbottom grass left now to deer and pheasants. In a cloudy topography, a strange image emerged: Rowe's face and mouth and body but Brother Giggons's voice: Multiply and replenish the earth. *Kids* or *children?* "Shoot, seems like all the same process to me." How many do you want? "A truckful." Oh, she had no idea what she was asking. Down a long hallway in her mind, deep in a back chamber, there was no separating lovemaking in the early years of marriage from morning sickness and labor pains and a kettle of water heating on the coal stove and diapers hung out in an endless winter, the cotton freezing so fast it crackled between the jaws of clothespins.

In her parents' bedroom, just two hours before the ceremony, her mother had tried to tell her something. "Honey, tonight you'll be man and wife, and you've both saved yourself for something that, the first time . . ." What is it, Mother? The truly consuming worries were dress and pictures and cake and gifts.

Spare me your pity, Mr. Glassworth. It so happens that *I've* found someone else, too. In a hotel not ten blocks from the Sugarhouse Fifth Ward church building where the reception was held, not twenty blocks from the home she grew up in, in a room well beyond the budget she was to live with for the next forty-nine years . . . What is it? "Honey, men and women feel differently about certain . . . things."

He was *so* eager. So eager and clumsy. "But, Honey—" Just tell me, Mother. You've got to admit: it's really quite lovely and flattering that he's so eager for *you*. And, despite hands foreordained to daily contact with raw textures, to the many fluids of cattle husbandry, he was always clean and tender—and teachable. And yes, yes, you must admit, after all, the desire was mutual. It was that. Just tell me. You don't get six kids from cold hormones. Just tell me. Men are so very eager—and stay that way for a *long, long* time.

"Can anyone in this room tell me how long forever is?" Ten years for a start on a basement and bedroom, three more to see the job finished. Thirteen years of childbearing, more than twice that many of childrearing. Forty years of mortgage. Forty-nine of manure. Who's blaming anybody for anything?

On freezing nights, when their mothers were too weak or negligent to suckle them, Rowe brought newborns in by the stove, cared for them with sweet devotion. Using rags that she proffered, he rubbed off the slime of afterbirth and coaxed them to take a nippled pop bottle full of foamy warm milk. "I'm sorry about your floor, Vida."

Yet she never minded so much. Amid the bright chandelier light and the pure white of the wedding dress and veil, she looked across the altar and saw decency and commitment. "I need to know how you feel about me, Vida." Never mind the aversion, during a certain period of pregnancy, to his touch and smell and even his voice. By the time she was carrying Mitchell, he understood and dutifully kept his distance—until one afternoon, with Lucas down for a nap, she approached and, facing him where he stood by the kitchen sink, took the water glass from him and set it on the counter. Then she undid the two cuff buttons, slid her hands deep, deep inside his shirt sleeves, and, without a word, persuaded him that his next chore of farming could wait.

Is that it, Mother?

Every fiancé is a gamble. The closest he came to musical ability was bellowing hymns while milking or feeding. *Come to*

*Zion, come to Zion! Zion's walls shall ring with praise.* But everything he did, he did with vigor. "I don't smell so sweet, Vida." So wouldn't a hot bath feel good about now? He was forever braiding, whittling, fashioning. Jump ropes. Dollhouses. Sailboats. Toy swords and rifles. Hugging, tousling, dandling, wrestling, patting cheeks, kissing foreheads. It wasn't all work and want.

Beside the row of barn boots in the washer room was a fruit crate full of balls of all kinds, a bat, several mitts. In the middle of one of forty-nine harvests, he took a full morning to mount a basketball rim and plywood backboard on a length of salvaged telephone pole. He spent several hours digging a posthole. "Why so deep, Dad?" "I want it to last a lifetime." On an afternoon bright as butter and honey, with no trucks coming, the children suddenly swarmed him and clung to his legs and arms as he lurched toward the rim, trying to bounce the scarred basketball. Across many autumns their laughter rang.

"Up and at 'em, cowboys. It's branding day. Lucas, you and Bern take the truck to the woodpile and fill it up. Mitchell can get the branding irons; they're hanging in the tool shed." "I hate branding, Daddy." "But I need you, Sweetie, just the same."

I need you, Rowe; it's time. The contractions are coming close together now. No, they didn't have so many just for the help or because they didn't know how not to have them. It wasn't that. It wasn't. After a miscarriage between Norene and Gabe, he mourned for a month. "I know I'm not the Prince Charming you had in mind, Vida; Payton would have given you a very different life."

A little late for that, isn't it?

It was Rowe she knelt across from in the Salt Lake Temple, Rowe she shared a bed with, Rowe she cleaved to innumerable times in passion and refreshment and hope and healing and love, Rowe she had accompanied on the long walk toward brisket-deep grass.

In shallow sleep, Vida smelled dirt freshly tamped around other pieces of telephone pole set for snubbing posts. On another far-away evening, with the tang of October in the air, he chugged into the yard in his old pickup, its springs sagging beneath the weight of a burden draped with a tarp. I'm trying to get supper on the table, Rowe. "Just come and look." Where on earth did you get this? "I have a few connections of my own in the musical world. It's beat up and out of tune, been sitting in the basement of the Elks Lodge for who knows how long. But it's solid oak; it'll outlast us both."

Sixteen calves, and it wasn't even noon. "We're making headway, cowboys."

With their new-morning chatter, magpies at roost in the big cottonwood mark the end of all sleeping and dreaming in the world. Long before the sun edges above the Bighorns, Vida Sloan, lying in her marriage bed, imagines the engine throb of trucks afar off and cattle ascending the mountain. *Come to Zion, come to Zion.* "Can anyone in this room tell me how long forever is?" Floating toward a wakefulness that shimmers like tears in candlelight, she reaches under warm bed covers, comes up against Rowe's thigh, ranges higher to locate the shoulder, elbow, forearm, all of it solid and familiar flesh. Then her hand finds his, and she holds on.

## Author's Acknowledgments

I am grateful to Paul Bowers for reading and commenting on most of the stories in this collection, and to Lisa Torcasso Downing for her careful editing of the entire volume. Their efforts spared readers the worst effects of my bad habits.

## About the Author

Darin Cozzens grew up in Ralston, Wyoming. He earned a B.A. from Brigham Young University, an M.F.A. from the University of North Carolina–Greensboro, and a Ph.D. from Oklahoma State University. His stories have appeared in *Greensboro Review, Cimarron Review, Weber Studies, River Oak Review,* and *Irreantum.* He has been a semifinalist for the Ohio State University Press Prize in Short Fiction and a finalist for both the Iowa Short Fiction Awards and Sarabande's Mary McCarthy Prize in Short Fiction. Recently, his story "The Treading of Lesser Cattle" was nominated for a Pushcart Prize. He has taught in Georgia, Arizona, and, for the past eight years, at Surry Community College in Dobson, North Carolina. He and his wife are the parents of four children.

www.ingramcontent.com/pod-product-compliance
Lightning Source LLC
Chambersburg PA
CBHW070020120726
47909CB00003B/1006